# Sunday's Child

## Clare Revell

**Sunday's Child**

Cover Art by Nicola Martinez

White Rose Publishing, a division of Pelican Ventures, LLC
www.pelicanbookgroup.com  PO Box 1738 *Aztec, NM * 87410

White Rose Publishing Circle and Rosebud logo is a trademark of Pelican Ventures, LLC

Publishing History
First White Rose Edition, 2014
Paperback Edition ISBN 978-1-61116-310-0
Electronic Edition ISBN 978-1-61116-309-4
**Published in the United States of America**

## Dedication

Dedicated to all the members of the Royal National Lifeboat Institution who volunteer to save lives at sea. Also to Cal who wanted to be the hero.

## Thanks to

Huge thanks go to
Hayling Island RNLI Station for letting me visit and spend several hours asking questions and taking photos. Not to mention the immediate answer to all my emails.
Particular thanks go to:
Jonathan Bradbury
Graham Raines MBE
The crew of Red Watch
Also to
@RNLI on twitter
Liz Cook at RNLI HQ
More information can be found about the RNLI at
http://rnli.org/Pages/default.aspx

## Special Thanks to

Editor in Chief Nicola Martinez for listening to my proposal for a seven book series and going with it.
Editor Lisa McCaskill for her patience, guidance and inspirational photos for the entire series.
You are both a blessing and a joy to work with. I'm so grateful to be part of the Pelican Book Family.

Monday's Child must hide for protection
Tuesday's Child tenders direction
Wednesday's Child grieves for his soul
Thursday's Child chases the whole
Friday's Child is a man obsessed
Saturday's Child might be possessed
And Sunday's Child on life's seas is tossed
Awaiting the Lifeboat that rescues the lost.

\*\*\*\*

## The Lifeboat Prayer

Merciful Father, all things in heaven and earth are held
within Your loving care, look with favor upon the Royal
National Lifeboat Institution. Protect and bless the crews of
all our lifeboats, our lifeguards and all who risk their own
safety to bring help to others.
Guide all who work for the Institution as volunteers,
supporters or staff that they may be faithful to the vision of
our founders, so that it may always be seen as a beacon of
hope and light to those who find themselves in peril on the
seas. Through the same Jesus Christ, to whom with You and
the Holy Spirit be honor and glory, now and forever.
Amen

\*\*\*\*

Oh, Lord, our boat is so small, and Thy sea is so vast. Please
protect us.

Praise for Clare Revell

*Monday's Child*
Traditional romance readers will love this story! However, the plot doesn't stop at romance. A few of my favorite things about this story were; the heart pumping explosive incident, the English, Scottish, and American accents I could actually hear as I read, and an underlining thread of faith. - JoAnn Carter

*Tuesday's Child*
As a hard of hearing person, I easily identified with the deaf heroine whose faith and love were her bedrock. I cannot begin to recommend this book highly enough. The suspense will make your hairs stand at attention. Get it, read it, you'll be happy you did ~ J. Wright

*Wednesday's Child*
Liam Page is wounded. The burdens he carries tug your heart. I love the ordained way in which he meets our more than worthy heroine, Jacqui Dorne. Their paths, we discover, were meant to intersect—not just on a professional but on a personal level as well. ~ Marianne Evans

*After The Fire*
Clare Revell has written a wonderful Christian mystery in *After the Fire*. From the beginning, I found myself drawn into the story. The descriptions brought the story to life, and the vibrant characters felt like they could step off the page. Second-chance-at-love stories are always fun to read, and this one did not disappoint. ~ EA West

Other titles by Clare Revell

Novels
*After the Fire*
*Turned*

*Monday's Child*
*Tuesday's Child*
*Wednesday's Child*
*Thursday's Child*
*Friday's Child*
*Saturday's Child*

Novellas
*Season for Miracles*
*Cassie's Wedding Dress*
*Time's Arrow*
*An Aussie Christmas Angel*

Dollar Downloads
*Saving Christmas*

Free Reads
*Kisses from Heaven*

Glossary

**LOM** – Lifeboat Operations Manager makes the decision to launch at the request of the Coastguard.

**DLA** – Deputy Launch Authority also able to make the decision to launch if the LOM not on duty

**DODO** – Drive On Drive Off rig used to launch the inshore lifeboat. The tractor tows the lifeboat in its cage into the sea.

**RNLI** – Royal National Lifeboat Institution. The RNLI is the charity that saves lives at sea. They provide an on call, 24-hour lifeboat search and rescue service and a seasonal lifeguard service on the beaches. It's staffed entirely by volunteers. Not part of the Coastguard.

**RHIB** - Rigid Hull Inflatable Boat. Also known as a RIB

**Bunny Suit** – the fleece onesie worn underneath the crew dry suits.

*And Sunday's Child on life's seas is tossed, awaiting the Lifeboat that rescues the lost.*

# 1

*And He saith unto them, 'Why are ye fearful, O ye of little faith?' Then He arose, and rebuked the winds and the sea; and there was a great calm. Matthew 8:26*

"Rainbow Lodge is a small, family run, Christian guest house on the banks of the River Thames. Providing bed, breakfast, and home cooked evening meals, it's a home away from home."

Hattie Steele tilted her head and looked at the computer screen. Designing the new brochure for the guest house she helped run alongside her twin brother and his wife, had seemed such a simple task when Steve suggested it. But it had taken up most of the day and turned into a mammoth job. Nothing else had been done, unless Penny or Steve had done it, but she doubted that. Pigs would fly first.

And try as she might, she still couldn't get rid of those annoying green squiggly lines from the text. She just had to take comfort from the fact that said green lines wouldn't be printed in the final version. She also liked the fact she could click 'ignore' and they vanished.

"Each room is ensuite, with tea and coffee making facilities. There is a large screen TV in the lounge. We also have a games room and a large garden, with barbeque in the summer months."

She added the photos she'd taken earlier and hit save. A few clicks later and she had something she was happy with. If only those green lines would go away. If she found them annoying, Aunt Laurie, a famous novelist, must hate them even more. She pushed the chair back, needing some tea, when a cup appeared at her elbow.

She grinned. "Are you reading my mind again, Steve?"

"Of course I am. How else do I keep tabs on my baby sister? You have a problem with that, Hattie?" Her brother grinned as he handed her the cup.

"Excuse me...*Baby sister*? You are five whole minutes older than me. How does that make me a baby?" She let the mock outrage drop as the scent of the tea filled her senses. She took a long sip. "What do you think of the brochure?"

"I think you're a genius, but then I'm biased."

"Uh huh. Be serious and you haven't even looked at it yet."

"I am being serious. You've saved us about a couple of hundred quid in design costs, if not more." Steve studied the screen, running a hand through his short blond hair. "You spelled facilities wrong. You have faculties."

"Oops. My bad." Hattie changed it. "Better?"

Steve nodded. "Better. It's nice to see you putting your God given talents to use."

Hattie tucked her hair back behind her ears. "According to you, God gave me more talents than I can shake a stick at. There's this, floor cleaning, silver polishing, cooking, organizing, and shopping. Not to mention changing the beds and making those new curtains you wanted in room twelve. I'm surprised you don't still make me do the accounts as well, like you used to do. I tell you, slaves had it easy compared to what I do all day every day."

He laughed. "I have an accountant to do the books, which is why you no longer do them. Speaking of cooking, the new guest, Callum Trant, is arriving before dinner now. He managed to get an earlier train. Is that going to be a problem? Remember I told you about his allergy when he booked. The last thing we need is someone like him getting sick or dying."

For a moment Hattie wondered why Mr. Trant was different to any other guest, but didn't pursue it. "I remember. No nuts of any description, especially macadamia and peanuts. It's fine. I never use nuts anyway and what few packets I do use, I always read carefully. There is nothing in the kitchen, or his room come to that, which can hurt him. And I have thrown out every jar of peanut butter and put all the plates and knives through the dishwasher. Not to mention scrubbed out all the cupboards and then thrown away the cloths I used. And I made his room up this morning when I did the rest of them. So, no, Mr. Trant arriving early won't be a problem." She winked. "How would you ever manage if I left?"

"You're not allowed to. Whoever you marry has to move in here, too."

"Just because Penny moved in when she married you, doesn't mean—"

"And his name has to start with a P."

Hattie twisted and gave her twin the horrified stare she'd perfected over the years. "*Excuse me?*"

"Well, I married Penny. And Mum and Dad were

Peter and Pauline. So it's a family tradition and you can't break it."

"I don't even *have* a boyfriend, let alone want one, and you're talking marriage? Thinking about it, I don't actually know any blokes whose names start with a P, unless you include Pastor Jack and I think Cassie would object to me marrying him."

"There's a chap starting with P out there somewhere."

"He can stay there. I'm planning on being the spinster aunt. *The* Miss Steele."

"Yeah, right, you'll change your mind when someone comes along and asks you out. I could set you up with someone if you want. There's this really great bloke I know that you'd adore and—"

"I'm good, thanks." She turned back to the computer, and hit save. Her brother took teasing her about her singleness to a whole new level and it grew irksome after a while. Though sometimes she did wish a swashbuckling knight on a white horse would gallop up and whisk her away from this place. If she ever did get married, she wouldn't stay here, that's for sure. "There. All ready to go to the printers, bar a final spell check. Either you or Penny can do that. I need to go make a start on dinner."

"Thanks, Hattie. I'll do it later."

Hattie stood and stretched, her curiosity finally getting the better of her. "What's all the fuss over this new guest anyway? Is he some kind of superhero or politician or something? Will him getting sick ruin your reputation quicker than anyone else?"

"Don't you know who he is?"

"If I knew I wouldn't ask. All I know is that his name is Callum Trant. Which is important because—?"

"Hattie." Steve looked at her, hands on hips, a mixture of amusement and shock on his face. "He's only the greatest footballer that ever lived. He played one hundred and twenty times for England, was capped ninety times, and scored thirty-seven goals at international level and another three hundred and fifty at club level."

"And this matters because...?" Brother baiting was her favorite pastime and he never failed to rise to it where football was concerned. The thing was, she really didn't understand this fuss over kicking an air filled ball of leather around a field. Nor did she want to.

"Because it's *football*. And because he's Callum Trant. *The* Callum Trant." Steve shook his head, sheer despair on his face. "Of course it matters. Wouldn't it matter to you if, oh I don't know, if say Beethoven came to stay?"

"Beethoven is dead. He has been for hundreds of years. And you can't put one of the greatest composers that ever lived in the same league as an over paid bloke who runs around a field all day complaining when he trips up."

"I can't believe you just said that."

She laughed and waggled a finger at him. "Oh yeah, I went there." She dropped her hand and slid it into her pocket, heading to the door. "In any event, you can't possibly compare what a footballer does with a soldier or firefighter, and they get nowhere near as much money. And I'm going to start dinner now while you lay up the dining room and I have you gobsmacked."

"*Soldiers*? Where'd that come from?"

"Those on the front lines don't make in a lifetime

what a top flight footballer makes in a week." She took a deep breath. "But I'm not getting into that now. I have fish to bone and potatoes to peel and…"

Steve's face fell. "Right. Potatoes…"

"You forgot? Ste-eve. You'd forget your own head if it wasn't screwed on. You'd best run to Asda and get some. A ten pound bag will do for now." She shook her head as her brother rushed out. Taking her tea with her, she headed to the kitchen. There would be twenty guests for dinner tonight now, plus the three of them. And she still had no idea what to make for dessert.

****

Callum Trant stepped out of the taxi and looked up at the cream three story guest house in front of him. A multi-colored sign declaring the name *Rainbow Lodge* arched over the front door. Net curtains hung at every window, with different colored shutters surrounding them. Flowers nestled in window boxes under each casement, each one a different color and matching the shutters. Each color of the rainbow represented. Someone had gone to a great deal of trouble to create the perfect first impression. It looked bigger than what the brochure said, but still a great deal smaller than what he was used to.

But that suited his new way of life better. He'd be the first to admit the stardom had gotten to him and turned his head, stifling his faith. This was why he'd retired and left the game completely instead of going into coaching or management. A few people on the mainland still recognized him, but he liked his otherwise incognito lifestyle. And to the people back home, well to most of them, he was simply Cal the

Carpenter.

"That'll be twelve fifty, mate."

Cal pulled the cash from his wallet and paid the taxi driver, leaving him a substantial tip. Picking up his case, and shouldering his bag, he headed up the stone steps to the arched door. Sun shone through the rainbow stained glass, casting a pattern onto the tiled floor of the hallway.

There was no reception desk, just a bell set into the wall with a rainbow tag saying *please ring for attention.*

He pressed and waited. There had been no accompanying ring. Perhaps it didn't work. He was about to press it again, when a blonde woman came through the door marked *private*. Her hair was pulled back in an untidy ponytail and she wore no makeup. A blue gingham apron tied over her jeans and open neck shirt did nothing to hide her slim figure and ample feminine curves. She wasn't amazingly pretty, but there was something about her that made him want to know her better.

Cal felt the familiar blast of heat surge through him and he did his best to quash it. That belonged to his old self, when women threw themselves at him and he took advantage. That part of his life, no matter how hard he tried, still raged like a wild animal within him. He prayed for help as his heart pounded and his pulse raced.

"Can I help you?" Her melodic voice rang in his ears like silver bells. That wasn't helping.

He rubbed his hand on his chinos before offering it to her. "Callum Trant. I have a room booked."

Her face broke into a smile. "Of course, we spoke on the phone. I'm Harriet Steele. Welcome to Rainbow Lodge and Headley Cross. It's a pleasure to meet you."

Her touch was cool and sent a ripple of peace through him. Not something he was expecting.

"Did you have a good journey?"

More than a little thrown, it took him a few seconds to articulate a response. "Nice to meet you, too. The journey wasn't too bad. Better than I expected at any rate."

"I'm glad. Let me show you to your room, Mr. Trant."

Before he could respond, she picked up his case and headed down the hallway. "The dining room is just there." She nodded to a room to the left. "The lounge is straight ahead. There is a downstairs bathroom just behind the staircase. The games room is through the lounge and the conservatory is just beyond that."

Cal glanced into the lounge as they walked. Huge sofas sat around a coffee table, laden with magazines and coasters. Ornaments lined the mantelpiece above an open fire. A TV hung on the far wall. It looked and felt as warm, welcoming, and cozy as his grandmother's house.

A fish tank nestled under the stairs, filled with tiny tropical fish, the filter humming and bubbling. The stairs themselves curved up and around to the first floor. Cream doors opened off beige walls, giving the place a comfortable feel. Each door had a brass number on it. He followed Miss Steele, and it was Miss as he'd noted the absence of a ring when he shook her hand, up another staircase to the second floor.

This floor had the same pale green carpet as was downstairs, but brown doors and cream walls. She unlocked room nine and went inside, placing his suitcase on the deep pile cream carpet.

The room was bigger than he expected, with a double bed, chest of drawers, wardrobe, and even a sofa. He turned around, taking in the décor and pictures on the wall. It really was lovely. A real home away from home, just like the brochure had said.

Miss Steele smiled at him. "Here you are. The ensuite is just through there, although there is another bathroom on the landing. You have tea and coffee making facilities over there on the dresser. We replace them daily, but if you need more, just ask. I've just put the kettle on if you'd like a drink now?"

"I'd love some tea, please. The buffet car on the train wasn't working."

"That could be a blessing in disguise. The last time I drank railway tea, it was hot, wet and tasted of nothing." Her smile shot straight through him. "Here are your keys. The silver one is this room. The gold one is the main front door. Its open all the time apart from Sunday's when I'm at church, and we lock up about half past eleven at night. I'll be right up with the tea."

"Thank you."

Cal turned to the window as Miss Steele left. The garden spread out beneath him. A swing for the kids, sandpit, and seating area nestled amongst trees and flower beds. A brick built barbeque stood against the corner of the patio. High fences around the perimeter ensured privacy. It was perfect.

He just hadn't expected to find the owner so—alluring, he decided was the right word. It was more than a little disconcerting, not to mention disappointing, how fast his body betrayed him. The body is willing, but the spirit is weak, wasn't that the usual saying? In his case, the spirit *was* willing, more than willing, desired to do God's will, but his body was weak and still strove after the old ways. But he'd be out all day, every day and would probably rarely see her.

He picked up his case and set it on the bed, starting to unpack. How long had it been since he'd had a proper break? He didn't remember. Straight from retiring from football, he'd gone back into the family building business and worked alongside his father and uncle.

Dad had always insisted he have a trade alongside his football career and he'd chosen carpentry. Keeping his hand in over the years, now stood him in good stead as the quality of his work meant customers were asking for him by name having been referred by friends and neighbors.

He picked up his wash bag and went across to check out the bathroom. Small, but functional and perfect for the long hot showers he loved to take first thing in the morning and last thing at night. He unpacked his toothbrush and other things, setting them on the glass shelf over the sink.

Then he headed back into the main room.

His older brother, Carter, helped out with the decorating side of the business in between cycling tours, which wasn't often. A professional cyclist, Carter competed for his country and last year had won the Tour de France. Something that meant more to Cal than all the caps, goals and medals he'd won himself combined.

A knock on the door made him turn. Miss Steele stood there with a tray in her hands. She smiled and came in, setting it down on the side. "Just leave it here when you're done. I'll pick it up later. Dinner is at six, evening drinks at ten and breakfast at eight. Is there anything else you need to know?"

"Thank you for this, and no I'm fine." Cal paused. He'd better ask as he needed to be safe rather than sorry later. "Did you get my email about my nut allergy? I didn't get a reply so I just wanted to double check."

Her smile wasn't fixed or condescending, rather genuine. "I did and I'm sorry you didn't get a reply. You should have done. I don't use nuts as a rule anyway, but will read all the packets carefully during your stay and I've made sure there is nothing in the kitchen containing nuts."

"Thank you." He turned back to his unpacking as she left. All of a sudden, two weeks didn't seem long enough.

# 2

Hattie returned to the kitchen with the intention of finishing dinner. Steve had bought the potatoes. She'd prepared enough to accompany the new recipe she was trying tonight. She'd made potatoes like this a hundred times and loved the way they looked piped onto the plates. It was so much prettier than plain mash.

Penny came in with a pile of serviettes to fold. "Well, is it him?"

Hattie sighed. "As I told Steve, I have no idea who *he* is, but Mr. Trant has arrived and won't be treated any differently to any other guest."

"But he's Callum Trant. The best footballer we've—"

"And you've been married to my brother for too long. I've already heard that way too many times today. Steve's corrupted you. Mr. Trant is retired and probably doesn't want constant reminders about it. So no asking for autographs over dinner."

Penny pouted and complained to her husband as he came in from the garden with a handful of rhubarb. "Steve, she's being bossy again."

"I don't care," he sing-songed back. "There's the rhubarb you wanted for the crumble tomorrow, Hattie. I'll put it in the fridge."

"Thank you." Hattie turned back to her

preparations. Experimenting with a new dish was no excuse to let her standards slip.

"So what's he like?" Penny persisted.

She turned the pastry before rolling it again. "He's a man."

"No. That's a shocker."

Hattie smirked. "Yeah, a man. Not like we have many of them staying here. If we have any at all."

Penny laughed. "Seriously, what's he like."

"He's tall, dark, handsome, fit and scores a nine, but charming and pleasant along with it."

Steve groaned. "Not the hunk rating *again*."

"You're just jealous because you're not on it," Hattie teased.

"Pfft. I don't need to be on it. I own it." He grinned at her. "You like him."

"I do not." She shot the retort back way too fast, even for her.

"Yes, you do. You're blushing. Why would you blush if you don't like him?"

She scrunched up her nose at him. "Because it's hot in here, that's why. Go pick on someone your own size."

Steve hugged her. "OK, shorty."

"Beast," she laughed, wriggling out from his arms. "I'm what an inch shorter than you?"

"A whole inch and don't you forget it."

"Fine, I won't. Now, go lay the tables."

"Yes, ma'am." Steve kissed her cheek, and fired off a mock salute, before grabbing the cutlery tray and heading out of the door.

She glanced back at the pastry. Twenty-three for dinner, so forty-six equal squares. Did she use her new lattice cutter on the top? Why not?

Having decided what to do, she worked quickly. The food was an important part of the Rainbow Lodge experience and she took great care to ensure it was right each time. And that meant three courses each evening. Tonight was melon boats to start, then a main of Russian fish pie, duchess potatoes, green beans and carrots, followed by hot trifle. The latter had to be one of her most popular dishes, made along the same principal as a baked Alaska.

Breakfast was cooked, with a different variation of the full English each day. She also offered packed lunches, and although not many people took her up on those, she always made new guests aware of the option at evening drinks.

She slid the pies into the oven and glanced at the clock. Precision timing as always.

"How are we doing?" Steve called.

"Starters are good to go, and twenty minutes on the mains."

"OK. Let's get them seated." He headed out and Hattie smiled as the gong sounded in the small hallway.

****

Having showered and changed, Cal followed the other guests down the stairs. He hoped it would be obvious where he was to sit. He filled his lungs with the delicious aromas coming from the ground floor. Whatever was cooking set his mouth watering in anticipation. He couldn't remember the last time he'd eaten for anything other than necessity. But just the smell of this meal had him wanting to eat.

A blond man stood at the door to the dining room

welcoming the guests. The likeness with Miss Steele was uncanny. Brother perhaps? The man held out a hand. "Good evening, Mr. Trant. I'm Steve Steele. Welcome to Rainbow Lodge."

Cal returned the smiled and handshake. "Thank you."

"Your table is number nine, right under the window. The same as your room number."

He crossed over to the table, nodding to a couple of the guests who smiled, obviously recognizing him. He sat, noticing the flowers and neatly laid table, with three sets of cutlery. The flowers matched the serviettes, each table a different color.

Once everyone was seated, Miss Steele spoke from the doorway. "Let's say grace."

*Wow, I wasn't expecting this, Lord, even though it's a Christian guest house.* He closed his eyes and bowed his head as Miss Steele prayed.

As Miss Steele and another woman began to serve the first course, Cal glanced around the room. A clock hung over the fireplace, texts and landscapes dotted the walls. In pride of place on the long wall, was a cross stich picture of the guest house. Around the edge was a border of nautical flags, spelling out the names of the lodge and the proprietors—Harriet, Steve, and Penny Steele.

Miss Steele put the starter in front of him. "Did you settle in all right?"

"Yes, thank you."

Her smile was genuine. "That's good. If you need anything, just shout."

He held her gaze, wanting to prolong the moment. "I was admiring the cross stich. It's beautiful. Did you do it?"

"No. I'm nowhere near talented enough to make something that amazing. One of the guests did it last summer. She and her husband have been coming for years now—ever since their honeymoon."

"It really is lovely. The flags spelling your names are a nice touch."

"You can read them?"

Cal smiled. "I have an interest in nautical things, so yes. And living on the coast it's hard not to know them."

"That's cool."

"You all have the same surname?"

"Yes, Steve's my twin and Penny is his wife. Enjoy the starter."

Cal looked down at the plate in front of him. The melon boat was beautifully arranged. The curved yellow shell, with cubes of melon, sails made of thin orange slices and cherries sat on waves made of curved lime slices. It looked much too good to eat. A lot of thought had gone into the presentation of the dish and he was almost tempted to take a photo of it and post it on his social media page.

Almost...

Instead, he ate it, savoring the ripe fruits and tangy lime combination. He didn't think it could be surpassed, but the fish pastry dish managed it. If this was a sign of things to come, he'd be putting on weight and need new uniform when he returned home.

Dessert arrived and curiosity got the better of him. He caught Miss Steele's attention as she passed him on her way back to the kitchen. "What is this? I haven't come across it before."

"Hot trifle."

He raised an eyebrow. They were two words he

wouldn't *ever* dream of putting in the same sentence under any circumstances. "*Hot* trifle?"

She smiled. "It's a firm favorite with the guests here. It doesn't have jelly in the bottom layer and has meringue instead of cream. And I promise not a nut in sight. Would you like tea or coffee to finish with?"

"Tea, please. I'm not a great lover of coffee."

"Nor me. Steve's the opposite. He hates tea and loves coffee."

"And the two of you are twins?"

"More like opposites." She laughed. "He's left handed. I'm right handed. So ordinary tea, Earl Grey or I have several fruit flavors if you'd prefer those?"

"Just ordinary is fine, thank you."

He smiled and watched Miss Steele head to the door, before he turned back to his dessert. It was by definition an opposite. Trifle should be cold not ho—

The thought cut off as he tasted his first bite. His mouth exploded with flavor such as he'd never imagined. It was perfect. Or as near perfection as it was possible to get this side of heaven. He had to get the recipe before he left. Yes, his waistline was definitely going to suffer. Mr. Steel was, without doubt, one well fed and very blessed man, to be married to a chef as good as this one.

He allowed himself a small smile. He'd never given himself the luxury of thinking marriage. He'd had his fair share of girls and was determined to stay single. For at least the next millennium. Women, in his experience, were only after one thing, and now he was right with God, that part of his life was over. He wasn't proud of it, but some mistakes were destined *never* to be repeated.

Besides, with his pager now going off any time of

day or night, three hundred and sixty-five days a year, usually at the most inopportune moment such as the middle of Christmas dinner, plus the dangerous nature of this other, voluntary job, no woman would want him now. Despite being a man in uniform and therefore swoon worthy as his sister constantly told him.

It was him, God, his carpentry, and his job as part of the crew on a lifeboat.

Launched in all weathers, but usually storms and gale force winds, the men and women of the Royal National Lifeboat Institution worked in conjunction with the coastguard, going out in the roughest of weather, where no helicopter or other seagoing vessel could, saving lives at sea, at the risk of their own. It was a very dangerous job, sometimes resulting in the death of the lifeboat crew, but he wouldn't change and do something safer for anything. Even though, unlike the coastguard, he and his crew mates did it for love, not money.

# 3

Breakfast served and over, the dishes finally stacked and the dishwasher set going, Hattie had five minutes in which to change before leaving for church, without being late. Steve and Penny had gone on ahead as they were giving out the hymnbooks. She finished her hair and dashed from the house, locking the front door behind her.

Church was a brisk fifteen minute walk away, or a more sedate thirty minute one. Today, she didn't have time for sedate. Not if she wanted to be on time. And she couldn't afford petrol in her car this week. Or next week either.

When she started working with Steve, she'd bought into the guest house with all her savings and had been under the impression she was a part owner. But the paperwork had never arrived and as the years passed, she just dropped the subject. She was paid a pittance. It was way less than the minimum wage, especially for the hours she put in and the lack of time off, but there was no point in saying anything, for fear of upsetting him. And it wasn't just because he was her twin, either.

He had a temper like none other, and had been known to sulk for days, ignoring her and then giving her far more work that she could cope with, by vanishing with Penny for days on end. Besides whenever she brought the subject up, Steve had an answer for everything. Each time she mentioned it, he had a very good reason for not paying her more. The roof needed doing or they needed to redecorate. Not that she ever saw any decorators or builders. She usually ended up doing that herself. But she had to ask for everything she needed. When it came to money, Steve kept tight lipped and his wallet padlocked. He dealt with that side of things— even going as far as controlling all the shopping and doing it himself— and always bought the cheapest things possible. Fortunately, she was a master at making something from nothing and her cooking skills only improved as a result.

As she kept up a brisk walk, her thoughts turned to her newest guest. He didn't seem anything like she imagined a footballer to be. And despite Steve's teasing, she wasn't attracted to Mr. Trant. Was she?

No, she wasn't. There was something about him, something she couldn't put her finger on, but he'd never be interested in her.

Besides, he was a guest and that was the end of it.

But still her imagination wandered. What would it be like to date someone like him? A world famous athlete who was a household name and got recognized everywhere he went. Did he get preferential treatment in theatres or restaurants? He was someone who'd been to places she could only dream about, never mind attempt to pronounce. The furthest abroad she'd ever been was a school geography trip to Interlaken in Switzerland when she was fifteen.

Holidays were spent with Aunt Laurie and Uncle Reg in their cottage on an island off the south coast of England. Someone famous would never fit into her quiet, boring existence, where the most exciting thing that happened was the washing machine breaking down or the freezer door being left open and the kitchen flooding.

She slid into the back row of Headley Baptist, and scanned the service sheet. Mrs. Jefferies was back in hospital again. She should go and visit her at some point. Aaron Field and Meaghan Knight were getting married in a few weeks. Perhaps she'd be able to take the afternoon off to attend the wedding.

There was a list of local churches on the noticeboard in the guest house, including this one, but she'd never run into any of her guests here. That was probably a good thing.

Enough of this—she wasn't here to worry about which church her guests attended. She opened her Bible to the passage Pastor Jack would be preaching on. Isaiah forty verses twenty-eight to thirty-one. She loved that passage and the imagery it provoked in her mind. *Those who hope in the LORD will renew their strength. They will soar on wings like eagles; they will run and not grow weary, they will walk and not be faint.* She read it through twice, closing her Bible as Pastor Jack rose to his feet on the platform.

Someone slid into the pew next to her just as the service started, but she didn't turn to look, knowing how much she hated the sidelong glances when she was late.

She stood to sing the first hymn, based on the passage she'd just read, and was more than a little surprised by the voice next to her. It couldn't be Mr. Trant, could it? She risked a sideways glance. It was.

\*\*\*\*

Cal had gotten lost trying to find the church. He'd perused the notice board after breakfast and found the list of churches. Admittedly, he'd done a search on churches in Headley Cross before leaving home and found the website for Headley Baptist, but he'd been pleased to find it listed at the guest house. Although this one was called a Baptist church, it was a member of the FIEC and thus more Evangelical than the strict Baptist church he'd grown up in.

His navigational skills had let him down after he left the map on his bed. He'd taken a left instead of a right somewhere and got hopelessly lost. He just prayed that the lads back at the lifeboat station never found out about this. He was the helm officer after all and he'd never live it down. Still, he'd found the church in the nick of time and took a seat on the end of a pew on the back.

And ended up sitting right next to Miss Steele. He felt rather than saw her glance at him during the first hymn. He turned his head towards her and smiled; the smile fading slightly as she blushed and looked down at her hymn book.

That was a reaction he hadn't seen in a while and had hoped he'd never see again. The 'Oh-Wow-I'm-Sat-Next-To-Callum-Trant' look that he hated so much, which had followed him around for so many years. Yes, adoring fans came with being famous, and most of the time he didn't mind. It was just women. He thought, hoped, that Miss Steele was different, but maybe all women were the same when it came to the adoring fangirliness. Unfortunately, all they would see would be the fame and fortune and not him. He turned back to the hymn, focusing his mind on his reason for being here.

As the children left after the first twenty minutes, he noticed a few of the older boys look at him twice and he smiled, flustering them. A few of the parents recognized him and nodded or smiled and he returned the smiles. Then he immersed himself fully in the service, finding the teaching speaking to him.

After the service, he sat in prayer for a moment. He straightened, reaching for the sheet, he'd tucked into the pew in front.

"How did you find the service?" Miss Steele's voice made him grin.

"Almost didn't," he said, playing on her words. "I got lost on the way here."

She giggled. "Oops. I'll have to put a better map on the leaflet."

"The map was fine—or it would have been. Except for the fact the leaflet it's on the back of is still on my bed."

"Ah. It's not much good there."

"No, not really." He rubbed the back of his neck. "But the real answer to your question is the service was good. Your pastor is a gifted man."

She smiled. "That he is. He's always full of joy and love and zeal for the Lord, no matter what is going on around him."

"Excuse me, sir?"

Cal turned. A kid of about fourteen stood there, several others partway down the aisle looking at him with anxious anticipation. He must have been elected spokesman and had hands shoved into his pockets, hopping nervously from one foot to the other.

Cal smiled to put him at his ease. "Hi."

"Are you Callum Trant?"

"Yes, I am."

The kid beamed and did a thumbs up at the others. "Told them you were him, but they didn't believe me. Can I have your autograph please?"

"Of course." Cal pulled a pen from his jacket pocket. Soon he had a whole gaggle of children there, but he kept signing, offering each one a smile and friendly word. After they left, he sat for a moment to compose himself.

"You could have said no."

He almost jumped, but caught himself in time. He'd forgotten she was there. "I could have, but that wouldn't have been the Christian thing to do. Jesus never turned anyone away when He was recognized."

"You're on holiday."

"Technically so was He, when He went across the lake to be alone. The crowds followed Him everywhere He went, but He still welcomed them."

Miss Steele nodded. "And He even fed them."

"All five thousand of them. So I can't begrudge a few kids an autograph. Besides, it doesn't happen as often now as it used to." He stood as rain started to pound against the church windows and laughed. "Another typical summer's day in England."

She nodded. "I'll see you at dinner. Don't forget it's an hour early tonight so I can make the evening service. Five o'clock rather than six."

"I'm looking forward to it. Oh, and before I forget, thank you so much for the extra tea in my room. I noticed last night you'd replaced the coffee with teabags."

"You're welcome. It makes sense as you don't drink coffee. Have a good day."

"You, too." He pulled his collar up and headed out into the storm. Lightning flashed and thunder roared shortly afterwards. The rain bounced off the pavement, splashing his legs. He walked the short distance to the café he'd planned on visiting for lunch. Storms here seemed almost tame by comparison to the ones he was used to at home. Yes, there was wind, driving rain, thunder and lightning, but with no twenty foot waves and his feet planted firmly on solid ground, there really was nothing to fear.

Was there anything on land that could rattle him?

*Falling in love* came the unbidden response. This was why he wasn't going to do it. He'd seen the fear in the eyes of the wives, girlfriends, and husbands as he and the others left parties, dinners and functions to go to sea.

He couldn't, wouldn't ever do that to anyone. Especially not to Miss Steele.

# 4

Hattie sat in church with her brother, seven days later, exhausted. She hadn't stopped all week. Every room was full, every bed taken and even with Steve and Penny working alongside her, the work never stopped.

However, half way through this week, Penny had gone to stay with her sister, Di, while her brother-in-law was away on maneuvers with the Territorial Army. One by one the children had fallen sick with chicken pox over the last several weeks, and now Di had gone down with it, too. Penny had had it, so she was the obvious choice to go and help. It just left them shorthanded.

The church was warm, and Hattie knew she'd be in serious danger of falling asleep during the sermon if she wasn't careful. This wasn't advisable, as Pastor Jack had a habit of randomly using members of the congregation as examples of his points. Never in a nasty way, but Hattie had a morbid fear of waking as he mentioned her name.

The previous Sunday evening, she'd stayed in and streamed the service over the internet. The service had gone seamlessly from Pastor Jack praying, to Pastor Carson preaching. The only problem was she hadn't heard the two hymns and Bible reading that came in between the two. And although she knew Pastor Jack's wicked sense of humor would love that, it was bound to end up in a sermon a few years down the line, if he ever found out. So it was best he never did.

Brown brogues appeared next to her black floral sneakers and she glanced up at their owner. Chocolate brown eyes sparkled at her and she smiled. "We must stop meeting like this. People will talk."

"Let them." He picked up her teasing tone and continued it. "I mean we see each other so many times a day as it is."

"Exactly my point," she said, trying not to laugh. "I do have my reputation to consider. This is a small town."

"Not as small as the one I live in."

His grin was infectious and oh so charming. They'd had celebrities stay at the guest house before, and she'd never been affected like this. What was wrong with her? She didn't even *like* football. So why did her pulse race, her breath catch and her stomach do cartwheels whenever she saw him?

He leaned closer to her. "Besides, surely being seen with me will do wonders for your street cred and your reputation. Everyone will want to sleep in the same room as the famous Callum Trant." He winked. "Although my brother would say that was infamous."

She tucked the service sheet over the edge of the book rack in the pew in front of her. "And you're so modest with it."

Cal grinned. "Modesty is one of my faults, I'm afraid."

Was he flirting with her? She found herself replying in kind. "Just one? How many faults do you have?"

"According to my sister, Jess, I have two. Sophie,

on the other hand, said she stopped counting at one hundred and fifty."

Hattie took off her cardigan and folded it before setting it on top of her bag under the pew in front of her. "Ouch. That's a rather big difference."

"That's the difference between sister and ex-girlfriend." He undid his jacket, revealing a white shirt and a plain navy blue tie with a crest of some kind on it. Not often these days you had a bloke wear a tie to church, unless he was preaching.

"Ah, yes, it would be. Not that I have a sister, except Penny."

"Sister-in-laws count just as much. But then, thinking about it, Jess's 'only two faults' is more of an insult than a compliment."

"How can two faults possibly be an insult, when too many to count isn't?" She furrowed her brow in confusion.

"Her favorite quote is *'women's faults are many while men have only two. Everything they say and everything they do.'* I get that at least twice a week, if not more frequently."

Hattie laughed quietly. "I shall have to remember that line and wind Steve up with it." She fell silent as the service began.

*He's so easy to talk to, Lord. My heart is running wild here reminding me he's a man, a striking man at that and I'm a woman. I admit I'm attracted to him. I don't think it's the fame thing. At least I hope I'm not that shallow. And he can't possibly be interested in me. Let my head overrule my heart here.*

Concentrating on the service was hard, but not just because she was tired. She was aware of Cal's every movement. The way his long tanned fingers held his

Bible and turned the pages. The angle his head was tilted at and the strands of hair falling across his eyes that her fingers itched to push back out of the way. And the way his left ankle hooked over his right knee, cradling his Bible.

She pushed a hand through her hair. She was here to worship God, not the attributes of the man next to her. Even if he was the first man to notice she was a woman and not part of the furniture. That's if they noticed her at all. She took a deep breath. If he was going to invade her thoughts this way, then she was going to pray for him.

As the service finished, she picked up her bag. All she wanted to do was go back home and sleep for a couple of hours before starting dinner.

Cal turned to her. "I was wondering if you had anything planned."

"Right now?" She held his gaze.

"Right now," he repeated. "Because if not, would you like to come for a walk along the river with me?"

"Me?" Flabbergasted, her mind froze and she was sure she had a stupid look on her face to match. And suddenly she wasn't as tired as she had been a few minutes earlier.

Cal nodded. "I don't make a habit of asking hoteliers out, but you're here and I'm here, the sun is shining and—"

"OK, thank you. A walk would be nice." She agreed quickly before he could change his mind.

"If nothing else it might enhance your street cred." He winked and her heart melted into a gooey mass on the floor by her feet.

From the other side of her, Steve caught her arm and squeezed it, an unspoken message that he needed a word.

"I need to speak to someone first."

Cal stood. "Sure. I'll wait outside."

Hattie smiled as he edged out of the pew and headed down the aisle. Then she twisted and raised an eyebrow at her brother. "Yes?"

His normally smiling eyes were hard and cold. "What do you think you're doing?"

"I'm going for a walk. I'll be back in time to make dinner, don't worry."

"He's a guest."

"I know that. What's your point?"

Steve's scowl deepened. "You're crossing a line. You don't date the guests. It's one of the rules, remember?"

"For crying out loud, it's not a date. I don't date anyone, do I? It's a walk." She reined in her irritation, remembering where she was. "Steve, is this just because of who he is?"

"Hattie, he lives differently to how we do. He's doubtless used to having a pretty girl on his arm and getting what he wants." He lowered his voice. "He's probably only after one thing."

"That's more than a little judgmental, don't you think? You don't know the first thing about who he really is. He's a Christian anyway." She lowered her voice. "He can hardly take me back to his hotel room now, can he?"

She stood up, pleased at the shocked look on her brother's face. "I thought you knew me better than that." Shouldering her bag, she stormed down the aisle, blinking hard.

Her own brother didn't trust her. Maybe she wouldn't bother to go back to the guest house at all and let him cope on his own. She hadn't even had ten minutes to herself all week, except when she slept, and he was begrudging her this?

But her sense of duty prevailed and kicked in hard. Just because Steve was being an idiot of the first degree, didn't mean everyone had to suffer. She loved her brother, she always would, but he really could be thoughtless at times. With him it was himself first, then money. Or was it money first, then self? It was hard to tell sometimes. Despite being his twin, she seemed to rate bottom of the pile.

She headed out into the bright sunshine and put her shades on to hide her tears. She shook hands with Pastor Jack on the door then crossed over to where Cal sat. "All done."

He nodded, sliding off the wall. "Shall we, Miss Steele?"

"Yes, let's." She glanced over her shoulder as she felt her brother glaring at her again, and then turned her attention to the bloke who wanted to spend time with her. Nothing would come of it, she knew that, but like he said, he was here and so was she. And it was *just* a walk. "And it's Hattie."

\*\*\*\*

Cal smiled at her. "Then you must call me Cal." He'd noticed the too bright and glistening eyes, as Miss Steele—Hattie he corrected— left the church, before she'd hidden them behind her shades. But being a gentleman he wasn't going to mention it. He assumed her brother had said something from the look he'd given the pair of them from the doorway, but again he wasn't going to ask.

"Cal?"

"Short for Callum. It's what my friends call me. And I'd like to think you're a friend, Hattie."

"Thank you, Cal. Did you get lost on your way here again, this morning?" Her voice wobbled slightly before she managed to get it on an even keel.

He laughed. "No, I remembered the map this time. I'm one of the rare breed of men who learn from their mistakes."

"Where are we going?"

"Along the river, if that's all right? And I brought a big enough picnic for two. Although I'm not averse to eating it all if needs be."

"Both sound wonderful." She eased her shoulders slightly. "I could do with a break."

"Busy week?"

"No more so than usual, but with Penny away since Tuesday, the work load increased a fair bit."

"I didn't think I'd seen her. She isn't sick, is she?"

Hattie pressed the button at the road crossing. "No, her sister is though. Her brother in law has gone away on maneuvers with the TA. Penny's gone to look after Di and the kids."

"Did she have to go far?"

Hattie nodded. "Not too far away. They live about forty-five miles from here. Normally Di manages fine by herself when Brendan's away, but with a small baby, and being sick, she needed a hand this time."

"I can understand that." He paused. "I know people sometimes mock the TA's, but they are just as important as the regular army blokes."

She nodded. "Yeah, they are. Brendan loves doing it. Says it gives him a focus outside of home and work and is a way for him to give something back to his country."

The lights changed and they crossed the road. "How many children do they have?"

"Five, including the baby. Penny says Di's rushed off her feet with the four little ones as it is, doesn't know how they'll manage with five. The oldest is eleven."

"Wow, that's a lot of kids." Cal glanced at her. From the look on her face it was a painful subject so he changed it. "So, where does an hotelier go on holiday? Another hotel or is that too much of a busman's holiday?"

"Definitely a busman's holiday and not my scene." She paused. "I was meant to go away fairly soon, but whether that will happen now I don't know."

"Oh?"

"Steve's talking about going to go and help Penny, the week I wanted to go away. And he doesn't like us all being away at the same time."

He glanced at her. Her shoulders had slumped and she looked downcast at the thought of missing out on her trip. *So much for picking a neutral subject, Cal Nice one.* "Won't that leave you on your own if he goes?"

"He's talking about possibly getting someone in to help, but..." She shrugged. "I'll just have to see how things go I guess."

"Is your holiday booked?"

"I'm staying with my aunt so it's flexible. As far as he's concerned, it's just driving to the coast and staying with family and not a holiday. Therefore it's not booked in the proper sense of the word and doesn't count."

"If it was booked anywhere else, or you had flights or something, you wouldn't be able to change it so

33

easily."

Hattie held his gaze. "I know. And yes, he does take advantage, but he's my brother and—"

He nodded. "It makes it harder to put your foot down and insist on some me time, doesn't it? But everyone needs a break. Even you. So pick another week, book it and don't tell him where you're going."

"That's an idea. Maybe I will."

"You could still go stay with your aunt, just don't tell him that until you get there."

Hattie nodded. "I might just do that when I get home. Thank you."

"You're welcome." A faint smile crossed her lips.

His heart leapt at the thought of having made her smile. The gravel path crunched under his feet as they began to walk along the river. He undid his jacket and checked his camera and phone were secure in the inside pocket. "I don't remember the last time I had a holiday."

"Really?" She sounded amazed. "Surely you'd have gone away during the off season?"

Cal laughed. He pulled off his tie and rolled it, before sliding it into his pocket. "There rarely is an off season in football anymore. Especially with all the European, and World Cup matches there are now. Not to mention the friendlies and even Olympics."

Her grin lit her face. "Even when England always got knocked out in the first round?"

"Especially then." He smiled back, moving aside to let a woman jogger pass them. "You may mock, but it's not easy having the hopes and dreams of an entire nation on your shoulders all the time. Every British tennis player will tell you that."

"True. It's been a long time since we won any

singles titles. At least on home soil."

He undid the first two buttons on his shirt. "But winning isn't everything. It's the taking part that matters."

Hattie looked at him, brows arched in shock.

"What's that look for?" He stopped and sat on a bench. He patted the space beside him.

She sat, her perfume wafting over him. "I just didn't expect to hear you say that. I thought winning would mean everything to you. The 'be all and end all' kind of everything."

"At one point maybe. You get so caught up in the whole—" he gesticulated, trying to think of the correct word "—shebang, that it's just a massive cycle it's not easy to break out of. It's like your whole life is dominated by being here simply to score and win matches. Some players are just so driven by the bonuses that they do anything to win."

"Like cheat and dive all the time to get penalties and free kicks?"

He took a deep breath, looking back out over the river and the ducks swimming on the surface. "Some do, I never did. The whole 'ref he tripped me up' routine used to annoy me something chronic and it still does. In fact, when I was captain, I used to forbid the team to do it. I'd make a point of telling them that if they go down, unless they're physically incapable of it, they get up and carry on."

"Too right. That's why I prefer rugby." She paused and put her hand over her mouth, blushing in a most delightful manner. "Oops."

He roared with laughter. "I'll pretend I didn't hear that."

She laughed with him. "Sounds good to me."

Cal opened his backpack and pulled out the sandwiches he'd bought. He offered her one. "I hope cheese and tomato is all right."

"Cheese and tomato is great, thank you. My favorite combination."

He smiled and pulled out two bottles of juice. He gave her one and said grace. He opened his sandwich and turned his attention back to the river. "It really is beautiful here."

Hattie followed his gaze. "It is. Have you seen the abbey ruins yet?"

"No, I haven't." He glanced at her. "I didn't even realize Headley Cross had an abbey."

"It was destroyed during the dissolution of the monasteries. The stones gradually got used in other buildings over the years, but there's still a fair amount left. The gardens are beautiful."

"I will have to go and see them. Whereabouts are they?"

Hattie tilted her head and pointed. "See that stone bridge just over there? Go under there and you're in the gardens. The abbey is just beyond them."

"I shall go and see them tomorrow. Thank you."

"Welcome. Then a little further downstream is the weir. That is really worth seeing, even on a calm day like today. During a storm it's incredible."

"I'm sure it is. How far along is it?"

"Not far. Five minutes if that. I'll show you once we've eaten."

"I'd like that. Have you always wanted to run a guest house?"

She sipped the juice. "No. I wanted to be a ballerina."

"Really? You dance?"

"Not anymore. I loved ballet and even though I say so myself, I was pretty good at it and used to get the lead a fair amount. But I broke my leg when I was fourteen. I fell out of a tree and after six weeks in a cast, I couldn't go en-point anymore. They didn't know why. The break had healed perfectly, without the need for surgical intervention. I just didn't have the strength in my lower legs any longer. I was heartbroken."

"I bet you were. Dare I ask why you were climbing a tree at the age fourteen?" He took another bite of his sandwich.

"I was trying to impress my brother's friend."

He tilted his head. "Did it work?"

Hattie laughed wryly. "Oh it worked all right. He was so impressed by my inability to climb a tree that he never spoke to me again. Of course, it didn't help that I landed on his brand new skateboard and broke it, either."

He pointed his bottle at her. "His loss."

"In more ways than one. I decided at that point that boys weren't worth it."

"Really?"

She finished her sandwich and rubbed her hands on her skirt. "Yep. I mean I ruined what could have been a glittering career."

"And a skateboard," he added, collecting the rubbish together.

"And a skateboard," she said wryly, brushing the crumbs off her lap. "And for what? To attempt to get the attention of someone who never spoke to me again, even after we replaced it. I have remained uninterested in the male of the species ever since." She stood. "Shall we go and see the weir?"

"Sure." He dumped the rubbish in a bin and slid

his back pack on again.

They started walking, his hand inches from hers. He had no compulsion to hold it, like the old Cal would have done. He was content simply to be with her, enjoy the moment and her company. "What did you do once your leg healed?"

"I left the dance academy and started at the local comprehensive school. I chose different exam courses, ones that didn't involve music or dance or sport. Then I went to college and did catering, purely because I liked cooking and the teacher said I was good at it. Steve always wanted to run a guest house, and when the lodge came on the market, he bought it on a whim. As I was a qualified caterer, he asked me to help. So I put all my savings into helping buy it and started working there."

*Wait a minute…She cooked? Was she really responsible for all the wonderful meals I've had over the past few days?*

"Do you enjoy it?"

"Most of the time. Some days I'd rather do something else, but I guess that's like any job and here we are at the weir."

"Yes, here we are." He leaned over the barrier, looking down at the fast flowing water tumbling and pounding over the rocks. "That is amazing."

"And it's relatively calm today."

"It must be awesome during a storm."

"It is. And after a lot of rain, as well. The water comes off the Downs and pours through here."

"Does it flood?"

"Sometimes, yeah. I've got some photos of the whole area under a good two feet of water that I took last winter."

Cal watched two children playing along the

water's edge. Their parents stood close by, keeping tabs on them. He automatically scanned the riverside for lifebelts and buoys and shook his head as both marked posts were empty. "Someone should tell the council that the lifebelts are missing."

Hattie followed his gaze. "The kids keep stealing them. They end up in trees or on roof tops, but I'll call them when we get in."

He nodded, deciding to do the same thing. The more people that complained, the better chance there was of the equipment being replaced. The problem was they needed to be accessible to everyone all the time and therefore couldn't be locked away to keep them safe.

The two children ran along the edge, tossing the ball back and forth. The water thundered and twisted beneath them.

He pulled out his camera and took several photographs, wondering about taking one of Hattie without her noticing. Deciding against it, he shot her what he hoped was a winning smile. "Pose for me? It'd make a good picture for your wall in the dining room. I noticed there isn't one of the weir there."

"Sure."

He lined up the shot and took several photos at differing angles. As he put the camera back in its case, there was a scream and a loud splash. Glancing down, he saw one child on the river bank and a brief glimpse of a dark head in the raging torrent below.

Instinctively he shoved the camera at Hattie, stripped off his jacket, and toed off his shoes. He climbed onto the railing, took three rapid deep breaths, prayed the water was deeper than it looked, and dived in.

# 5

The water was cold and sent ripples of shock searing through Cal. His fingertips grazed the base of the river bed as he pushed upwards. He surfaced and glanced around, not seeing the child. One of the adults on shore pointed to his left. The current was stronger than he realized, trying to pull him downstream towards the weir. And if it was having that effect on him, being such a strong swimmer, then a child wouldn't stand a chance.

He caught a glimpse of something red, and swam hard in that direction. It vanished just as he reached it and he dived down to search. Grabbing hold of it, he kicked for the surface. Terrified eyes looked at him. He drew in a deep breath. "You're all right. I've got you. Hold on to me tightly."

"O−K..."

Cal started for the shore. The weir was getting closer and the last thing he wanted to do was go over it. Rescues were second nature to him and inch by inch, with telegram prayers, he gained precious distance between him and the weir.

Finally, he was within touching distance of the bank. Arms stretched towards him and he handed the child to his parents. He hauled himself up. Water streamed from his clothes, and dripped from his hair into his eyes. He rubbed both hands over his face, his breathing coming hard and fast. A crowd had gathered and applause broke out.

Ignoring them and the way his body shook as the adrenaline began to drain from his system, he hunkered down next to the child whose mother was now sobbing and holding him tightly. He sucked in a deep, teeth-chattering breath. "Are y-you OK?"

"Y-yes." The wide-eyed child coughed, clinging to his mother.

"Th-that's good. I'm Cal..." He held out a hand.

The child held it tightly. "T-T-Thomas."

Cal grinned. "That's a good name." As he stood, Thomas's father touched his hand.

"Thank you so much for saving him."

"You're w-welcome." He shook the man's hand. "I'm just g-glad I w-was there."

"Cal!"

He turned as a panicked Hattie came running over to him, carrying his shoes and jacket. He attempted a reassuring smile. "We're OK, j-just wet."

An ambulance with lights and sirens going pulled up, and he moved out of the way. "I need to g-get back and ch-change."

"Shouldn't you get checked over too?"

He shook his head, glad all the attention was now on Thomas and not him. "Let's just g-go. I d-d-don't want a f-fuss." He shook hard as he put his jacket and shoes on, cold despite the warmth of the sun.

Hattie looked concerned, but she didn't argue as he took the pack from her and they slid away.

As they walked, Cal's breathing gradually slowed, but he couldn't stop shaking.

Hattie touched his hand. "You're freezing."

"It's n-nothing a hot s-shower won't f-fix."

She nodded. "Are you a lifeguard or something?

You knew what to do and did it without thinking. Almost as if it was second nature to you."

He chuckled. "Not exactly, but I have done lifeguard training." He managed a whole sentence without stuttering, but didn't imagine it would last. "And like I said, I live by the s-sea, so swimming is kind of an essential thing to know."

"Good thing you were there."

He shrugged. "I'm sure s-someone else would have reacted. It's just I got there first. The council r-really needs to get that lifebelt back. It was touch and go as to whether we got pulled by the c-current."

The cold, wet shirt stuck to his skin, and he shivered hard.

"Are you all right?"

"Just c-cold. Sorry to cut the walk s-short."

"Don't be silly. I'm just thanking God that you and the little boy are all right. I thought you were going over the weir at one point."

"Yeah, m-me too."

By the time they reached the guest house, Cal was frozen and, despite the warmth of the sun, couldn't feel his hands or feet. He shivered continually, his teeth chattering.

Hattie unlocked the door. "Go and run a hot bath. I'll bring up a tray of tea and some warm soup in twenty minutes or so. I'll put your wet things through the washer and drier too. And don't argue. The river isn't the cleanest thing to go swimming in."

"Thank you." He headed up the stairs, hoping he'd be able to unlock his room, never mind turn the taps and remove his clothes. In which case he'd stand under the shower fully dressed until the feeling returned to his hands.

He was glad the little boy was all right and grateful the Lord had spared both their lives. He just hoped the incident was over and done with now and no one got wind of it.

****

Hattie gave him just over twenty minutes before she carried a tray of tea and hot asparagus soup up to his room. She knew it was his favorite because he'd mentioned it at dinner a few nights ago. She balanced the tray on one arm and knocked on the door. Not getting an answer, she let herself in.

The bathroom door was shut and she smiled at the voice raised in song coming from behind it. He really did have the most amazing singing voice. She set the tray on the side with a note asking him to knock on her door when he came down and reminding him to bring his wet clothes as well. She wouldn't have been surprised if he wasn't going to bother.

She returned to the kitchen. Steve's note still leaned against the bread bin. She'd found it there when she got back from the weir.

*Hattie, I've gone to help Penny and stay overnight. I'll be back in the morning at some point. Steve.*

Short, sweet and to the point. Not to mention taking the biscuit. It left her having to do everything. And, of course, she'd put a roast in the oven to slow cook before leaving for church. It was just like Steve, though. She'd dared to take a couple of hours to herself, and he didn't like it, and this was pay back. Sometimes knowing him so well was a curse.

*What do I do, Lord? Do I leave the meat and do cold cuts tomorrow and serve the guests a salad tonight? Or do I prove to him I can manage and just do it?*

She pulled over the booking diary and checked ahead. There were two weeks when only two rooms were taken. Cal was right. She needed a break. Steve and Penny could manage those weeks, or find someone else. Two could play at that game. She crossed out the rest of the rooms and picked up the phone to call her aunt.

"Hello?" Her aunt's cheerful voice made her smile.

"Hi, Aunt Laurie, it's Hattie. How are you?"

"Hello, dear, I'm fine. How are you?"

"Been better, rushed off my feet today."

"I keep telling you, you work too hard. You need more staff than just the three of you at this time of year. Steve takes you for granted."

Hattie sighed. "Especially today. But I love him anyway."

"I know you do. Are you still coming to visit in a couple of weeks? I know you weren't going to mention it right off, but this isn't your normal day for a chat either."

"Steve wants to go away with Penny then—or rather go and help her with Di's kids. Brendan's away on maneuvers and Di's sick. So between that and the new baby, Di needs the help. Penny left on Tuesday. I don't begrudge her going. She's the only one of her siblings who's had chicken pox so Di's need is greater than mine."

"What about you though? Won't that leave you alone when Steve goes? Or will he get someone in to help this time?"

"I'll just have to manage." Hattie shrugged. "Anyway..."

"You need a rest. And a holiday, just as much as

anyone else."

"You're the second person to tell me that today."

"Then take it as the Lord directing you to take time off. When are you coming? Pick a different week—actually two weeks."

"You know me too well. I have the diary open in front of me. How does the last week of September, and the first week of October sound?"

"That looks wonderful. Can Steve spare you?"

"Probably not, as he insists I'm indispensable." She sighed. "But it's tough. They have four people booked in those two weeks, and if I can do twenty-three alone, they can manage four between the two of them."

"Twenty-three? Alone?" Her aunt sounded incredulous. "I know you said Penny is away, but where's Steve today then?"

"We had a disagreement and he took off, same as he always does. The thing is, I wanted to go out for a couple of hours and he didn't approve. And if it sounds like I'm complaining—"

"It's because you are. What did you do? Date a guest or something?" Her aunt's tone was teasing, but she'd unwittingly hit the proverbial nail on its head.

Hattie paused. "It's been a rough week. I haven't stopped for a minute. Steve and I had a fight after church, because someone asked me to go for a walk with him. OK, he's a guest, but I know the rules. It was just a walk. And he ended up jumping in the weir to save a kid's life."

"Steve did?"

She laughed. "No, the guest. His name's Cal and he's kind of cute for an ex-footballer. But it was just a walk, nothing more. Thing is, Steve knew I was doing a roast, and he up and left me to feed twenty-three anyway. Just to prove a point."

"Will he be back to help you serve?"

"No. His note said he *might* be back for breakfast. Though if he is, it'll be a miracle. But I'll manage tonight. I'll set it out buffet style. It won't kill them, just once."

"A buffet roast?"

"Like the carvery. I'll plate the meat, then they do the veggies themselves."

"Ah, yes, with you now. Anyway, dear, I shall let you get on. I'll see you at the end of September. Don't let anyone stop you from coming. If Steve says something, tell him to take it up with me."

"I will." After a few minutes more, Hattie hung up, a smile on her face. Somehow talking to Aunt Laurie always made her feel better. She pulled out the heated hostess trolley and plugged it in to start warming up. This would also cut down on the amount of dishes she had to wash up afterwards.

She busied herself with chopping veggies and making the quick setting jelly for the mandarin tarts. The cream could wait until the last minute before being piped on. She kept half an eye on the time, needing to adjust when she did things to ensure everything was done, but there just wasn't enough time. The doorbell rang just as she finished the tarts. Wiping her hands on her apron she went to answer it.

Cal stood there, tray in his hands and a carrier bag looped around his fingers, looking decidedly warmer than he had. He smiled at her.

She smiled back. "Hey. You look a lot better."

"I feel it. I thought I'd bring this down for you."

"Thank you. There was no need though." She took

the tray.

"Well I figured I was coming this way anyway." He held out the bag. "The wet clothes you insisted on having."

Hattie set the tray down and took the bag. "Thank you. I'll have them back to you tomorrow if that's OK."

"Tomorrow's fine, thank you. Something smells good."

"Thank you. I'm hoping it'll taste good, but I'm running late."

"That's probably my fault for taking you for that walk."

"Not at all," she said honestly. "Steve's gone to see Penny, and I'm trying to do everything by myself."

Concern flickered in his handsome chocolate eyes. "Can I help? I'm pretty good in the kitchen, if I do say so myself."

"I can't ask you to do that. You're a guest."

"You're not asking. I'm offering."

She thought quickly. She would never be ready by five on her own. By six maybe, but everyone would be expecting the meal at five. "Can you carve?"

"Like a pro." He grinned.

Hattie swallowed her pride and nodded. "Then, please, some help would be good. I've never been late with a meal yet, and I'm nowhere near ready."

"Sure. Show me what you need me to do."

Hattie picked up the tray again and led him into her part of the house, down the short passageway to the kitchen. She set the tea tray down on the side and put the bag on the floor to deal with after dinner. She was aware of his eyes glancing around, taking in the décor and furniture and she was glad the house was clean and tidy.

She checked the oven and pulled out the meat. Then she stabbed the veggies with a knife to see how cooked they were. "I figured self-service for the veg from the heated trolley tonight. I can do dessert same as usual. But there won't be a starter as I don't have time."

"What were you going to do?"

"Ganoush with ciabatta toast, but I don't have time to make the ganoush now."

"You have the ciabatta bread already?"

"I made it this morning."

"What about salad?"

"I have baby tomatoes, but that's it."

"So make bruschetta."

She looked at him. Something that simple hadn't occurred to her. "Seriously?"

He grinned. "Why not? I love it. Toast the ciabatta on one side and top with the tomatoes. If you're doing a roast, it's not going to be too heavy either. And it's something you can put on the table before people come in."

"Sounds like a brilliant idea. Thank you."

His smile melted her again. She'd knock the evening meal off his bill for this. His lips started moving again and she forced herself to concentrate on what he was saying. "...And as for tea and coffee after the meal? Fill the flasks like you do at breakfast and set them out when you bring dessert through. People can serve themselves when they want that way."

"You are just full of good ideas tonight. Want a job?"

He laughed. "I'll think about it." He began carving, neat deft strokes that were far quicker and far better than Steve could do.

She sliced and toasted the bread and added the tomatoes. She didn't know why she'd never thought of this before. Such a simple idea, yet the food looked so pretty, especially with the small sprinkle of herbs on the top. She took them through and looked at Cal in surprise. She thought he was still in the kitchen. "How did you get in here?"

He winked. "Through the door whilst you were busy singing and making the bruschetta. I finished carving and thought I'd lay up in here." He took the tray. "I'll do this, you go and get the other one."

"Thank you." She paused, mortified. "Singing? I was singing?"

"Very nicely as it happened."

"Oh." Her cheeks burned. Why would the floor never open up and swallow her whole when she wanted it to? "I'm sorry."

"Don't apologize. I liked listening to you sing. I'll even give you a hand with the dishes afterwards."

"There's no need."

"You're on your own, there is every need." He grinned. "I might even be persuaded to sing along next time."

She went and got the other tray, not sure what she'd done to deserve someone being this nice to her. And not just any someone either. He really was nothing like the Callum Trant she'd read about on the internet. That Callum seemed to do nothing but wine, women, and party. Almost every picture and article she'd read had him linked to a different woman.

But Cal was the total opposite. Almost as if he was a changed man. Perhaps he was. Maybe God had worked in his life, turning him around completely. She didn't much care for the footballer, but the man who'd given up part of his holiday to help her, the man who'd leapt into the raging water to save a child he didn't know without so much as a second thought...? Now that was a man she could care for.

She went back to the dining room, and Cal took the tray from her, finishing the tables off.

"I can't find my camera. Do you still have it?"

"Yes. I put it in my bag for safe keeping. Come back with me, and I'll give it to you."

He walked with her. "Thank you. Can I ask a favor?"

"After all your help this afternoon getting dinner ready, you can ask anything."

He smiled. "Don't tell anyone about this afternoon."

"About you helping me out in the kitchen?"

"No, I mean about me rescuing that kid. I don't want the press getting wind of it and turning it into something it isn't."

She tilted her head, confused as she opened the door. "Why ever not? It's something to be proud of."

"I don't want a fuss made and if word gets out, then people will realize who I am and it'll be splashed all over the papers. The kid and his family don't need that." He paused. "Besides I've done my fair share of being headline news. It's someone else's turn now."

She smiled, and pulled his camera from her bag. "OK, Mr. Anonymous Hero, my lips are sealed."

"Thank you." He kissed her cheek.

Flustered, she looked at him. It should be her thanking him for his help, not the other way around.

"I'll go before someone sees me and then you can ring the bell for dinner. The meat is in the trolley keeping warm."

"Thank you." She watched him leave, her hand covering her cheek. She could still feel the imprint of his lips. He made her feel like a normal person and even though she was working, time with him had flown by and she'd loved it. It was just a shame it could go no further.

# 6

By the time his two week holiday was over and it was time to go home, Cal was convinced his trousers were a little snugger around the waist. He'd certainly eaten better than he had in a long time, and far more than he'd normally eat. But that's what holidays are for, right? He could easily lose any excess weight when he got back in the gym.

He was going home both spiritually and physically refreshed. He was going to miss the Steeles—Hattie in particular and not just her cooking either. If only things were different. He'd enjoyed the Sunday afternoon they'd spent together immensely. In fact, he'd go as far as to say it was the highlight of his time there. He couldn't remember the last time he'd been with a woman and not wanted anything more than just friendship. Not that he'd turn away anything else if it came along, but the likelihood of seeing Hattie again, was microscopic.

Cal pulled himself up short. That sounded wrong, even to him and he was the only person privy to his thoughts. Well, that wasn't true either as God knew what he was thinking. He didn't mean the kind of relationships he'd had before. His whole life had changed since then. He was a new creation and proud of that fact.

He'd hoped to say goodbye to her in person, but Steve had been there and said Hattie was out. So he would write instead. On the station concourse, he spent ages looking at the cards, so long in fact that he almost missed his train. He chose one of the weir, paid and then got on the train with seconds to spare. He stored his large case in the luggage rack by the door and then made his way down the swaying carriage to his reserved seat.

For once there was no one sitting in it. Putting the small case in the overhead rack, he set his rucksack on the table and then slid into his seat. He looked out of the window as the train pulled out of Headley Cross. Once the houses were replaced by countryside, he set the card on the table and pulled out a pen.

By the time he got further than *Dear Hattie*, he was half way home and the lid of the pen was chewed beyond recognition. *Oh come on, Cal. At this rate you'll be home before you say anything. How hard can it be?*

*Very* he replied, before deciding he was clearly insane for having a conversation with himself.

He glanced down. *Thank you for a wonderful time* he wrote. *Definitely the best holiday I've had in years. I will be back. Cal Trant.*

Then he closed his eyes, knowing he couldn't sleep past his station as he lived at the end of the line. He woke just as the carriages rattled over one of the twin bridges that separated Penry Island from the mainland. The locals called the rail bridge Nessie, after its humped high girders and the road bridge Spiky after its suspension pillars.

He gazed from the window as his island home grew nearer. He'd lived here all his life and loved it. One of the bigger islands off England's south coast, the sea around the northern edge turned to mud flats at low tide. The rest of the island had an idyllic mix of both sand and shingle beaches, incredibly good for surfing, but hid a rip tide and sadistic current, which caught many a sailor and swimmer unawares.

Cal lived in one of the smaller villages on the eastern edge of the island, within sight of the bridges, where everyone knew everyone else and all the small details of their lives. Most times he hated it, but it did have its advantages. If someone hadn't been seen for a day or so, neighbors checked on them. That level of care and friendship had saved several lives last winter.

The train was buffeted by the wind and Cal glanced up at the sky. It looked as if a huge storm were building. He'd best drop off his case, then drive down to the lifeboat station and pick up his pager.

Although he wasn't on duty until Tuesday morning, it wouldn't hurt to let them know he was back on the grid.

The carriage was empty as he pulled down his small case and went to retrieve the larger one from the luggage rack. Rain pounded the windows as the train halted and he quickly stepped down onto the platform.

Carter stood waiting and enveloped him in a manly hug. "Missed you, bro."

"Nah. You just missed having no one to tease."

"You know me too well. Come on, there are heaps of things to tell you."

"Heaps?" he asked, amused. "I was only gone two weeks. How can heaps possibly happen in a dead end village like this one?"

Carter took one of the cases and started walking. "Joanne in the post office is expecting again. So is Mrs. Firth. Peter Johansson had a heart attack, but he's doing better now and should be home next week. Dr. Kneebone, my orthopod, says my knee is fine now. So I can start training again tomorrow."

Cal trundled the other case behind him, stifling the grin at the doctor's name. So apt, but Carter never got the joke. "Can we go via the base and pick up my pager. I'm back up crew until Tuesday and there's bound to be a call out tonight."

"Blue Watch is on duty until Tuesday at 0700 and you're still officially on leave."

"I know, but old habits—"

"Speaking of old habits, how was your holiday?"

"It was really good. You'd love it there. There are plenty of places to go riding, including some fairly steep hills called the Downs. And the lodge was amazing. The woman who helps run it and does the cooking—"

"She's pretty. Harriet Steele, blonde, bit younger than you, of Rainbow Lodge, Headley Cross."

Cal stopped dead under a shelter. How did he know? "I'm sorry?"

Carter pulled a folded newspaper cutting from his pocket. "*Lifeboat hero is never off duty*," he read. "*Found on Eliza Craig's blog, and printed with her permission, these photos show the dramatic moment that one of our dedicated lifeboat crew, and former England footballer, Callum Trant, leapt into a weir to save the life of her six year old son, Thomas Craig.*"

"*What?* Let me see that." Cal snatched the paper and read the rest of the article in dismay. There were pictures of him in the water, one with Thomas and one with Hattie.

"So? What's the story behind the one in the paper then?"

"You read it here. There's nothing much else to tell." Cal gave the paper back. "We went for a walk after church, the kid fell in the water, and I pulled him out. End of story. Can we go home now?"

"You wanted to pick up your pager."

The change of subject wasn't going to fool him for an instant. He hesitated. "Has everyone seen this?"

"Oh, yeah. Jim from the *Courier* made sure of that. And Alba helped a lot."

Cal sighed. Jim was a member of White Watch, which meant everyone at the station would have seen it. And then some. Probably also framed it and put it on the noticeboard for good measure. And Alba ran the village store and spread the local news faster than a speeding bullet, jungle drums or the internet. "Then, no, I don't want to pick up my pager. Like you said, I'm on holiday until Tuesday." He ignored the stunned look on his brother's face and headed back out into the rain towards his brother's car. "They can tease me about it then."

Carter followed him. "You like her."

"I *like* a lot of women."

"No, Cal. She's different. I can tell."

Cal stopped, the driving rain sticking the hair to his head. "It's not like I'm ever going to see her again. It was a few conversations as she served meals and one walk that got interrupted." And one afternoon spent cooking in her kitchen, but he wasn't going to mention that. She also had a very protective older brother.

"And…"

"Yes, OK, fine. I admit it. She's not like any of the others. She's different."

Carter smirked. "I think you've finally grown up, little bro. Women are not objects to be desired and used and thrown aside."

Lightning split the sky and thunder crashed

overhead almost immediately. It was as if a cosmic light bulb switched on over his head like in the cartoons he'd watched as a child. Lost for words he just nodded.

Carter thumped his shoulder. "That's great. Now, let's get out of this storm before we drown. I want to see your photos. And I don't care what you say; I want to know what this Hattie is really like. You can also tell me all the details about the rescue you did. And more importantly, those cycle routes. Maybe you and I go check them out."

"Me? On a bike?"

"Yes, you, on a bike." Carter laughed. "It'd be just like when we were kids."

"OK." Cal followed him slowly. He'd just have to make him promise not to tell anyone. The last thing he wanted was anyone else finding out. Though on reflection, if it was all over the internet and in the *Courier*, that would be like shutting the barn door after the horse had bolted.

# 7

Hattie sat in the kitchen nursing her tea, the menu for the coming week on the table in front of her. It had been a month and she still couldn't get Cal Trant out of her mind. What was it about the former footballer that held her attention after so long? There was no chance she'd see him again, not unless he rebooked for next year. And even then, Steve would prevent her seeing him. He'd probably refuse the booking.

She just wished she knew what her brother had against her dating, or just seeing a bloke as a friend. If she didn't know better, she'd think he was trying to set her up with Markus Kerr. She hadn't seen him in years, not since the last family holiday to Penry Island to stay with her aunt. Now, Steve managed to bring Markus into the conversation at least twice a day. And his name didn't even start with a P.

The postcard Cal had sent of the weir was still attached to the fridge with a magnet. Alongside one Aunt Laurie had sent of the local lifeboat station. She looked down at the menu again, only glancing up as Steve came in and called her name.

"Hattie, when do you go away again?"

"Day after tomorrow," she replied. And it couldn't come soon enough. She loved her job, but needed a break. Plus, Steve had been on her case ever since Cal left. She put this down to him being his normal irritating self. She'd never known anyone to sulk and hold a grudge the way Steve did. She hadn't even had an afternoon off in the last month. "You know that very well. You've only got two rooms booked, that's a total of four guests. I've done your menus to fit around the shopping you've already bought. You'll be fine."

"That's the thing. I've just got off the phone with a late booking. A returning client wanted to bring a small conference or house party. He'd been let down by the hotel he'd originally booked and needed somewhere quickly. We had the rooms vacant, and somewhere they could use for the talks, so he took them."

Hattie stiffened and her grip tightened on the mug. She hadn't heard the phone ring, but this was just typical. "I knew you'd do this," she hissed, trying not to let her anger erupt.

"What?" Steve looked at her innocently, but she wasn't falling for it. Not this time. "The rooms were empty," he continued, "and the church needed them and—"

"They were empty for a reason, Steve!" she yelled. "I need a holiday. I've already cancelled it once. I have put eighteen months solid into this place whilst you and Penny have been away for days on end at least three times this past year, if not more than that. I do the lion's share of the work around here and I'm worn out."

"That's not fair. We work just as hard as you do."

"That's codswallop and you know it! I'm not cancelling again. I'm not going to lose my holiday, forfeit my deposit, travel costs or anything else any more. If I could go early I would."

She barely paused for breath. "I am tired of being

taken for granted. You assume I'll just forgo my holiday to run around after you time after time, when you both go away and don't bother to arrange any extra help at all. You drop additional guests on me, expect me to make some marvelous meal out of nothing and work three hundred and sixty-five days a year for what amounts to pocket money. I'm tired of it."

Steve looked stunned that she'd finally snapped and let him have it with both barrels. His jaw dropped. Then he put his hands on his hips and glared at her belligerently. "What am I meant to do? I can't let them down, not after one hotel has already cancelled on them. I promised them those rooms. I need your help."

"You should have thought of that when you saw the weeks blanked off with *Hattie away* across the top of the pages." She took a deep breath. It was time she put her foot down and stood up to him. "Hire someone."

"Where from?"

"I don't know and I don't care." She slammed the cup down. "You know what? I'm going to leave now. Well, as soon as I've packed. I'll drive and find a Travelodge or something for the next couple of nights." In reality, Aunt Laurie wouldn't mind her going a couple of days early, but if Steve knew that's where she was going, he'd badger her until she relented to remain here and work. She pushed the chair back and stood.

"What about dinner?"

"You're a big boy. You do it." She stamped out of the kitchen and let the door slam shut behind her. Angry tears burned her eyes as she ran up the stairs. How could Steve be so selfish? What was wrong with him? Was this her fault, because she had never stood up to him before? No, she decided. It wasn't her fault. It was bullying, pure and simple and it ended. Here and now.

She pulled her suitcase down from the top of the wardrobe and dumped it onto the bed. Packing wouldn't take her long at all; as the case was still ready from the last time she'd tried to go away. Picking up her phone, she sent Aunt Laurie a text. *Leaving here in a few. See you tonight if that's OK. If not I'll find a hotel for a couple of nights. Will explain when I see you.*

Two minutes later came the reply. *Of course, it's all right. Come when you like, stay as long as you like. Don't let Steve stop you. He can be a right 'charmer'. I'll keep some dinner for you. Talk when you get here.*

Her heart warmed. Aunt Laurie really was a saint. Perhaps it was her that her mother referred to when she often commented 'oh my sainted aunt'. *Thank you, Lord, for people like her. I didn't mean to yell at Steve, but he does this every single time, well You know that, and I just can't take it anymore.*

She didn't look up at the knock. "Come in."

"Hattie..." Penny's voice came from the open doorway. "Steve said you're leaving..."

*What a surprise. Steve sends Penny to sweet talk me. Well, it isn't going to work this time. Lord, give me the strength I need for my no to be no and my yes, yes.* "Yeah, I'm taking my holiday. You remember, something I haven't had in over a year."

"But it's early. You're not meant to be leaving until Saturday, and then I thought..."

"Thought what? That I'd just cave and do what he wants again? Did he tell you what he did? I'd booked the next two weeks off over a month ago, having already cancelled the holiday once because you were away and he decided to go and join you, right? Something he knew all too well. It was written in the diary. The rooms were blanked off so you'd only have four guests between the two of you, and now he goes and fills *all* the rooms."

Penny moved into the room, holding out her hands in what Hattie assumed was a placating gesture. Well, that wasn't going to work either. "Hattie, I don't understand. Didn't you know about the house party? Steve rang Bill three weeks ago and offered a special rate if he'd bring a group up for the two weeks you were supposed to be away."

Hattie's throat constricted and her stomach lurched. She narrowed her eyes, straightening. "He. Did. *What*? Three weeks ago? Really? And for the two weeks I'd booked off."

Penny nodded. "Yeah, I was there when he made the call, but he told me not to say anything. Besides, he said you wouldn't mind staying on and helping."

Her temper flared. That was the final straw that broke the proverbial camel's back. Or, in this case, hers. "How *dare* he? So, he did it deliberately and then lied about it to my face, as well. I'm not putting up with this any longer. I quit. I'll be back at some point for the rest of my things, but I'm not doing this anymore."

"Hattie, you can't quit."

"I just did." She pulled down another bag, filling it with random things she didn't want to leave behind. She wouldn't put it past Steve to take all her stuff to the tip in a fit of rage. He'd calm eventually, he always did, but by then it would be too late for her treasured possessions.

"Hattie, you're his sister, his twin. He needs you."

"No, he needs a slave. I ceased being his sister a long time ago. He refuses to give me time off, he doesn't pay me."

"He said you wouldn't mind staying. He said that you didn't take time off by choice, you never went anywhere and therefore didn't need the money."

"Apparently he says I don't mind about a lot of things that I don't know about." She drew in a deep breath, wishing she had a brick wall to hit her head against. "I suppose it never occurred to you that the reason I don't take time off, is because someone cancels it or arranges stuff like this so I have to stay here. And on the odd occasion I do get an afternoon to myself, the reason I don't go anywhere much is because I don't have the money to do so? Do you realize that I barely get two hundred quid a month? That's a fraction of what you two get. I wasn't expecting to make a killing. I thought this was a good investment, but not even being paid to work here is really taking the biscuit."

"Hattie…" Shock resonated in Penny's voice, mirroring the look on her face. "I had no idea. I'll write you a check for something."

"No point. He'll stop it. You know that. I don't even know the password for the bank accounts." She pushed her shaking hands through her hair and lowered her trembling voice. "Sorry. I don't mean to rant and take it out on you. I have to go. Before he locks me in my room, steals my car keys and prevents me from leaving."

"Promise me you'll wait twenty minutes."

"I'll be here as long as it takes me to pack. Not a second longer." As Penny left, Hattie carried on packing. She threw things into the bags, taking out her anger on the inanimate objects. She didn't have much and managed to fit all her clothes and most of her books and pictures into her three matching suitcases.

She didn't often lose her temper, but this time Steve had driven her past the point of no return.

Steve appeared in the doorway. "Penny says you've quit. You can't. I forbid it."

"You forbid it?" She laughed shortly. "You're too late. I already have. Or would you like it in writing?"

He scowled. "When were you going to tell me?"

"It's time you remembered I'm your sister and not your slave," she snapped. Steve at least had the decency to blush. "I'll be back for the rest of my things in two weeks." She paused. "I love you to bits and always will, but I can't work with you any longer."

She pulled up the handle on the biggest case, trying to read the expression on his face. "You're not going to say anything?"

"What's the point? You'll come around. You always do."

"Not this time." She shouldered her bag and headed to the door. "Could you bring the other cases for me please?"

"Sure." Steve picked up the other two cases. "When will you be back at work?"

"I won't be. Apart from collecting the rest of my things after my holiday is finished. Weren't you listening?" She backtracked to her desk and pulled a piece of paper towards her. She scribbled 'I quit' and the date in big letters, and tucked it into his shirt pocket. "There, now you have it in writing."

"Where will you go?"

"I'll find somewhere. Getting a job won't be a problem." She headed to the stairs. At least with her qualifications and experience she hoped it wouldn't be.

She'd be without a reference which wasn't going to help any.

"Where are you going now?"

"What is it with all the questions?" Hattie stood still. "Why does it matter? Is this so you can ring and cancel my booking before I get there? Like you did two years ago?"

He shook his head and passed her, heading down the stairs.

She closed her eyes. How did they find themselves here? She couldn't back down because if she did, he'd crow and walk all over her, and nothing would change. She had to make a stand. *Just hope he forgives me. If I lose him because I didn't do what he wanted, what will I do? Falling out with him is like falling out with me.*

She mentally shook her head at herself. *No! Don't do this. Stand your ground, he is in the wrong. There's nothing for him to forgive, as I've done nothing wrong. He's the one who needs to apologize.*

Slowly she headed out to her car. Her luggage stood next to it, Steve nowhere to be seen. She loaded the cases into the boot and glanced up at the Lodge. She'd put seven years into this place and now it was over. She shook her head and climbed into the car. As she was about to shut the door, Penny ran over to her.

"Hattie, I didn't know. I promise. I don't know what's going on with Steve and the finances, but I will get to the bottom of it. He had no right to treat you like that. It was unforgivable of him."

"He's my brother. Of course I'll forgive him, but I just don't want to be around him right now or work with him anymore."

Penny held out an envelope. "Take this as part of what he owes you."

"I can't."

"He owes you thousands, Hattie. This isn't enough—it won't even begin to cover it. I'll get the accountant to go over the books and raise a banker's draft which he can't stop, for all your past wages and your original startup money. I'll send it to Aunt Laurie. You can get her to send it to wherever you are."

Hattie hugged her. "Thank you."

Penny returned the hug. "My pleasure. See you soon, I hope."

Hattie nodded and drove away, not looking back.

# 8

Cal headed back into the crew changing area. It had been a long rescue, made longer by the inept sailor who'd given the wrong co-ordinates. They'd found him by grace rather than anything else. He toweled down, then stripped off his dry-suit with the integral boots, and checked it over before hanging it back on his named hanger. Did he leave his bunny-suit here or wear it home again? Nah, he'd risk it. He pulled off the fleece onesie undergarment and hung it on the peg with his dry-suit.

As he dressed, Phil, Trevor and Sam, the other crew of his boat came in. He glanced up. "What kept you?" he teased.

"Tom caught us," Sam said. "And the paperwork is ready for your autograph."

"Thanks." He let the sarcasm hang there. He no longer got to *sign* anything these days: instead he had to *autograph* it. He had hoped the teasing would have stopped completely now, even if the newspaper cuttings were still displayed proudly on the office wall, but it hadn't.

"You're welcome. Tom also wanted a word before you leave." Sam dried off.

"Oh?" Tom Milligan was the LOM, otherwise known as the Lifeboat Operations Manager and the officer in charge of the lifeboat station.

"Yeah. Something about a press interview he needs you to do."

He sighed. "Uh huh, right. Haven't you lot milked this to death already?"

"Seriously. Maybe you're going to be the new face of the Penry Island RNLI."

Cal tossed the towel he'd used at him. "That's you, that is."

"I'm tired of being Mr. RNLI. It's your turn." Sam good naturedly threw the towel back and grinned. "Tom really did want to see you."

"OK. I guess I have to go up to Ops to sign the paperwork anyway." Cal tugged down his sweater. "Don't take this the wrong way, but I really hope I don't see you guys later."

"Back at ya." Trevor laughed. "The wife has plans for tonight. We have the kids sleeping at Grandma's. It might be our last evening alone before the little one arrives."

"She's not due for another six weeks. You guys really don't get out much, do you?"

Trevor winked. "My mistress, the sea, is just too demanding of my time."

Cal grinned. "She is that. Have fun." He headed up the stairs to the huge operations room. Filled with radar and radios, it connected them to the boats and coastguard, as well as the Met Office, the three emergency services and other RNLI stations along their stretch of coastline, and head office at Poole Harbor. He signed what he needed and then headed to the office.

The door was open. He tapped on the frame and stuck his head around it. "Tom, you wanted to see me?"

Tom looked up. His eyes sparkled in welcome and his blond hair, tinted with grey looked too perfect, as always. "Yeah. *The Courier* wants to do an interview and a piece on river safety. I figured you'd be the man to do it."

Cal rolled his eyes. "Me? Haven't I been in the press enough already?"

"Not really," Tom teased. "Besides, people still remember your rescue in Headley Cross, and it won't hurt to reiterate the need to take care out there."

Arguing wasn't going to work, best just to agree. "OK. When?"

"Two o'clock tomorrow afternoon. He'll want pictures of you in full kit too."

"I'll be here. See you then. Hopefully not again tonight." He winked and headed outside to where he'd parked his truck next to the shop.

Some of the RNLI stations had a small shop attached to them, selling RNLI merchandise, again all staffed by volunteers. Laurie Dillon, the shop manager was unlocking her car, her normal smile replaced by a worried frown. He shot her a smile. "Hey, Laurie. You're leaving early tonight. What's up?"

"Hi, Cal. Family problems. My niece is coming up to stay unexpectedly early after a fight with her brother. I'm hoping I can sort things out."

"That doesn't sound good."

She shook her head. "No. They've fallen out before, but never enough for her to just up and leave like this. Oh, while I think of it, can you chase up that quote for me?"

"Hasn't Dad sent it yet?"

"No, or if he did, it hasn't arrived."

"I'll swing by the office on my way home and

hand deliver a copy myself later."

Laurie smiled. "Thank you. See you later."

Cal nodded and crossed to his red truck. He'd pick the quote up now, in case he got called out again. This was possible the way the week was going.

Red Watch had started their duty shift at 0700 Tuesday, with a shout almost immediately.

Training on Wednesday evening had turned into the real thing after a paddle boarder got swept out on the rip tide. Today they'd had three shouts already and it was *only* Thursday afternoon.

At the office, he found the quote and slid it into an envelope. Then he checked the diary. Glancing at the clock, he realized it had gone six and decided just to go home via Laurie's to give her this. Then maybe have something to eat before the pager went off again.

****

Hattie pulled up on the driveway of her aunt's house. She didn't remember any of the two hour drive from Headley Cross to Penry Island. That on reflection wasn't a good thing, but nothing she could do. Her heart ached and tears were still perilously close to the surface. She stepped from the car, straight into the warm embrace of Aunt Laurie.

"I've got you." Aunt Laurie's gentle voice opened the floodgates, bringing forth a tsunami of tears. Aunt Laurie guided her inside the cottage, and sat with her on the sofa, still holding her.

Finally Hattie looked up. "I'm sorry. Didn't mean to get here and cry all over you."

"It's fine, dear. What happened?" Her aunt handed her a tissue.

"Steve wanted me to cancel again. He booked in a house party and lied about it, in order to make me stay. I hate him."

"Hate isn't a nice word," Aunt Laurie chided. "You may not like him, but you'll never hate him."

"I'm so tired of this. I haven't had a proper day off in forever." She took a deep breath, reigning in her emotions. "Penny said she'd send a letter here for you to forward to me. They don't know I'm staying here and I don't want them to."

"I'm not going to lie for you if he rings."

"I'm not asking you to. I'll just leave the room if he calls and then you won't know where I am."

Aunt Laurie gave her the look she knew so well. "That isn't going to help."

Hattie sighed. "I know I need to talk to him, but not yet." *He needs to apologize first,* she added silently. She wasn't in the wrong here.

Aunt Laurie nodded. "OK, dear. Bring your things in from the car and I'll put the kettle on. I made up the pink room for you."

"Thank you." She got up and headed out to the car. Opening the boot, she pulled out the smallest case and set it on the path beside her.

A red truck pulled up on the main road as she pulled out the next case. She tugged at the largest one, but it refused to budge. Figured, just as it started raining as well.

The gate squeaked. Footsteps walked down the path towards her. "Can I help you with that, ma'am?"

"Thank you. I seem to have gotten it stuck somehow." She looked up into familiar eyes and shock of dark hair falling over his forehead. "Cal?"

"Hi, Hattie." He grinned at her. "I wasn't

expecting to see you here."

"Me either. Uh—see you here, that is." She stood there. She must look a sight. Her face would be red and blotchy and her mascara streaked. What would he think of her? "Thank you for the postcard."

"You're welcome."

Aunt Laurie laughed from the doorway. "Are you two coming inside or just playing statues in the rain for the rest of the night?"

Hattie's cheeks burned. "I'm coming." She picked up both cases as Cal pulled the other from the boot.

Did he live here on the island? What was he doing at her aunt's house? A thousand questions whizzed through her brain in the time it took her to walk up the garden path. But she didn't ask any of them. Instead, she smiled at him as he set her case in the hall. "Thank you."

"Welcome." He reached into his jacket pocket and pulled out an envelope. "Here's your quote, Laurie."

"Thank you." She took it and grinned. "I know I don't have to introduce you to my niece, Hattie."

Cal smiled. "No." He cast a glance over her cases. "You always travel this light when you go away?"

"No." She took a deep breath. "I've had enough." She noticed the look Cal and Aunt Laurie exchanged, but wasn't going to comment. "Steve finally pushed me too far."

"I don't blame you," Cal said gently. "I've seen the way he takes you for granted close up. A break will do you both good."

"This is more than a break. I've quit. But he doesn't believe me."

He raised an eyebrow, the expression so comical she would have laughed under different circumstances. "Really?"

"Yes, really."

"What will you do?"

"I don't know. Figured go out and explore the island tomorrow, maybe. Then help out in the shop or something. Then find another job. Preferably one miles and miles away from Steve."

A fleeting look crossed Cal's face, mirrored exactly on Aunt Laurie's. Almost akin to consternation, but not quite, and again would have been funny under different circumstances. He cleared his throat. "That doesn't sound like much of a holiday. You need some proper time off. Find someone your own age to have fun with."

*I'm not five!* The thought crossed her mind and almost made it over the threshold of her lips, but she managed to bite it back just in time. "I'm sure I'll do fine. Besides, I bet all the kids we played with here when we were growing up have moved off the island long ago. I won't know anyone my age to have 'fun' with."

Aunt Laurie looked up from the piece of paper in her hand. "The quote is fine, Cal. When can you start?"

"Next week, do you?"

Hattie grabbed one of the cases and headed up the stairs to the pink room, leaving the others to talk. Cal must live here and obviously knew her aunt. But why hadn't either of them said anything? She stopped. Where Cal lived had never been mentioned and she hadn't bothered to look up his records back at the lodge.

That didn't alter the fact it was good to see him again. Did he feel the same way? Maybe she'd have the chance to find out. Right now though, all she was certain of was the fact she didn't want to go home. Ever.

She tossed her bag to the bed and dumped the case on the floor. The room hadn't changed since she was a kid.

As she turned, her handbag fell off the bed and the envelope that Penny had given her fell onto the floor. Hattie opened it and blinked hard. "Oh…"

She slumped onto the bed, stunned at the sight of red notes filling it. However much was there in here? She pulled out the white bank receipt. *Five grand?* Her phone beeped and she glanced at it. Penny not Steve, so maybe she'd read it.

*'I'm guessing you opened the envelope by now. The money is yours. Please keep it. There is more to come via your aunt. Don't call tonight. Steve in a foul mood. But he'll live. üP'*

She allowed herself a small smile. Penny's signature always looked like a poked out tongue. *'I can't accept it and nor can you two…'* She typed quickly and got an almost instant reply.

*'Don't be silly. You're owed every penny of it. We can more than afford it. The rest will follow.'*

*'Rest?'* She replied. *'I don't understand.'*

*'I'll explain later. Gtg and serve dinner. Luv you sis. Xx üP'*

A knock on the open door jerked her head upright. Cal stood there with the rest of her bags. "Laurie asked me to bring these up."

"Thank you. Just dump them anywhere."

Cal put the cases and bag down and perched on the edge of the bed next to her. "Are you all right? For someone with a lot of cash on her lap you look like the world's ended."

"Maybe it has." She swallowed hard, all her nerves coming alive at his nearness. "Penny gave it to me as I left. Said I was owed it and there was more to come. I assumed all my money went back into the business. I just had, well, pocket money I guess you'd call it. Steve took care of all the finances. But maybe that was another ploy so I couldn't leave. Once he knows I have this, he'll want it back."

"You should pay it into the bank first thing. It's not a good idea to keep that much cash lying around the house."

"I'll do that tomorrow."

He smiled. "I'd better go. Dad's expecting me for dinner tonight. I'll see you around, I hope?"

"Sure."

Cal touched her hand lightly, sending ripples of warmth running through her. "Just put all this into God's hands, Hattie. He'll work it out, even if you can't see a way right now." He stood and headed out.

Hattie watched him go. He was so different to Steve. He genuinely seemed to care, and his faith almost shone through him. But it was just infatuation on her part, nothing more.

Aunt Laurie's voice floated up the stairs. "I'm just going to get some milk."

Hattie jumped up. "I'll go." She ran down the stairs. "Just milk?"

"Please." She held out a two pound coin. "Thank you, dear."

"I've got money." Hattie smiled and hugged her aunt. "I won't be long."

"You remember the way?"

She laughed. "It's not been that long. Left out of the path. Left at the top of the road and over the crossing. Five minutes there and five minutes back."

"And a twenty minute catch up with Alba behind the counter." Aunt Laurie grinned.

"Is she still there? Wow."

"Yeah, she is. So see you in half an hour. Dinner will be ready then."

The corner shop and post office was just as Hattie remembered it. Magazines and papers lined the shelves under the window by the door. Laundry, bathroom and kitchen stuff on the other wall. Behind the main counter were all the other groceries, fridge, and stationery supplies. But her favorite section by far was the shelves next to the small post office counter.

Jar upon jar of every sweet you could imagine and then some. All the ones she remembered from her childhood.

Bonbons, fruit salad, rhubarb and custard, pear drops, jellies, chocolate éclairs, lime éclairs, toffees, fudges, and even shoelaces and the chocolate buttons with hundreds and thousands on them. *Wow. This place really hasn't changed at all. Time stands still here.*

"Harriet, is that you?" The deep voice was familiar, yet at the same time wasn't.

She turned to find a tall, ginger haired man with green eyes grinning at her. Oh, but she'd recognize those eyes anywhere. Part of her hoped he wouldn't still live here. For all she knew he'd tell Steve he'd seen her and that wasn't at all a good thing. Of all the people she could run into here, it had to be him. The one bloke Steve was determined to set her up with and marry her off to, purely on the basis he was the richest man on the island. "Hello, Markus."

Strong arms enveloped her in a bear hug. "My goodness, you've changed."

She hugged him back, not wanting to be rude. Maybe if she were nice to him, he'd keep her secret. "So have you."

He kissed her cheek. "Let me look at you. Still the same on the inside no doubt, but far prettier on the outside."

"Flatterer." She grinned, pulling back from the over familiar and too long hug. "Think you've changed more. You're a lot taller now for one thing."

\*\*\*\*

Cal edged towards the door, not wanting to see any more. His heart had leapt when he saw Hattie at Laurie's place. For a few short moments, he'd allowed himself to hope he could see her again. And properly this time. But it looked as though she was on more than friendly terms with Markus.

He was almost out onto the street and safety when Alba called to him. "Cal, here a minute."

He slowly went back over to the counter, glad Hattie and Markus were too wrapped up in talking to each other to notice him. "What's up, Alba?"

"That package came for your dad yesterday. I meant to get Fraser to bring it over, but he had to go to the mainland. The wee bairn was taken sick."

"I'm sorry to hear that." Cal knew full well that the 'wee bairn' was thirty-two with his own gardening business on the mainland, but guessed all kids remained kids in their parent's eyes, no matter how old they got. "I hope he feels better soon. I can take the parcel if you like. I'm heading that way now."

"Thank you. Bring your truck around back into the yard."

"Will do." He turned around to find Hattie standing right behind him. He smiled. "We must stop meeting like this. People will talk."

"Let them." She grinned at him. "But we do seem to be making a habit of bumping into each other. But it's a wonderful habit to have."

"It sure is."

Markus came up behind her, a paper and box of washing powder in his hands. "Callum."

Cal nodded. "Markus."

"You and Harriet know each other?"

"Yeah. We've known each other a while." Well that was true, just not as long as Hattie and Markus had evidently known each other. Cal took a small measure of comfort in the fact that Markus called her Harriet and not Hattie. Not that he could read too much into it, as Markus was formal with almost everyone. Very old school, he still addressed the majority of the village folk by their title and surname, except people his own age or his own circle of friends. Cal wasn't in either category, but because he was famous, Markus considered them to be on first name terms.

Cal smiled at Hattie. "I'll see you around. A lot."

Hattie returned the smile. "I'm looking forward to it already."

He headed to the door. "I'll be around back in two minutes, Alba."

"OK, dear."

Cal turned for a final glance at Hattie. Markus had his arm around her waist. He sighed. For the first time in his life, the boot was on the other foot and he wasn't sure he liked it. He'd always had his pick of women, sometimes more than one at once, but now? The one he wanted to get to know better was in the arms of another, even if there was nothing between them.

He didn't like the sudden rush of grief that filled him at that thought. He didn't want to lose her. Was she even his to lose? He didn't know, but he was going to fight for her one way or the other.

# 9

Hattie finished her breakfast. "That was lovely, thank you, Aunt Laurie. Want me to do the dishes before I go out?"

Her aunt piled the plates on top of each other and shook her head. "No, dear, you're on holiday, but thank you for the offer. I have plenty of time before I leave for work. Where are you going?"

"I bumped into Markus last night. I haven't seen him in years. He's taking me out on his boat this morning, around the headland to the lighthouse."

"Markus Kerr?"

Hattie nodded. "Yes. He seems to have done well for himself."

"Self-made money at the expense of those less fortunate than himself," Aunt Laurie commented dryly. "He made a fortune with that haulage company. And the prices they charge for the taxi's to the mainland and back are ludicrous."

"He'd say justifiable overheads."

"Aye, well, it's not as if they're lacking a pretty penny or two."

"I guess so. Anyway, it'll be good to catch up with him and it should be a fun day out on the water. Actually, I only agreed in exchange for him not telling Steve where I am. They seem to have been in touch rather a lot over the past several months. If I didn't know better, I'd say Steve was up to something."

"Like what?"

"Matchmaking." Hattie grimaced. "He drops Markus's name into the conversation several times a day, tells me what a good bloke he is, what a good catch he'd be. It makes him sound like a fish."

"Is that Markus or Steve?"

Hattie laughed. "Markus."

Aunt Laurie looked out of the window. "It might be better to go for this boat trip around the headland tomorrow instead of today."

"Why?"

"There's a storm coming."

Hattie followed her aunt's gaze and studied the view out of the window. The sun sparkled on the water and the leaves hung motionless on the trees. "Are you sure? There isn't a cloud in the sky or a breath of wind by the looks of it."

"Trust me. There's a storm coming. A bad one, too."

"Then I'll take my raincoat. I'm sure Markus is a perfectly good sailor or he wouldn't skipper his own yacht. And if he thinks there's a storm coming, we'll probably not go. I'll be back by dinner and I have my phone."

"OK. Cal is starting work here on Monday. He's a carpenter and will be doing the paneling in the den and then finishing off all the details on that side of the house. So it'll be a little untidy and noisy for a week or so."

"Cool. You've needed to get that done for a while."

Aunt Laurie nodded, pushing a hand though her grey hair. "Since the fire. But it takes time and money and with your uncle gone…"

Hattie hugged her. "I know. It's hard."

"It is. He did all the decorating and having someone else do it, seems wrong somehow. But I guess your Dad's right. It's time to at least make that half of the house livable again."

"Can I help? I could do all the soft furnishings for you. I've got some money—long story—but I'd like to help."

"I can't take your—"

"I'm offering. At least let me get the material and make them. We could go shopping on your day off. Please..." She tried the puppy dog eyes. That had always worked when she was little.

"Thank you. I'd like that."

Hattie smiled. It had worked, just like she knew it would. Aunt Laurie had struggled since Uncle Reg had died in the fire two years ago. The fire had destroyed half the cottage. The rebuild was done, the new wiring in, but the rooms stood in limbo and untouched. "I'll see you later."

****

Cal set the ladder against the wall of the cottage. The wooden shutters the owner requested, had driven him mad with their intricate carvings, but he had to admit they looked incredible. Small hearts whittled out of them and interwoven ivy carved into the wood to connect them. He just hoped the customer would think they looked good.

He ran up the ladder and unhooked the old shutter and passed it down to Rob. Being a family business, Rob was his cousin as well as his colleague. Only a couple of years between them, they got on like a house on fire, spending most of the day in a combination of laughter and merciless teasing. Cal replaced the two old hinges with new ones and then took the new shutter. As he fitted it, he spied Hattie walking along the path. "Morning, Hattie," he called.

Hattie shielded her eyes against the bright morning sun. Her smile rivaled it for brightness. "Hello, Cal. How are you?"

"I'm good. You?"

"Yeah, I'm OK."

He watched the way her hips moved and the bag on her shoulder swung in time with them. He could tell she'd taken time with her appearance as he took in the white jeans and red, white, and blue striped shirt she wore. A red and white scarf knotted around her neck, and pristine, white canvas deck shoes complimented the outfit. "You look lovely."

"Thank you." Her cheeks colored, making her look even prettier. "I'm off, out for the day."

"Very nice."

"It should be. Markus is taking me out on his yacht along the coast a ways."

Cal looked at her, his heart sinking. He glanced up at the sky. "There's a storm coming," he said gruffly, a huge surge of something, was it jealousy, rocking him. His fingers whitened on the edge of the ladder. "Best go another day."

"Aunt Laurie said the same thing, but there isn't a cloud in the sky." Hattie waved a hand. "However, I have my raincoat in my bag, and I don't get seasick."

He nodded, somehow keeping his face straight. She was wrong, a storm was brewing, he'd seen the forecast, but more than that, he could feel it in the air. "Have fun."

"You have a good day, too." She waved and headed off.

He waited until she was out of earshot. Then he yanked the old shutter out of its hinges, almost ripping the bracket from them. "Markus is an idiot!"

"He knows the weather as well as you do," Rob said calmly, taking the shutter. "He won't sail if he's got any sense. Or if the forecast shows we have bad weather coming in."

Cal laughed bitterly. "This is Markus Kerr we're talking about. A box of rocks has more sense than he does. Especially where women are concerned."

"You really don't like him, do you?"

"I don't like his type. They think of no one but themselves as they put others at risk whilst trying to impress women, whether it's boats or a fast sports car on these narrow roads or something else." Was he being judgmental? No, based on Markus' track record that was how he operated, and Alba still had a dented fender to prove it.

Cal knew he was no saint, but he always acted with decorum, using his charm to impress, not speed and recklessness.

"She does have a point," Rob's voice dragged him back from his musing. "The sea is flat calm. It's a perfect day for a sail."

He *humphed*. "I'm telling you, there is a storm coming. A big one, and you know how fast they can blow in off the sea. Pass me up that shutter."

"Here you go and I bow to your superior knowledge of the sea and the weather. You know, couz, I'm sure I've seen her before."

He took the shutter from Rob. "She's Laurie's niece. She spent most of her summers here growing up.

And Laurie has probably shown you photos of her over the years."

"I know that, but…Photos. That's it." Rob grinned. "She's the woman in the paper."

If Cal could have slapped himself without risking life and limb he would have. He really did need to keep his mouth shut and stop reminding people about that news report. Especially now Hattie was here on the island. "Which woman in particular? There have been numerous photos of me and women in the paper over the years."

"You know full well I mean the woman that was with you at the weir when you rescued that kid a few weeks back. You're jealous because she's going out with Markus and not you."

"It doesn't matter if I am." He slotted the shutter in place. "If Markus is after her, there is nothing I can do."

"Rot. She likes you, I can tell."

"And you know this how?"

"Seven sisters, mate. What I don't know about women ain't worth knowing."

Cal smiled, despite the annoyance filling him. "Careful that doesn't get taken the wrong way."

Rob grinned. "You're not my type. I prefer blondes. That one was pretty nice actually."

"Shutter fastener."

Rob laughed and handed them up to him. "Here."

Cal bolted the shutter into place. "There. Let's do the rest before my pager goes off. There's bound to be at least one call today."

"It's getting so you may as well live there this week."

"Tell me about it." He ran down the ladder and

repositioned it. "Hasn't been this bad since Christmas when we got called out during dinner and didn't get home 'til almost two days later. We slept on the base, alternating with the relief crew. But it comes with the job. If I didn't enjoy it, I wouldn't do it."

Rob nodded. "Never something I fancied doing. Shore crew yeah, but in the boats?" He shook his head.

"You don't swim."

"Exactly."

"You should learn," he said, sliding the bolts into his pocket. "Especially living by the sea."

"I don't intend to go on a boat."

"Even so. I should teach you." He climbed the ladder again. "OK, next shutter."

****

Hattie sat on the deck of the yacht, the wind blowing through her hair as Markus steered through the waves. Yacht wasn't the right word for it. The boat was more like a cabin cruiser and huge. Well, in her inexperienced eyes it was huge. Kitchen, bathroom, bedroom to name a few; not that those were the correct terms for rooms on a boat. Markus had called them something else—galley, cabin and... some funny word she couldn't remember.

The breeze had picked up a fair bit since they left the harbor, but Markus said it was normal and nothing to worry about. She leaned back in the deckchair and studied him.

He really had grown into a fine looking man, from the gawky, spotty kid she remembered from the summer holidays when she was young. He'd always hung around her aunt's house, theoretically to play with Steve, but seemed to pay more attention to her than her brother.

Her mind shifted back to the tall, dark haired man she'd spent so many hours thinking about. Had Cal always lived here? Why didn't she remember seeing him around the place?

Markus grinned at her. "Enjoying the view, Harriet?"

"It's really pretty along here," she said returning her gaze to the coastline. She knew that wasn't what he meant, but wasn't going to give him the satisfaction. "It hasn't changed much at all."

"It has further around to the west. There was a huge landslide there about six months ago. All the winter rain undermined the cliff and a sizable chunk fell. Even took the cottage on the cliff edge with it. Fortunately, it hadn't been lived in for years."

"Wow."

"I can take you to show you if you'd like."

"Yeah, I would." She paused. "Markus, you did mean what you promised, right? I don't want Steve knowing I'm here. Not for a couple of weeks anyway."

He looked at her. "I still think hiding from your own brother is a little off, no matter what he did, but sure. I'll keep schtum for you." He put the wheel hard over and the cruiser responded to his touch. "So, we'll go and see the cliff fall. After that we'll go to the lighthouse."

Hattie watched the sea, looking for the seals he'd promised she'd see, but her thoughts returned to Cal. Had he made those shutters himself? The carving on them was wonderful. If he had, then maybe she could ask him to make shutters for Aunt Laurie's cottage. The ones there needed replacing—the ones the fire hadn't destroyed anyway. Maybe Cal could replace all of them. Perhaps incorporating her uncle's family crest or their initials intertwined.

There would be no harm in getting a quote anyway. She could put money towards them. Or pay for them outright.

"There," Markus called. "Seals at eleven o'clock. See them?"

Hattie shielded her eyes against the sun and turned her head. "Wow." She watched, enthralled, as the seals leapt over the waves, playing with each other.

"I heard they mate for life."

Hattie shook her head. "That's seahorses. Or swans."

"I was close. Still starts with an S. But the point remains though. It's a neat thing. Only loving one person for your entire life."

She glanced at him. "So you'd stay faithful even after death of your wife?"

"Yes, I would."

"Even if she died really early rather than when you were both say eighty or ninety?"

"Your aunt did."

"Uncle Reg only died two years ago, and they were married for over forty years and devoted to each other. I think that kind of love is wonderful, but it doesn't mean you have to rule out someone else coming along. Our pastor back home remarried after seven years of widowhood."

Markus looked at her. "Would you?"

"Remarry?"

"Mourn me forever 'til you died."

"That's a little presumptuous, don't you think?" Hattie raised an eyebrow.

He grinned and pointed to the coast. "That's where the cliff fell. See?"

Hattie looked where he indicated. The jagged cliff with its rough edges was a different color where the new rock had been exposed. "Wow. Was anyone hurt?"

"A woman was trapped, but they got her out. It caused a riptide on the beach over there."

"I bet it did." She pulled her sleeves down. It had gotten cold and the sun had vanished behind a thick bank of leaden grey sky.

Markus glanced up at the sky. "It's clouded over."

*You think? Talk about stating the obvious.* "Should we head back? Aunt Laurie said there was a storm coming."

"Nah, we're fine. I'm not afraid of a little rain. We'll head further out. I know a great picnic spot by the lighthouse."

"Are you sure?"

"Perfectly sure." He smiled and headed further out into open sea.

Twenty minutes later, Hattie had to admit that Cal and Aunt Laurie were right. Rain pounded the deck, and crashed against the windows. She clung to the rail on the side of the cabin as the boat heaved over another huge wave. Her raincoat wasn't as waterproof as she'd thought. She had gotten drenched clearing the deck of furniture as Markus had asked, and her hair hung in rat's tails about her face. Even her cast iron stomach was more than a little unhappy now.

Markus spun the wheel, trying to bring the boat about to face into the waves, but the wind was too strong and tossed them violently to one side.

Hattie cried out involuntarily as she flew across

the cabin, hitting the rail on the far wall.

Markus tried to regain control. Another gust of wind tossed them against a buoy with a resonating crash. He swore and tried to turn them away from it. The engines cut out, leaving the boat at the mercy of the wind and waves.

Hattie clutched her arm, gritting her teeth. Pain rocketed through her. She staggered to her feet.

"Hold this while I go below and check the engines. Just keep the compass pointing east if you can."

"OK." She staggered to the wheel and clung onto it, trying to use her good arm to hold it steady.

The waves grew in size as Markus headed below. With no engines there was no way she could control the boat one handed. It was all she could do to stay upright and keep the needle pointing east. The waves tugged the boat away from the buoy towards the open sea.

Markus came back up. "We're taking on water." He looked out of the window. "Where's the coast gone?"

"That way. I can't hold her steady with one hand, sorry." She gasped as her injured arm caught the wheel. "What do we do?"

"Call for help and hope they get here before we sink." Markus grabbed the radio. "There are lifejackets under the seats. Put one on."

Hattie pulled up the seats and tugged out two lifejackets. She struggled into one of them. She closed her eyes. *Please, help us. Don't let me drown. I'm not scared of dying, but drowning...*

Markus fiddled with the radio. "Mayday. Mayday. This is the *Petunia Bay* calling Mayday."

# 10

Cal grinned over his glass at Rob. "And you got away with it?"

Rob nodded. "Aye. Mara washed the same dish six times before she realized."

"I love it. I'll have to try that on Jess one weekend." He cut into the steak and mushroom pie, inhaling deeply. The food in this pub really was second to none. "Don't forget I have that press interview at two. I'll be back afterwards."

Rob laughed. "My cousin the hero. Mr. RNLI himself. Maybe we should start selling signed photos of you in the office."

"For the dart board, maybe."

"Spoilsport."

The pager went off. "Told you." Cal put down his knife and fork. He pulled the pager from his belt and looked at it. "OK, got to go. See you later."

"Stay safe."

"I always do."

Rob caught his arm. "I mean it, couz. We've lost entire crews out there before, but since Porthness last winter, I worry all the more. You're more than my cousin—"

Cal hugged him. "I promise I'll be back later." He smiled and ran out into the storm. He leapt into his truck, with its sticker proudly bearing the RNLI flag with *lifeboat crew* on it and drove the short distance to the base. A thousand scenarios flooded his mind. Torrential rain hit the windscreen and even with wipers on full pelt, visibility was practically zero.

The wind buffeted the truck and he knew all too well the problems that faced them in open water. *Lord God, protect whoever it is out there until we can get to them. Protect us as we go out to help them and if it's Your will, bring us all home safely.*

Parking in his usual space, he ran around the building. A flurry of activity met him. The tractors already had engines running and the Atlantic class boat, his boat, was already being prepped.

Tom stood there with clipboard in hand, checking in the crew as they arrived.

Cal glanced at the ten foot waves already building in the harbor, then turned to Tom. "Looks bad out there."

"There's no way that a chopper can reach them in this. Everyone else is in now and kitting up."

Cal nodded and ran into the crew changing room. Phil, Sam, and Trevor were almost ready. "Afternoon."

"Hey, Cal."

Sam, one of the local doctors, grinned. "You really know how to avoid having your photo taken, huh?"

He stripped quickly. "Yep. The paper can wait. Never would be a good time for the interview."

"You know that isn't going to happen. This will just make the interview more exciting. I bet he's outside now, snapping away, taking pictures of the boat and the tractor and the shore crew. He'll want to know details of this rescue, too. What it's really like out there in the wind and rain and so on."

"That's an easy one. It's rather wet and windy." Cal zipped his bunny suit and pulled on his dry suit.

"How are we doing?"

"Two minutes before we beat our record," Sam said.

"Easy." Cal pulled on his life jacket and grabbed his helmet. "Let's go."

The others followed him out. As helmsman, the boat was his, but he never pulled rank. If he needed to do something, he did it. They were more than a team, they were a family, and they always had each other's backs. He turned on his radio. "OK, Tom. What have we got?"

"The *Petunia Bay*, a cabin cruiser, lost both engines. And she's taking on water after colliding with a buoy. She's now adrift in the shipping lane. Porthness are sending the all-weather boat as back up, but it'll take them a while to get down here."

Cal listened as they ran into the storm and climbed up into the boat. Once they were seated, the tractor started down the shingle beach into the water. The waves crashed far higher than usual, rain poured, and the wind rocked them in the safety of the cage. He checked the dials in front of him. Everything on and working. "Green across the board. Did you guys catch all that?"

"When will they ever learn to check the weather?" Trevor asked.

"Wish I knew. But we have a job to do." He raised a hand so the tractor knew they were ready.

As soon as the tractor stopped, Cal opened the throttle and took them out into the water. The waves were worse than they appeared as the small boat powered its way through them. The wind tossed them as much as the waves towered over them.

Cal kept one eye on the radar and the other on the

water. "I'm heading for their last known position, but they could be anywhere."

"Unless he had the sense to drop anchor. That would at least slow them somewhat."

Cal shrugged. "Maybe, though it wouldn't do them much good in this." He aimed the boat between the waves as much as he could. Not that it made much difference. It was going to be worse the further away from the shore they got.

And it was.

The twelve foot waves towered above them, doing their best to swamp and overturn the little lifeboat as it cut through the water towards the last known position of the *Petunia Bay.* He watched the radar, but nothing was showing.

"Where is she?" Sam called. "I can't see anything."

"If she was taking on water, she could have gone down. Or capsized anyway." Trevor twisted in his seat.

"Flare," Phil yelled. "Seven o'clock."

Cal turned the boat and headed into the heart of the storm, keeping the bow of the boat into the breaking waves. Visibility was down to five feet.

"There's another flare," Sam yelled. "But doesn't look the same direction."

"Radar's got something." Cal squinted at the screen.

"There. Two o'clock, there's a light."

Cal aimed the boat at the faint light he could see between the towering waves. As he grew closer he could see the hull of the boat with a figure clinging to it. "Phil, toss the rope to him. If he catches it, bring him in that way. If not rope up and go get him." He touched the mic button. "Penry base this is *Ray of Hope.*

Found the *Petunia Bay*. We will need assistance to tow the capsized boat out of shipping lane. One in the water."

"Roger that, Cal. Will send out the RHIB."

Cal brought the boat around, bringing it in closer to the wrecked cruiser. He watched the figure on the boat catch the rope. Then he brought the lifeboat right alongside the upturned hull.

Phil and Sam grabbed the man and pulled him into the safety of the lifeboat.

"Is there anyone else with you?" Sam asked.

"Harriet. Where is she? Did you pick her up, too?"

*Hattie's out here?* A stab of fear filling him, Cal turned in his seat, hoping he was wrong. The soaked figure was as unmistakable as his clipped posh accent. He wanted to berate the man for being stupid, but now wasn't the time. "Where did you last see her, Markus?"

"Didn't you find her yet?"

"We barely found you. Where did you last see her?" *Oh, God, keep her safe out here.*

"Before we capsized. The boat flipped over so fast. When I came up she was gone."

Trevor turned the searchlight on the water around them.

"Sam, check Markus over." Cal yelled, fear twisting his gut.

"I'm fine. Harriet was hurt before she went into the water. She hit her arm on something, and couldn't use it."

"You're being checked over regardless. Trevor, rope up in case you need to go in. If she's hurt she won't be able to hold onto the rope."

"Aye, aye."

Did he imagine a faint call for help carried on the

wind? "Aim that light over to the right." The search light caught sight of something yellow floating on the waves in the distance. Cal turned the boat around on a dime. *Please let it be her.*

"There!" Sam yelled.

Cal nodded and accelerated the boat towards the small yellow shape the light picked out. He came in close to the figure and Trevor dived over the side into the maelstrom. Waves crashed over and around them, spray threatening the stability of the boat.

Trevor reached the figure in a few short strokes and grabbed her.

"Haul them in," Cal yelled.

Phil and Sam hauled on the line as Cal held the lifeboat as steady as the storm would let him. A huge wave broke over them. Four attempts later and they still weren't on board.

Another wave picked up the lifeboat, tossing them on top of the figures in the water.

Cal immediately cut the engines. He wasn't going to risk the people in the water being cut to shreds. "You still got them?"

"Yes," Sam said, the lifeline tight in his grasp.

Cal leaned over the side. "Anyone see them?"

Trevor came up the other side of the boat, still holding Hattie tightly. "Take her."

Cal reached out and grabbed her, pulling her into the boat.

Phil pulled Trevor onboard. "Got them. Go, go, go."

Cal restarted the engines, praying the lifeline wasn't caught up in them. "Are they all right?"

"Sam's checking them now."

"Markus, is there anyone else?"

He shook his head. "No. It was just the two of us."

Cal turned the boat and headed back towards the shore. "Penry lifeboat station this is *Ray of Hope*. Two survivors located and retrieved. Request ambulance standing by for our return. Conditions prohibit the harbor. Making for your location."

"Roger, Cal. Bert is on his way to your position now in the RHIB to tow the cabin cruiser back."

"Tell Laurie one of the injured is Hattie."

The boat dropped off the top of a huge wave, water cascading down on top of them. Hattie screamed from somewhere behind him. Torn between doing his job and needing to make sure she was all right, Cal prayed hard as he headed the boat back to the protection of the lifeboat station.

Docking backwards on the tractor wasn't easy under normal flat calm training circumstances. But tonight was nigh on impossible. It took five minutes he didn't have to line up and reverse the lifeboat onto the trailer, but finally the tractor began to back out of the water and onto the relative safety of the beach.

Blue lights flashed in the pouring rain and the paramedics stood by the boat house ready to retrieve Hattie and Markus as soon as the tractor reached them.

He turned in his seat. "Hattie, are you all right?"

"Just cold," she said quietly, her face white against the bright yellow of her lifejacket. She clutched her arm in its makeshift sling tightly.

He didn't believe her for a second. He reached down to her, pushing her soaked hair from her face. "No you're not."

"I am now," she said. "Because you saved me. Your doctor doesn't think it's broken, just bruised. But he wants it x-rayed to make sure."

He held her gaze. "What are you doing tomorrow night?"

"Nothing," she looked confused. "Why?"

"Have dinner with me." He ignored the scowl on Markus's face.

She smiled. "I'd like that. Thank you."

"I'll pick you up at seven." He glanced up, seeing Laurie by the base with Tom and Dick, the DLA, standing alongside her. "Markus, are you hurt?"

"I'm fine."

"Almost there, then the paramedics will take you both to hospital to get you checked over."

The tractor came to a stop and Cal rose. He gently helped Hattie to her feet. "Let's get you out of here first."

She cried out as she stood.

"Hattie?"

"My arm's a little sore," she whispered. "But I'm fine."

He nodded, helping her to the edge of the boat. "It's a big step over, then a ladder. But we'll help you. Sit on the edge here."

Hattie sat slowly, biting her lip. Cal steadied her, reluctantly letting go as Tom lifted her down.

Laurie ran to her as soon as she could, her face wracked with concern and fear.

"I'm fine." Hattie gave Laurie a one handed hug. "I'm OK. Cold and I knocked my arm." She allowed the paramedics to take her over to the waiting ambulance.

Cal glared at Markus as he reached him. "You should know better."

"I didn't know this storm would blow in from nowhere."

"Any idiot knew that storm was coming."

Markus leaned forward and got right in his face. "Who are you calling an idiot?"

"If the cap fits…"

"And it was improper of you to ask my date out." Markus lowered his voice, his eyes glinting in anger.

"Oh? Was it proper to sail in a storm and nearly drown her then?" Cal's hands clenched into fists and he longed to knock the self-satisfied look from Markus's face, but he didn't. Instead, he glared at him a moment before getting back to work. He had things to do before he could go home. And that included handing over his passengers to the shore team. "Just get off my boat and go and get checked out."

He turned away and started overseeing the refueling, while the shore team hosed down the tractor and the sides of the boat. Just as they finished and were about to disembark, Tom ran over. "You have to go again."

Cal nodded. "That doesn't surprise me in the slightest. However, it's really bad out there. We almost didn't make the rescue this time."

Tom nodded. "I know and believe me, if there were another way I'd take it."

"What is it?"

"Oil tanker with a very sick crewmember — suspected ruptured appendix. It's not possible to winch them off as it's too windy, and we're the nearest vessel. I'll have a med team standing by for your return."

"OK. We have Sam anyway. Where is the ship?"

"I've loaded the coordinates into your GPS. Its five miles off shore to the south west. The captain can't risk coming in closer and being tossed into the harbor wall."

"We're on it. See you later." He turned back to the others. "OK, we're going out again. Tanker medevac."

****

Hattie watched from the ambulance as the tractor pushed the lifeboat back into the raging sea. She pulled the foil blanket tighter around her. "Where are they going?"

The paramedic glanced up at her. "Called out again most likely. It'll be a long night." He looked at his partner. "OK, let's get them to the ED. Closest one is at Yarborough Infirmary."

Aunt Laurie looked at Hattie as the paramedic shut the door of the ambulance. "Cal knows what he's doing. He'll be fine."

"I hope so. He asked me to dinner tomorrow night."

"When did he do that?"

"When I was on the lifeboat."

Markus coughed to get her attention from the other side of the ambulance as it pulled away. "I can't say I'm happy about Callum asking you out while we were still on our date." He paused. "I hope this hasn't put you off sailing."

"Not at all." And it wasn't a date, more of a bribe, but she wasn't going to tell him that any time soon. She'd just have to find a reason not to go out with him again. Even as a friend.

"Cool. Then maybe you'll come with me again."

Hattie raised an eyebrow and shivered with cold. "The boat sank."

"We have another. Besides, the insurance will

cover it."

Aunt Laurie scowled. "It covers stupidity, does it?"

Markus returned the scowl. "It is hardly my fault the yacht sank, Mrs. Dillon."

"Anyone who lives here knew there was a storm coming. You should have double checked the weather before leaving the harbor."

"I did. The storm warning had been lifted."

"Obviously not."

Hattie closed her eyes, tuning them out. Images of Cal on the lifeboat in his uniform filled her mind. Cal was a member of the lifeboat crew. Why hadn't he said anything? Was that why he didn't want her telling anyone about the kid he rescued back home?

She didn't understand why he'd kept quiet. This was such a brave, honorable thing to do.

For a moment, out in the sea, lost and alone, she thought she was going to die. She was sure she was going to die. Not that she minded that, but she didn't want to drown. Then she thought she was seeing and hearing things. The huge waves kept crashing over her, her wet clothes pulling her under. There had been a light and a voice calling her name. His voice calling her name. Then the lifeboat appeared, plucking her from the jaws of death.

Just like Jesus had. He was her Lifeboat. When she'd been tossed on life's seas, alone and friendless, going under for what she thought was the last time, Jesus had reached out and saved her.

She smiled at the picture images that thought gave her.

"What's so funny?" Markus asked.

"Just thinking how Jesus is like a lifeboat."

He rolled his eyes and looked away. "If you say so."

Aunt Laurie smiled. "It's a lovely picture. You should tell Cal. He'd like it."

"You must have known he works on the lifeboats."

"Of course."

"And you didn't tell me."

"You didn't ask, dear." She paused. "You mentioned a Cal in passing that had been a footballer and I knew who you meant. I didn't imagine you'd bump into each other again the way you did."

"Nor did I. He was a guest at the lodge. But why didn't you say last night that he worked on the lifeboats?"

"Because it wasn't my place to tell you." Aunt Laurie grinned. "That walk of yours made the headlines here. It was a lovely picture of you both."

Shock ran through her, freezing her to the seat. "What photo? What headline? When? He asked me not to tell anyone. How did the press find out?"

"It's all over the internet," Markus answered. "It has been for well over a month now. You and Callum and the kid he rescued from some river in Headley Cross."

Hattie closed her eyes. That was the last thing either of them wanted or needed. Especially now. She sucked in a deep breath and looked at her aunt. "Why didn't you tell me?"

"I assumed you'd know. That it would have been news in Headley Cross."

"No…At least not that I'd seen, but then I've had so little time to read the papers or watch television lately." Hattie let out a long breath. "But it explains

Steve's attitude. He didn't approve of me taking that walk with Cal in the first place. He still treats me like a child. Even calls me his baby sister, despite the fact he's only a few minutes older than me. If he saw those photos..." Her voice drifted, things falling into place.

Steve would have known Cal lived here. That's why he cancelled her initial stay with her aunt, to prevent her from seeing him again. He could take brotherly love and looking out for her too far.

Aunt Laurie touched her arm. "Sweetheart?"

Hattie forced a smile, cradling her arm. "Just thinking, it's time I spread my wings. And high-time Steve realized I'm a grown up now and not just some kid sister he needs to protect."

"Not that you ever needed protecting." Aunt Laurie laughed. "I remember a child with pigtails who used to beat up kids who insulted her brother at one point."

Hattie grinned. "Someone had to look out for him."

Markus cleared his throat. "Maybe he has someone in mind for you and Callum doesn't quite fit the bill."

"Perhaps. But I'm quite capable of making my own decisions. And like I told him, right now I'm content with being Miss Steele."

Or was she? Because all she could think about was a certain tall, dark haired gentleman in uniform currently in peril on the sea.

# 11

Hattie's arrival at the hospital ended the conversation, along with a rush of doctors, nurses, x-rays and check-ups. Her arm wasn't broken, just sprained. This meant no cast, for which she was grateful, and she sat on the edge of the gurney waiting for the nurse to strap it up.

"In a way it's a shame it's not broken," Aunt Laurie said wryly.

Hattie looked at her in shock. "I'm sorry? Why?"

"Because then you'd have to have six weeks off work. Steve couldn't argue with a plaster cast."

"He'd find a way. But I'm not returning to work anyway, remember? I quit." She paused. "So, going back to this picture in the newspaper. Did you keep it?"

"I did. It's a lovely picture of you."

"Were you going to tell me?"

"I didn't see the need. The teasing here had died down. Cal was mortified when the picture was published and when you didn't mention him again, I assumed you'd forgotten all about him."

She smiled. "How could I forget someone like Cal? I'm sure the press ran the story only because of his former profession."

"Probably. Although they put a different spin on it, and used his lifeboat duties as the main thread."

"I want to see it." *And him* she added.

Aunt Laurie looked at her. "I thought you were seeing Markus."

Hattie's cheeks burned. Had she said that out loud? She hadn't intended to. More than totally flustered, she sat there. "Um, uh…"

"You can't date them both at the same time. That isn't fair to either of them."

"I'm not dating either," she said finally. "Markus asked me sailing, and Cal asked me to dinner. Neither constitutes a date and both are on different days. I'd class it as spending time with a friend. Besides, I had my reasons for going sailing with Markus and romance doesn't really come into it."

"Hmmm. Are you sure it's not because Steve isn't here to keep tabs on you?"

"Steve's my brother, not my father. I'm tired of living under his shadow all the time. I love him and love being his twin, but I need to be me. Need to be who God wants me to be. Does that make sense?"

"Yes it does. Just make sure you don't get hurt in the process."

\*\*\*\*

Sitting in the privacy of her aunt's lounge that evening, Hattie read the newspaper article slowly, taking in every word. The reporter had jazzed things up a little, made a huge song and dance over who Cal had been and highlighted the fact he worked on the lifeboats.

She glanced up as Aunt Laurie came in with a tray of food they'd picked up from the takeaway on the way back from the hospital. "Thank you."

"Welcome. That article makes quite dramatic

reading." Aunt Laurie sat next to her and gave thanks for the meal.

Hattie smiled at her. "It wasn't quite as melodramatic as this makes out."

"So tell me what really happened."

In between mouthfuls of curry and rice, Hattie gave her aunt the potted, but accurate version of what happened. "Needless to say, the lifebelts got put back the following day."

"I bet they did." Aunt Laurie picked up the phone as it rang. "Hello. Oh, hello Cal. We've been in about twenty minutes. Yes, she is. She's right here." She handed Hattie the phone. "It's for you. It's Cal."

She grinned, having worked that one out. "Hello, Cal. How are you?"

"Doing OK. Thought I'd call before the pager goes off again and see how you're doing."

"I'm fine. My arm isn't broken, just sprained my wrist. Be back to normal in no time."

"Good."

"I should have listened to you. Not gone out. Then you wouldn't have had to risk your life—"

His calm voice cut her off. "It's fine, Hattie. We went out anyway."

She paused, pushing down the guilt filling her. "Why didn't you tell me you worked on the lifeboats?"

"It never came up."

"But even after that rescue in Headley Cross, when I asked if you were a lifeguard…"

His light laugh echoed down the phone. "We do provide lifeguards on the beaches during the summer months, but I've never done it. I'm too busy going out to sea several times a week. Besides, I knew if I gave them my name, it'd be all over the papers. Ex-England footballer saves kid."

"I honestly thought it was because—"

He cut her off. "Because I was ashamed from going from a famous footballer, to being part of the lifeboat crew and an unsung hero? No, that would never happen. It's my past I'm running from, not my present. I love going out on the lifeboats."

"Even on days like today?"

"Yes."

"Don't you get scared out there?" She finished her meal and set the fork down on the plate.

"Too much adrenaline to get too scared until it's over most of the time, but yeah sometimes it can be a little intimidating. But if I can do some good, save one life, then it's worth the risk and the danger."

"You saved me tonight. Thank you."

"Welcome." He paused. "And the pager's gone again. I must go. I'll see you tomorrow. Night."

"Night." The phone in her hand went dead. *Stay safe. Lord, the sea is so huge and their boat so small. Protect them.*

\*\*\*\*

Hattie was almost to the lifeboat station, with the bag of shopping, when what she feared would happen, happened. The flour she'd carefully balanced in her sling finally slid out and landed on the pavement. At least it didn't explode everywhere. Sighing, she put the shopping bag down, and was about to bend when a familiar voice from behind stopped her.

"Allow me." Cal bent and retrieved the flour. "Here you go." He grinned. "Though I don't know where you'd like it, and I'm too much of a gentleman to tell you where to put it."

She smirked, trying to hide the reaction seeing him caused to surge through her. "Thank you. You must be my hero and knight in shining armor. Always there when I need you."

He pretended to tip his hat, color touching his cheeks, making him look vulnerable. "That's me. But I really don't like being called a hero."

She tucked the flour back into her sling. "Did they tease you a lot over the newspaper article?"

"Yeah, and it'll be worse when the new one comes out."

"New one?"

"Tom had a press photographer take photos yesterday in between shouts whilst a journalist did a new in-depth interview on what it's like to be part of the lifeboat crew. Tom wants me to be the new face of the lifeboat station here."

"Mr. RNLI?" She chuckled. "Sounds fun."

"Oh, please, I had enough of that yesterday. He wants the pictures put all over the base internet sites as well. Where are you headed?"

She nodded. "Not far, just going to the shop. I figured I'd help Aunt Laurie for a bit. I can only sit at home for so long. I picked up a few bits that I know she needed on the way."

"Then let me carry your bag for you. I'm headed that way myself."

"Thank you. And speaking of yesterday?"

Cal picked up her shopping bag and started walking with her. "You're not reconsidering dinner, are you?"

Hattie shook her head. "No, no, nothing like that. I just wanted to double check that you meant it and it wasn't a heat of the moment or a let's irritate Markus thing."

Cal grinned. "There was nothing hot about that storm at all." He winked. "And as far as irritating Markus goes? I honestly don't think that's possible."

"Have you tried?"

"Not personally, but Carter, my brother has. He made it his mission in life to send flowers to every single girl that Markus ever paid any attention to. It cost him a small fortune."

"Bet it did. What happened?"

"He ended up falling in love with and marrying the florist. They have two kids now."

She chuckled as she walked with him, his nearness almost overwhelming. "So you meant the offer of dinner then?"

"Sure did. We can either go out or I can cook."

"You cook?"

"You know I do. How about beans on toast?" He winked at her. "We'll go out. Do you like fish?"

"Love it."

"Great. We'll go to the best fish place on the island. I'll pick you up at six. And while we're on the base, I'll give you a tour of it."

"I'd like that. Thank you."

Cal smiled and pushed the door to the store open for her. "Hi, Laurie," he called. "Found Hattie, walked over with her."

Aunt Laurie smiled. "That was kind of you."

"Actually he's being modest," Hattie put in. "He rescued me again."

Cal shook his head and put the bag behind the counter. "Here's your shopping. Hattie, are you ready for the tour?"

"Sure." She put the flour on the counter. "Where first?"

He grinned. "This is the shop and this is our shop manager, Laurie Dillon."

She shot him a withering look. "No, really? I thought this was a bus stop."

"Ha, ha, ha. Come on."

She waved to her aunt and followed Cal the short distance from the shop into the lifeboat station.

"This is the Atlantic class boat, *Ray of Hope.* But you got up close and personal with her yesterday. And over here in the other cage we have *Katherine* named in memory of Daniel Froe's wife. He wanted a more lasting tribute to her than a park bench."

"It's a good idea. Bet they cost a lot of money though."

"A fair bit yeah. You're talking between upwards of fifty thousand quid for a class D RHIB, like the *Katherine,* to several million for the biggest all–weather ones."

"Wow."

He nodded. "It's not just the boat, you see. It's all the onboard equipment and so on as well. And then our uniforms and other gear as well. It's not a cheap thing to keep running by any means."

"And you rely solely on donations? Do you get paid for saving people?"

"We're purely funded by donations, yes." Cal nodded, running his hand along the side of the boat. "And, the answer to your other question is no. We don't get paid as such. We get a monetary reward for loss of earnings, but we don't keep it. By a mutual decision, it goes into a crew fund for the kids. Dinner at Christmas, a party, pantomime, Santa, and so on.

We're just one huge family here."

Hattie smiled. "That's a lovely thing to do."

"Last Christmas we ordered a fish and chip supper for everyone on the twenty eighth of December—crew, partners, and kids. One hundred and fifty portions in total. Originally, the chip shop wasn't going to be open, but they did for us. Let's face it, they'd have been mad to turn down one hundred and fifty orders. I went to collect it, with Tom and Sam. Another chap came in while we were there. He asked what all the food was for and when Tom said it was for here, the guy paid for the lot."

"That's amazing. Show's how highly people think of you."

"Most of them. Although contrary to popular belief, the fourth emergency service is *not* the car rescue people."

Hattie grinned. "It's the coastguard. Even a land lubber like me knows that one."

"Anyway, the RHIB has a crew of two or three, depending who's around. The other one, my one, has a crew of three or four."

"Do you have any female crew?" she asked as she followed him down a short passage.

"Three shore crew and a female helm on white watch. Our youngest crew member is seventeen, the oldest is forty-three. We have to retire from the boats at fifty, but usually then become shore crew or do what Tom did and become the LOM or DLA. This is the crew changing area. We all have our own suits, helmets and so on. The boots are integral which saves time when changing. Except when Sam decides he's going to fill them with talc before a training exercise. Normally that's reserved for the newbies, but Sam just likes doing it anyway."

She laughed. "What happens if the suits get torn?"

"Your kit, you mend it."

"Seriously?"

He nodded. "They get looked after a lot better that way. The boats are launched via this rig called a DODO." He pointed to the tractors and cages. "That stands for drive on, drive off. We always reverse into the cage so we can just go straight out."

"Cal, can't you keep away?"

Hattie turned at the new voice. A tall, blue-eyed man with salt and pepper hair stood in the doorway.

Cal grinned. "Nope. Just giving a friend the guided tour. She's on holiday here. This is Hattie Steele."

The man held out a hand. "Tom Milligan, lifeboat operations manager. How are you finding Penry Island?"

"It hasn't changed since I was a kid. We used to come and stay with my aunt all the time. She runs the shop next to the base."

Tom clicked his fingers. "I knew I recognized the name. You're Steve's sister. He used to play with my Derek. How is he?"

"Fine." She smiled. At least she assumed he was fine. He wasn't sick, she knew that much. "He's married and runs a guest house on the mainland."

"Say hi to him next time you see him."

"I will."

"Cal, when you get a moment, can you look over those press photos please? You need to pick one for the RNLI mag and for the website."

"Tom, I told you a dozen times already, Sam is the face of Penry Island station, not me." Cal's tone changed and tinged with irritation.

"You are now. So choose a picture or two—or I will. They need it by one at the latest. The newspaper article gets printed today, should be in tonight's paper."

"And that one can go on the dartboard, too."

"It will not. I shall frame it right alongside the other one."

Cal sighed. "Fine. When I get the chance, I'll look at the photos. Right now I'm a little busy." He looked at Hattie. "Let me show you the rest of the station."

"Sure." She followed him to the stairs.

"All these pictures on the walls are of rescues we've done. One of the local artists does them for us, based on the reports we write and interviews afterwards. This is my grandfather—Sidney Trant."

Hattie read the text below. "Wow. That's some rescue."

Cal nodded. "That picture depicts the rescue. He got the MBE for his part in it."

"I can see why." The painting depicted a huge tanker, dwarfing the small lifeboat beside it. Lines ran between the two ships with a figure in lifeboat uniform in the water. "And they got everyone off?"

"Yes. And they secured the ship so it could be towed to safe harbor after the storm." He sighed as his pager went off. "Here we go again."

Tom appeared on the landing above them. "Cal!"

"I'm right here. What have we got?"

"Child gone missing—Dylan Wills age four. Reports say he either fell from or was swept off the pier. I need both boats to respond to this one."

"I'm there. Excuse me." Cal hurtled down the stairs.

113

Hattie turned back to the picture on the wall. She didn't have to imagine what being out there in a storm was like. She knew only too well. "Are this number of launches in a week normal?"

"No. We normally get one or two a week. This is pretty exceptional. Probably won't get any next week at all. Or we don't get out to sea at all except training."

"When's that?"

"Every Wednesday evening and Sunday morning. That way each crew trains twice during their duty week. Would you like to come and watch the launch?"

"Yes, I would." Hattie smiled and followed him down the stairs and out onto the beach.

The DODO was already outside the station, warming the engines and the shore team rushed around prepping the boats. Cal appeared already kitted up as the rest of the two crews ran in from the car park.

Sam rolled his eyes. "How'd you manage that one, Cal?"

"Already here," Cal grinned. "Hurry up. Four year old boy in the water off the pier somewhere." He climbed up into the boat and set about checking the equipment.

Tom smiled at Hattie. "As helm officer, Cal's in charge of the boat. Phil is training to be a helmsman, so during training, Cal becomes the instructor."

"They're good at what they do."

Tom checked his clipboard, marking off the names. "They're a team. It makes a difference to just being four men in a boat."

"The way Cal described it is a family."

Tom nodded. "Very much so. It's like being a father to twenty-one teenage boys at times."

The other members of the team ran past them and climbed into their respective lifeboats. The tractors instantly made their way down the shingle beach.

"It's so different to yesterday." She rubbed her arm, trying to equate the sea now with the huge life threatening waves from the previous day.

"It should make the rescue easier, but not necessarily. There are a lot of eddies by the pier. And the tide's about to go out. Which means the child could be pulled out to sea."

"How much fuel have they got?" She watched Cal guide the boat from the cage and speed off into the water.

"Two and a half hours' worth. But that should be plenty. The RHIB can last three hours."

"What if they don't find the child?"

"They'll come back and refuel. I'll have a relief crew standing by after the refuel if a third launch is needed."

"Isn't five hours a long time to be out there?"

"Three hours is the maximum in the winter, but today it's not too bad."

Hattie watched as the boats vanished out of sight. *Keep them safe and let their mission be a success.*

# 12

At exactly six o'clock. Cal rang the doorbell. He wiped his hands on his slacks, surprised at how nervous he felt. He'd taken out loads of women over the years, but this? This was different. He knew he carried a lot of baggage from the past on how to treat, or rather how *not* to treat women and at some point he needed to sit down and talk it through with Carter and or pray about it. Maybe on reflection he'd just pray about it.

The door opened and Laurie stood there. "Evening, Cal. My, you scrub up well."

He smiled, hating the way his cheeks betrayed him. "Thanks." His voice came out a lot gruffer than he wanted and he coughed to clear his throat. "Is Hattie in?"

"She sure is. Come on in." Laurie opened the door wide and as he stepped over the threshold, she turned to the stairs. "Hattie, Cal's here."

"One moment," came the reply. "I'm having a crisis."

"Need some help?"

"No. I just need a couple more minutes."

Cal smiled. "Mind if I take a quick peek in the den?" he asked. "Have a look before starting work on Monday?"

"Course not. You know where it is."

He nodded and headed through to the side of the

house that the fire had destroyed. The main repairs to the structure had been completed and the breeze block walls were in place along with the wiring. Floors were also in, but nothing else. He needed to plaster the walls, add coving, skirting, door frames and doors.

The original door and frame still stood in place, blistered and blackened. He wasn't sure why it was still there, but his first job would be to rip it out and put in a new one. The room felt chilly and he wondered if plastering then plasterboard would be a better idea. It would better insulate it and help the new heating. The radiators sat unconnected in the middle of the room. Dad could fit those once he'd finished and then Brian, the decorator could put the paper up. Unless he did it. Not exactly part of his job, but it wouldn't take long and he knew Laurie had it all ready and waiting.

A cough in the doorway dragged his attention back and he turned. To be almost floored by the vision of beauty that stood before him. Wow, wow, wow. Lost for words he just stood there.

The white floral dress swirled around her body, highlighting her very feminine curves, which were all in the right places. Her hair framed her face, her blue eyes sparkled and was that a hint of make-up? Some fragrance wafted on the air and he inhaled deeply. Whatever it was he liked it. He liked it a lot. He let his gaze run down her body, past her shapely legs to her ankles and the flat shoes she wore. He hated women who wore heels just to tower over him or to look good. Not to mention those who pretended to be able to walk in them when they blatantly couldn't.

His gaze slowly made its way back to her face and he smiled. "Very nice. Worth the crisis. Even the sling matches."

She shook her head. "I laddered my tights, three pairs of them. Then I splodged my nail varnish."

"Splodged?"

"Splodged, smudged or whatever the correct word is, I did it. I had to redo two of them. Doing things one handed isn't easy."

He grabbed her nails and inspected them. "They look fine to me. Oh, go you. Metallic paint with funky patterns on them."

Color burned in her cheeks and she looked at him shyly.

He kissed her fingers, his lips lingering on her warm skin.

"Did you find the little boy?" she asked.

"Yes, we did. He's fine. The hospital is keeping him in overnight just to be on the safe side. Think his mum found it harder than he did." Then he grinned. "Shall we go before my stomach starts rumbling?" At that instant his stomach did rumble and it was his turn to blush.

"Perfect timing." Hattie laughed. "Might be a good idea if we went now, before mine joins in and we have a symphony going on."

"Ya think?" He let go of her hand and indicated the door. "After you."

"Thank you." She glanced towards the kitchen as they headed down the hall and shot Laurie a smile. "See you later. I've got a key."

"OK, dear. Have fun. I won't wait up."

Cal grinned. "How long do you think I'm going to keep her out?"

"I know your type," came the laughing reply. "Dancing all night."

He opened the door. "You got it."

"Come for lunch tomorrow after training. It'll be ready about half one."

"Sounds great. Thank you. Bye, Laurie."

Hattie looked at him as they exited the warm house into the chilly night air. "I'm sorry. She does like to tease something chronic."

"It's fine." He slid his hand into hers, unable to wait any longer to touch her somehow.

"Have you ever done that before?"

"What? Held someone's hand? Or taken a girl out for dinner and dancing and not brought her home until the wee small hours?"

"The latter."

He hesitated and opened the truck door. "Yeah, I have. Only usually I didn't get them home until after breakfast the following morning." He winked. "Don't worry, I'm a reformed man."

"Just as well, or Aunt Laurie really would have something to say." She smiled and settled back into the seat. He ran around the truck and got in the other side. Starting the engine, he flipped on the lights. At least it wasn't raining. He wanted to take her for a walk after dinner.

Hattie looked sideways at him. "I've never been dancing."

"Never? And I'm sure you told me you studied ballet until you were fourteen."

"Ballet's different—that's an art form. Good little Baptist girls don't dance," she said, sounding as if she were quoting someone.

"Then I think it's time you went dancing," he grinned. "Good job you're not wearing heels. Or don't good little Baptist girls wear those either?"

"Nope." She grinned.

He stopped at the lights. "Boyfriends?"

"Never." She pretended to shudder at the thought. Then she sighed. "No, I'm pretty much a wallflower."

"I happen to love wallflowers."

She laughed. "I told Steve I was planning on being the maiden aunt."

"Man wasn't made to be alone, you know," he told her. "Whether it's a husband, wife or just a very good friend, there is someone for everyone out there. Even you, before you say anything else." She didn't look convinced and he carried on. "Trust me, on that one. If not, look at it this way. In the two days you've been here, you've had two blokes ask you out."

"That's what Aunt Laurie said, but I don't see them as dates."

His heart sank. "Oh? Then what would you call this?"

"I'd call it going to dinner with a great guy I like a lot. And yesterday was sailing with a childhood friend which I had an ulterior motive for doing." She paused. "Oh, and also getting rescued by a great guy I like a lot."

He winked. "Just don't tell that great guy you like that you're going out with me then. He may be the jealous type."

Hattie burst out laughing, rocking back and forth in the seat in obvious delight. Once she calmed down she smiled. "Thank you. I don't remember the last time I laughed like that."

"I aim to please." He pulled into a parking space at the back of the restaurant. "They don't just do fish here, but the fish is to die for. Although, thinking about it, dying for it would be a waste of a good piece of fish." He got out of the truck and ran around to open the door for her. He took her hand, guiding her from the truck.

Her smile made him go weak at the knees and her perfume filled his senses like nothing else ever had. Why was she so different? Was God leading him towards her in a way He hadn't before. She was definitely unlike any other woman he'd dated. He'd go as far as saying she was a lady, not a woman.

He escorted her into the restaurant and followed the waiter to the table. Pulling out the chair for Hattie he smiled at her, before he sat opposite.

"Here's your menu." The waiter handed them both huge cardboard folders. "Can I get you something to drink?"

Cal looked at Hattie. "What would you like?"

"Grapefruit and bitter lemon, please."

"And I'll have orange and lemonade, please." He looked at her as the waiter left them. "Is that the bloke you're having dinner with?"

She giggled. "Nope. I'll let you know when he shows up. You can hide under the table."

"I might have to. If he's that jealous he might have brought a gun with him."

"Hmmm…men in uniform," she said a wistful expression crossing her face.

Cal hid behind his menu so she wouldn't see the smirk on his face. "Oh, please," he complained halfheartedly. "Not another female who likes the uniform. What about those blokes who don't wear one?"

"Even pastors wear a uniform of sorts—a suit and tie." She tilted her head. "But this time I did mean the waiter." Her foot touched his ankle for an instant and he laughed.

"OK, I asked for that one."

She grinned and studied the menu. "Mind you, I've seen your uniform."

"And?"

She looked at him as if deep in thought, distracted by the reappearance of the waiter.

"Your drinks. Are you ready to order?"

"Please. I'll have the potato skins to start with, with the cheese and chive dip. Then the…" she turned over the menu "…grilled monkfish with black olive sauce and lemon mash and baby carrots."

Cal smiled. She'd picked things she could eat one handed. "And I'll have the seared wild salmon, Dijon sauce, new potatoes and green beans. With the scampi to start with." He looked at him. "I'm allergic to nuts."

"I'll make sure the chef knows." The waiter took the menus and vanished.

Hattie looked at him. "Did you bring your pager?"

"I did. Along with my EpiPen. All I can say is I'm glad its Saturday and the week's almost over. I've never known a week like it."

She nodded slightly, running a finger around the rim of her glass. "How often do you fund raise?"

"We have an open day a couple of times a year and the shop's always open, except on a Sunday."

She nodded.

"But I don't want to talk about work." He gazed into her eyes, content to lose himself in them. "I'd rather talk about other things. Like you."

"You know about me. I have a twin brother who's determined to run my life for me. I quit my job and am currently not sure what I'm going to do with the rest of my life."

He tilted his head. "And you're also an amazing cook. You should come and work here."

Her eyes lit as she smiled. "Maybe, but I prefer home cooking to high end dining. Cooking the food that is, not eating it."

He kept the light flow of conversation going throughout the meal. She was so at ease with him, as if his past didn't matter. Impressed his pager hadn't gone off at all, he paid and then taking her hand led her outside. It was decidedly chilly now and he pulled his jacket collar up. "Do you fancy coming for a walk?" he asked.

"Love to."

"Then let's drive a little way and walk along the beach."

****

Hattie removed her shoes and left them in the passenger seat of the truck. Sliding her hand into Cal's she walked with him onto the sand. It was cold between her toes, but she didn't want it any other way. Sand had to be walked on barefoot, not in shoes or sneakers or sandals. Waves crashed onto the shore to her left, the familiar sound comforting, yet at the same time frightening. She guessed that being thrown about in them changed her perspective a little. She shuddered and Cal stopped walking, turning her to face him.

"What is it?" His tone was gentle, concerned, his eyes searching hers. "I'm not going to hurt you."

"I know. It's not you."

"Then what is it? They say a problem shared is a problem halved."

"I've always loved the beach. Could sit here for hours, or walk on the sand and in the waves, but now? After yesterday, it's just..." She broke off. She was going to sound like a fool and didn't want him to think her stupid.

"Go on." His voice encouraged her. Maybe he wouldn't laugh.

"What if the waves drag me out there and pull me under?"

"They won't. You'd have to go a very long way out for that to happen. Or go out in a storm. Just standing on the water's edge is perfectly safe. Besides, I'm right here, holding you and I won't let anything happen." He tugged her hand. "Come on. Just as far as our ankles, no deeper. Probably not even that if it's cold."

She hung back, not letting go of him as he led her down to the water's edge and stood just in reach of the waves. His face was comical as the cold water rushed over his feet and he jumped back to her side. "Cold."

She smiled at his antics and when he took her hand again, pulling her with him, didn't argue. The waves dashed over her feet, sending shock waves running through her.

"See," he whispered, his arm going around her and pulling her close. "You're quite safe."

She nodded. "I'm just being stupid."

"Not stupid," he replied. "It's normal to be a little nervous after what you went through. You need to get back out there on a boat again, just to prove to yourself that you can do it. It doesn't have to be for very long. I'm sure Markus would oblige. He owns more than enough boats."

She looked up at the stars twinkling in the jeweled

sky. The twin bridges outlined against it a little further along the coast. "I guess so. But I don't want to talk about Markus, right now."

He pulled her into his arms. She leaned against his chest, listening to his heart beating. His voice rumbled above her. "You don't?"

"No. Those shutters you were hanging the other day. Did you make them?"

He grinned, confusion in his eyes for a moment. "Yes, I did."

"Would you be able to do some for Aunt Laurie's house? The ones she has left are so old now, that I figured we may as well replace the lot, not just the ones destroyed in the fire."

"She didn't mention them."

"I know, this is my idea. I can pay for them. It doesn't have to be anything fancy. Just Uncle Reg's family crest..."

His laugh was infectious and she joined in. "That's a good one, Hattie. Though I think a crest is a little beyond me. How about hearts and their initials intertwined?"

"That sounds good. Let me have the bill for those. I don't want her knowing what they cost."

"I'll work it out and get back to you." His finger ran down her cheek, sending rivers of warmth through her chilled body. "You're cold."

"A little."

"Then let me warm you up." His hands pressed against her back, holding her close as his lips brushed against hers and she closed her eyes, conscious thought leaving her.

Finally he pulled away leaving her breathless. He smiled, the stars forming a halo around his head. "I should get you home before Laurie comes after me with a baseball bat."

"Does she even have one?"

"I don't know, but I'm not going to risk it." He kissed her lightly. "Perhaps next time we go dancing."

Joy filled her, bubbling up from her frozen toes to the tips of her eyelashes. He wanted to take her out again. "I'd like that."

He grinned. "So would I."

# 13

Monday morning, Hattie looked at Aunt Laurie over breakfast. "Did you want me to hang around to let Cal in?"

"He rang earlier. He's not going to be able to start today after all. You know Mrs. Edgemont on the harbor? Patricia's grandmother?"

Hattie nodded.

"Well, her husband decided to go up into the attic yesterday and put his foot through the bedroom ceiling."

Hattie tried not to laugh. "But Mr. Edgemont is like eighty-two. What was he doing in the loft?"

"Goodness only knows. Anyway, the short story is, Cal can't start for the next two weeks as the entire attic is riddled with woodworm. He needs to replace all the ceiling joists then board the attic floor again."

"Mr. Edgemont's accident is a blessing in disguise, then. The whole thing might have come down on them during the night or something." She pushed aside the disappointment filling her. She'd hoped on seeing him for the bulk of the day, talking to him as he worked.

"But he did say he'd drop by later to pick you up. Around seven or so. He said something about tripping fantastic lights or some such thing."

"That sounds like fun. I need to get my head around what I'm going to do in the future. Only thing I

do know is that I'm not going back to Headley Cross."
She sucked in a deep breath. "Would you mind if I
stayed here a little longer. I can pay rent for the room,
help out with food and so on. I could also work in the
shop like I said I was going to."

"You will not," Aunt Laurie said firmly. "You are
on holiday. Let your arm rest, go for walks, do some
thinking."

"OK. It'll give me time to get all those curtains and
cushion covers made. They'll be ready to go straight in
your new rooms then. Do you want to come with or do
you trust me?"

Aunt Laurie grinned. "I'll come with. I don't start
work until midday today. Besides, after the last time I
let you decorate..."

"Oh, that was years ago and Steve's idea." Hattie
halfheartedly complained. "And what's wrong with
lime green and orange? You had one of those bubble
chairs decked out in that."

Laughter filled the room. "That was left over from
the seventies. And I was glad to see the back of it." She
broke off as the phone rang. "Hello." She listened for a
moment then held out the phone. "It's the hospital, for
you."

****

Cal arrived just before seven. His stomach roiled
within him and he wished he hadn't eaten. Or at least
had something plain like eggs on toast, rather than the
curry he'd fancied on his way home. He rang the bell
and waited.

Hattie answered the door, her face pale and her
arm in a...cast?

Shock flooded him. "What happened?"

"Hello to you too, Cal." She opened the door properly. "Come in." She left him in the hall and went back into the lounge.

Shaking his head, he shut the door and followed her. Laurie had rung earlier and said Hattie was out of sorts, but he hadn't expected this. "What happened?"

"The hospital rang. The consultant was checking the files from the weekend and decided he didn't like my x-ray. They called me back in and redid it and my wrist is broken after all."

"It could be worse."

She raised bitter, anger filled eyes to him. "How could this *possibly* be any worse?"

He sat next to her. "You could be on crutches as well."

She scowled. "That's not possible."

He grinned and waited patiently for the penny to drop.

It took a while before she relaxed slightly and a faint smile crossed her lips. "Yeah, I guess so."

He hugged her, planting a kiss on her cheek. "But as you're not, I'm taking you dancing."

"I can't dance like this."

"I beg to differ. The last time I checked, people dance with their feet, not their wrists. You'll be fine, I promise."

"I don't know how to dance other than ballet and I told you, I can't do that anymore. Not since some dumb accident when I was fourteen."

"No problem. I booked lessons for us tonight and Thursday."

"Lessons?" A wonderfully puzzled look crossed her face, making him want to kiss her even more. "Just because I don't know anything but ballet, doesn't mean I need lessons."

"We both do." He gently pulled her to her feet. "I have something special planned for Saturday. Now go put on a pair of flat canvas shoes and a skirt. We need to be there in twenty-five minutes."

They arrived at the hall just in time and he led her onto the dance floor. Most of the other couples were much older, but he didn't care. For the next couple of hours this was just him and Hattie.

"What are we doing here?" she asked.

"Ballroom dancing."

"You're kidding?" Amazement filled her face, her eyes sparkling. "Like on the television?"

"Without the judges I hope, but yeah. It looks so easy and effortless on the TV and I've always wanted to learn and as you don't know how to dance properly..." He broke off and grinned.

She shook her head at him. "And this connects to Saturday, how?"

"I'm taking you to a tea dance."

Her face lit up like the full moon on a clear night. "Oh, wow." She hugged him as tightly as she could with one arm. "Nanna met Grandad at one of those. I had no idea they still did them."

"Maybe not on the mainland, but here on the island, the Palladium does them once a month. If you'd like to come, of course."

"I'd love to. But my arm..."

"Won't be a problem."

No stranger to footwork, Cal found the first dance they learned was easy and soon they were both dancing like professionals. Or they may as well be. Hattie laughed and smiled and relaxed in his arms, following his lead effortlessly. He lost himself in her eyes, the scent of her perfume and her presence. He had easily the most beautiful woman in the room in his arms, but his reaction to her body flush against his, stunned him. He thought being a Christian would help him control himself, but he wanted her and it took every ounce of restraint he had, not to mention a shed load of telegram prayers, to simply drive her home afterwards.

He opened the truck door and walked her up the path to the house.

Her eyes sparkled like stars. "Thank you for a wonderful evening."

"You're welcome."

"It was nice not having to share you with your pager."

"Actually, my pager came too." He chuckled, low and long. "But you know what they say. Love me, love my pager."

Hattie tilted her head. "I thought that referred to dogs."

He lifted his hand and ran it slowly down her cheek. "Hattie…"

Her eyes darkened as she studied him. She leaned into his touch. Did she feel the same tightening in her belly that he did? "Yes?"

His lips covered hers. As she responded, he deepened the kiss, tasting and possessing her. His arms held her against him and he lost all track of time. Until the porch light flicked on, illuminating them.

He pulled back. "I think that's my cue to leave," he said regretfully. "Same time on Thursday?"

She smiled. "I'll be ready and waiting. Good night."

"Good night." He watched her go inside and then headed back to the car. *Better watch it, Cal* he told himself. *Or you'll be in too deep. Don't mess with the affairs of the heart.*

*Too late* came the reply. *You're already drowning.*

****

Hattie stood in the queue in the bank. She'd kept the money under the mattress long enough and decided that Wednesday was the day to pay it in and open a new account. One Steve wouldn't know about. Right now, the envelope was tucked into her sling as her purse was too small to fit all the notes it. Aunt Laurie had dropped her off and gone to work. After her shift finished, they were going fabric shopping.

She was going to give her aunt's address as her place of residence, with her old address as back up. Holding the ID in her other hand, she moved up in the queue at the customer service desk. Why she had to queue for a scheduled appointment she had no idea.

Markus moved away from the cashier and smiled at her. "Hello, Harriet. How's the arm?"

"It turned out to be broken after all, so I can't work for six weeks."

"I bet Steven's not happy."

"It's got nothing to do with him. He doesn't even know I hurt my arm, never mind anything else. I'm done working with him. I'm staying here for the time being. I might even find a job on the island and settle here full time."

"You can't quit the guest house. He depends on you."

"It's too late. I quit last week before I left."

"Does Steven know where you are?"

She moved up in the queue, shivers running up her spine and a hollow pit in her stomach, as his comment unsettled her. "No, and that's the way it's staying. You promised not to tell him if I went out with you and I'm expecting you to honor that promise."

"Do you have time for lunch?"

Hattie blinked. "That's a change of subject."

Markus grinned. "I guess so. But you do have to eat."

"True. OK, once I've paid this in."

He glanced at the envelope in her sling and his eyes widened for a moment before they narrowed. "Wow, that's a lot of cash to carry around."

"This would be why I'm paying it in." She reached the counter. "Hattie Steele. I have an appointment with Mr. Clyde at eleven."

"I'll take you through."

"Harriet, I'll wait outside for you."

"Sure." She followed the woman down the corridor to an office, shoving aside the thought that Markus's parting comment sounded more like a threat than a promise.

Twenty minutes later, and almost five grand lighter, she exited the bank into the bright, chilly sunshine. She always found it ironic that during winter the Earth was closer to the sun than in summer, yet the temperature was decidedly colder.

Markus leaned against the wall, chatting on his phone. "Here she is. I've got to go. Speak to you later." He smiled at her and held out a hand. "Let's go."

Hattie slid her free hand into her pocket, out of his reach, and walked with him. He led her into the first eatery they came to, which happened to be a fast food outlet. She ordered chicken strips and chips and a lemon soda. Markus paid and carried the tray to a table.

He spent most of the time touching her hand, or rubbing his foot against hers, his eyes fixed on her. She found it disconcerting at first and downright creepy after ten minutes of it. "I was thinking, Harriet."

"What about?" She pushed back in her seat, as far away from the table as she could politely get and picked up her soda, drinking slowly.

"About when we were kids and you used to come up here for the summers. Steven and I used to joke about being brothers, and you and I getting married before we reached thirty."

She looked at him over the cup, suddenly finding the chicken in her stomach too greasy. Steve had said the same thing several times over the past few weeks. And she'd felt just as uncomfortable. "Really? I don't remember that."

"We did. Of course, we were only kids, but I always knew we'd end up together. And you coming back here to stay has to be fate. I like you, Harriet. I like you a lot."

She raised an eyebrow. "Don't take this the wrong way, but I don't believe in fate. And I don't feel that way about you."

"Steven would like it."

"Then marry Steve. Oh wait, you can't. He's already married." She put the cup down, wiping her hands on the paper napkin. "Besides, your name doesn't start with a P."

Markus frowned. "What's that got to do with anything?"

"He said I have to marry someone whose name

starts with a P."

His frown turned into a grin. "Didn't I tell you my given name is Peyton Markus?"

Hattie buried the laugh. He wouldn't find it amusing and this really wasn't the time for humor. "Isn't Peyton a girl's name?"

He sighed. "It's a family name, handed down to the eldest child. So that's one plus in my favor."

"I can't marry you, Markus. For one thing, you haven't asked." She stood up. "Thank you for lunch. I have to go and run the rest of my errands now."

He grabbed her hand. "Is there another reason? I can fix the not asking you very easily. And I already have Steven's permission to ask you."

Her stomach plummeted and she felt sick. "Wait a minute. You asked Steve? When did you speak to him? You promised not to say anything."

"Whist you were in the bank. So, sweet one, what's to stop you from marrying me?"

She held his gaze. *My heart lies with someone else* she whispered silently. "I can't because I don't love you. Or trust you." She tugged her hand free. "Thank you for lunch. I'll see you around." *But not if I can help it.*

She hurried from the shop and almost ran down towards where she said she'd meet Aunt Laurie. By the time she got there, she was shaking.

Her aunt hugged her, sitting her down on a bench. "Goodness, child, whatever is the matter?"

"Markus said he'd spoken to Steve, so presumably Steve knows I'm here. That means he'll be down here begging me to go back. Or pressuring me to marry Markus."

Aunt Laurie handed her a tissue. "Marry Markus?

Where did that come from?"

Hattie took a deep breath and used the tissue. "I bumped into Markus at the bank. He asked me to lunch, said he'd spoken to Steve and asked his permission while I was paying in the money. Steve said yes. He'll insist on my marrying Markus now. And before you say he wouldn't do that, you know he will, or he isn't my brother."

Aunt Laurie hugged her. "No one can force you into marriage, dear. It's illegal in this country. Now dry those eyes and let's go fabric shopping. Then I feel a cream tea coming on with huge scones and clotted cream."

Hattie smiled slightly. "Sounds good."

"And you can tell me all about this date with Cal and the fantastic lights. I'm intrigued."

"Dancing," Hattie said, getting to her feet, thoughts of Cal whirling in her head, blowing away her fear. "He took me ballroom dancing."

# 14

Cal picked Hattie up at four on Saturday afternoon, and whistled softly. "Look at you."

She did a twirl. "You like?"

"I more than like." He was bowled over by the way her shirt fitted, the way the skirt flowed around her ankles, showing off her matching sneakers. Even her sling matched. He kissed her gently. "You look amazing."

"Thank you. So do you."

Laurie appeared in the hallway. "You kids have fun."

Cal grinned. "We will. And I promise I'll have her back by ten."

"Or parked out the front by ten," Hattie added, elbowing him.

His cheeks burned, the sensation worsening as Laurie laughed. "No parking outside my house," she told them. She winked. "I know the two of you far too well."

He cleared his throat. "I assure you my intentions are entirely honorable."

"I'm glad to hear it. I'd hate to have to find my baseball bat." She grinned and waved as she shut the front door.

"You told her about that?" Cal asked, mortified.

Hattie giggled. "I merely asked if she had one. She asked why and I said to make errant men behave themselves. How was I to know she would assume I meant you and not Uncle Reg?"

Cal chuckled and led Hattie over to his truck and opened the door for her. "Does Laurie ever quit with the teasing?"

"Nope." She shook her head, her blonde hair spiraling around her face, showing off her neck and the ribbon fastened around it. "Especially if she likes or approves of someone."

"I'm glad she approves. It makes seeing you so much easier." He ran around the truck, got in and started the engine.

"How are the Edgemont's repairs coming on?"

"They're getting there. Another week should see them finished. It helps not being on call this week and only back up crew next week."

"So we have to share you with the pager." She rolled her eyes.

Cal mimicked the expression right back at her. "Are you dissing the pager?"

"No, no, I wouldn't dare to diss the pager." She tried to keep a straight face and failed.

"Good. Because my pager is as important as say, your right arm is." He grinned, knowing it was her left arm that was broken.

"Oh, funny ha ha. It's a good job I like you."

"Like you too." He concentrated on the driving for a moment, his brain whirling. If he were honest, he more than liked her and had long since stopped fighting it. "So, have you decided what you're going to do long term?"

"Stay here. Aunt Laurie said I can stay with her until I find a place of my own, and then said not to rush finding somewhere. I think she likes the company. I need a job, but not sure what. Maybe in a café or somewhere, and although there's no rush there either, it won't hurt to start looking and see what's around."

"I'm sure something will crop up. God's timing is always perfect."

"Yeah."

He parked the truck and led her into the Palladium. The huge, decades old hall was surrounded by pillars holding up the gallery. A massive stage filled the front section and he could almost imagine the old time music hall performances that must have occurred here in years gone by. Tables and chairs set around the edge of the hall, the large floor in the middle cleared and ready for dancing. Lights glimmered overhead, the orchestra played quietly.

Cal handed in their coats and took the number in exchange. Taking hold of Hattie's hand, he led her over to the table which matched their number. He could tell by the huge grin on her face how much she enjoyed eating her sandwiches and cake off the bone china plates. Even the tea tasted different from the bone china cups.

She giggled and stuck out her little finger as if she were having tea with the Queen. And when they danced, it was as if they were floating on air. The lessons had paid off as he no longer trod on her toes. He was disappointed when the evening came to a close and it was time to take her home. He debated a late evening walk, but she looked shattered.

He escorted her to the door of her aunt's cottage.

"Thank you, Cal. I had a lovely time," she said, trying to hide a yawn.

"So did I." He wrapped his arms around her and

kissed her. "I'll see you tomorrow in church."

"Count on it. Good night." She let herself in, softly closing the door behind her.

He looked at the closed door for a moment then headed back to his truck. He wasn't sure where God was leading either of them; he just prayed that they were both going in the same direction.

**** 

Hattie found the next week flew by in a whirl of dancing lessons, volunteering at the shop and looking for work. She loved spending time with Cal and made excuses to drop by where he was working, bringing lunch and various cakes and nibbles from recipes she'd found stuffed in a folder at the back of one of Aunt Laurie's kitchen cupboards. Some of them she recognized as Nanna's.

She offered him the box of apple muffins and watched hesitantly as he bit into it. Barely able to wait while he chewed and swallowed, she asked, "Well?"

"You should sell these for a living."

"Don't talk with your mouth full," she quipped, doing the same thing she was accusing him of.

He swallowed. "Well, don't ask questions while I'm eating, then. And you can talk."

She grinned. "That's do what I say, not do what I do."

"Yes, *mum*." He chuckled. "Being serious, you should sell these for a living. Or some of your desserts. Or both. Or open a patisserie or your own café or something."

Hattie pointed her finger over the top of the cake at him. "That's rather a lot of 'ors' in the same sentence."

"Yes. Or you could open a guest house."

"Or not." She shoved the cake box under his nose and he took another one. "Maybe I just type up Aunt Laurie's unfinished book manuscript."

"Laurie writes?" The look of incredulous amazement made her want to laugh.

"Not since Uncle Reg died, but she's a bestselling author. Have you heard of Lee Fredricks?"

"Yes. He writes naval action books. I have all of them at home. Why?"

"That's Aunt Laurie."

Cal choked on the piece of cake. Hattie thumped him on the back and handed him a bottle of water. He chugged for a moment then looked up. "Wow. I never knew…she kept that one quiet. I honestly thought Lee Fredricks was a bloke."

Hattie laughed. "It's her initials. Laurie Elizabeth Emily and Fredricks was her grandmother's maiden name."

"Wow. That is going to take some getting used to. And you say that she's got a part written one?"

"Yeah. She stopped writing the day Uncle Reg died. Maybe if I type it up, she'll write the rest of it. She handwrites the first draft completely."

"Wow."

Hattie nodded. He still had that awed look on his face. "So I take it you're a huge fan."

"She has to be one of, if not my all time, favorite author. She has been for years. I might just have to ask for her autograph when I take you home."

"You will not. She'll kill me for telling you her secret."

He grinned and took another cake. "Have you

heard from Steve yet?"

"No."

"You need to call him."

"Not yet. I'm hoping Markus didn't tell him after all; else he'd have been here by now. Or he's just biding his time to catch me off guard."

"Speaking of Markus and his ongoing marriage proposals..."

She sighed. At least Cal hadn't been judgmental when she'd told him. "I haven't seen him all week which has actually been really nice as he seemed to be stalking me. Not in a creepy way, just kept appearing almost everywhere I was for a day or two. He's away on business or something. No doubt as soon as he gets back, he'll ask again."

"What will you say?"

"Same as always." She held his gaze. "I don't want to marry him. End of. Now can we please talk about something else?"

"Sure." He gripped her hand tightly, his gaze making her feel like she was the only girl on the planet. Something that Markus never did.

*And let's face it. Markus has taken you out twice, First time you almost drowned and the second time it was lunch. He hasn't kissed you, held you, laughed with you...*

"Hattie, can I ask you something?" His voice was low and serious. Had she done something to upset him?

"Sure."

"Would you go out with me?"

"We are out. And we've been out most nights since I've been here."

He ran his hand down her cheek, setting her skin ablaze where he touched her. "No, I mean date properly. Will you be my girlfriend?"

"Yes." A tsunami of joy overwhelmed her. His lips claimed hers and she lost herself in the sensations and emotions flooding her soul.

He broke off and leaned his forehead against hers. "Maybe you should just stay here with me."

She frowned slightly, her joy tempered. "What do you mean?"

"Stay here with me," he repeated.

"I won't live with you." Heat flamed in her cheeks. "I can't. It wouldn't be right."

"I'm not asking you to live with me. I'm asking you to marry me."

"Marry?" Shock ran through her. He'd only just asked her to be his girlfriend and now he was proposing?

"Yes, marry me. I don't need an answer right now. Think it over. Take as long as you need." His fingers moved slowly through her hair. "I love you, Hattie."

He kissed her, long and slow, until she lost all sense of who she was.

When he broke off, she smiled. "Is that an incentive for me to say yes?"

He grinned. "It can't hurt. I—I don't give my heart easily or often, but you… I fell for you the day I first walked into your guest house."

"Steve's guest house," she corrected.

"OK, Steve's guest house. And when I left I never thought I'd see you again. You coming here must be a God-thing."

She waved the empty cake box under his nose. "And my cooking has nothing to do with it? Or Aunt Laurie being your favorite author?"

Cal grinned. "Nope. I know this is sudden,

especially with Markus asking you as well. I'm not doing it to annoy him or to compete. I just didn't want you to marry him—without letting you know how I felt."

"Shut up."

He raised an eyebrow. "I'm sorry?"

"I said shut up." She kissed him lightly. "You can't propose in one breath and talk about Markus proposing in the next. I'll let you know next week or so. If that's OK?"

"More than OK. Take as much time as you need. I'm not going anywhere."

She nodded, half surprised she wasn't floating, she felt so light and giddy. He wanted to spend the rest of his life with her, and although her gut instinct was to say yes, she had to wonder if it was what God had planned for her.

# 15

Hattie sat at breakfast with what she knew was a stupid grin on her face, but she had no wish to change it. She spread a thick layer of marmalade on her toast.

"You look happy," Aunt Laurie commented. "Happier than you have for a while."

"Cal proposed last night."

"He what?"

Hattie grinned. "I told him I'd think about it."

"What about Markus? Hasn't he also proposed?"

"Markus?" Hattie shot elbows to the table. "He's rich, but he's... He's just a friend. And Steve's friend at that. But, Cal?" She paused, chewing on the toast, images of her tall, dark man in uniform dancing in her mind's eye. "They're complete opposites. Cal makes me feel alive. His kisses are like honey and fireworks. I spend every minute thinking about him and wanting to be with him, and when I am time just flies by."

Aunt Laurie smiled. "Cal isn't exactly poor, either."

Hattie looked at the toast in her hand and caught a stray chunk of marmalade with her finger. "No, but he doesn't flaunt it like Markus does. Besides, between you and me, Markus gives me the creeps at times. He suddenly sneaks up on me from nowhere."

"Sounds to me like you've made your decision."

"I told Cal to give me a week or so and he said take as long as I need. I mean he only asked me to be his girlfriend last night."

Aunt Laurie winked. "Before or after he proposed."

"Before he proposed. But admittedly that was after I discovered his favorite author is Lee Fredricks."

Aunt Laurie raised an eyebrow. "You didn't tell him, did you?"

"It might have slipped out. He was well impressed. The thing is," she continued, changing the subject quickly. "I don't want to rush into anything and find out ten years down the line that I made the wrong decision. Want my head to catch up with my heart and end up on the same page. I also want to pray it over, make sure God thinks it's the right thing to do."

"Sounds like a good plan."

She chewed for a moment. "When did you know Uncle Reg was the right man for you?"

Aunt Laurie drank half her coffee before she answered. "I just knew. But what sealed it was when he climbed a tree in my grandmother's garden to rescue her cat Snowball. In the rain."

Hattie laughed. "Oh, sweet."

"Only Snowball didn't want to be rescued and jumped from the tree to the windowsill and went back inside the house. So your uncle sat on the branch and launched into a version of *Singing in the Rain* which he made up on the spot." She smiled. "I knew then."

"You miss him, don't you?"

"Every day."

Hattie smiled. "You should finish the book, dedicate it to him. Even rename the hero after him."

"Maybe I will." She got up as the doorbell rang. "Wonder who that is."

"You won't know 'til you get there." Hattie leaned back in her chair. She finished her tea and stretched her good arm. Then she got up to clear the table.

"Hattie." Cal crossed the room in four strides, devastation on his face. His shoulders slumped and his normal tanned complexion was ashen as he fell into her arms.

Her tummy tied itself in knots of concern as she embraced him, she seached his anguished face. "What's happened?"

"Carter's been knocked off his bike during a time trial in Denmark. One of the support vehicles clipped his back wheel. Dad, Jess and I are flying out there today at some point to be with him and Rose, his wife. His manager is organizing flights now. We just have to get to the nearest airport on the mainland."

"I'm so sorry." Her heart thudded in her throat. "Is he OK?"

"It doesn't sound good. He's in intensive care." He hugged her. "I wanted to let you know before I left. Especially after last night, I didn't want you to think I was running out on you—"

"Shh...." Hattie put a finger over his lips. "Don't worry about that now. I know how you feel about me. Right now, what matters is Carter and you getting out to Denmark to see him. Let me know how he is."

"I will. I'll have my mobile with me and you've got the number. I love you." He kissed her with more passion than she was expecting.

She kissed him back. "Love you too."

\*\*\*\*

It was Wednesday before she heard anything.

A brief text apologizing for the delay in response, but getting a signal where they were was nigh on impossible. Carter was out of intensive care, but still critical.

She missed Cal more than she was going to admit to anyone. Not even a job interview lifted her spirits. She wasn't even sure she should go, just in case she messed up, but she did. She came out, even more miserable than when she went in. She'd blown the interview, but didn't care. She just wanted Carter to be all right and for Cal to come home.

"Hello, Harriet." Markus's voice made her jump. "What's the sad face for?"

"Markus, you startled me. I didn't see you."

"Is everything all right?"

"No, not really. Cal's brother's in the hospital in Denmark. He was run over. I was thinking about him and Cal."

"I'm sorry to hear that. Can I interest you in a spot of lunch? We need to talk."

"No, thank you. I have a lot of things to do before meeting Aunt Laurie later." She pulled up her collar against the drizzling rain.

"I don't need much of your time. I missed you while I was away. I like spending time with you and even if you can only spare me twenty minutes for a lunch date, it would mean the world to me."

"I said no, Markus. I'm with Cal now."

Something nefarious flashed in his eyes for a brief moment before he covered it. "I see."

"So, I'm sorry, but I can't do a lunch *date* or any other kind of date. I'm spoken for." The rain came down harder and she wished she had an umbrella.

"It's just lunch or are you on one of these

newfangled diets where you skip meals?"

"Markus…"

"Harriet, I have to insist. We can talk here in the rain or we can go and sit somewhere private and discuss it alone. Or we have lunch in a public place and talk, because we are having this conversation one way or the other, whether you like it or not."

"OK, fine. Twenty minutes." She agreed reluctantly, as she wasn't really interested in what he had to say. But his request sounded more like a threat than anything else, which made lunch in a public place definitely the better and safer of the three options. She had no intentions of being alone with him, ever.

Markus put a hand against the small of her back. His touch nauseated her, but every time she tried to move away, he compensated, keeping the contact as he guided her two shops down and into the restaurant. Quickly getting a table, he pulled her chair out for her. "How are you keeping?"

"Fine. Still looking for work, nothing's cropped up yet though. I was just coming out of an interview when I almost walked into you."

"How did it go?"

"I don't know."

Too worried about Cal and Carter to eat, Hattie chose the salad and just picked at it, while Markus devoured a very rare steak, peas, and chips. Looking at the steak, she decided it if was any rarer, it'd get up and walk out of the building under its own steam.

Markus touched her hand. "I saw Steven whilst I was on the mainland. It was great to catch up with him. I told him about seeing you and that we'd been out a couple of times. Told him you said hi."

Hattie shriveled inside. "You told him where I

was? You promised not to."

"I had to. He's concerned about you. He was on the verge of calling the police to report you missing. So I put his mind at rest."

She nodded stiffly, not going to deign to reply.

"He was telling me he's probably going to have to close the guest house."

She frowned. "Why? Because he's concerned about me?"

"He can't keep it going since you left. Plus, the accountants are all over him like a virus for some reason. He wouldn't say why."

She could guess though. And no doubt Steve would blame her for that as well. "He's more than capable of running it. He just needs to employ someone to help rather than expecting them to work for next to nothing. I wasn't even a partner in it, did he tell you that?"

"Then change that. Buy into it and run it with him."

"You do it if you're that fussed," she snapped. She'd already bought into the guest house for all the good it had done, but Markus didn't need to know that.

"Have you thought about my proposal? I want to marry you, Harriet."

She tilted her head. He changed the subject more frequently than she changed her shoes. "I've already answered you, but once again, the answer is no."

"Why?" He sounded like a petulant child, always used to getting his own way.

"I don't love you and it wouldn't be fair on either of us. And like I said earlier, I'm with Cal now."

She got to her feet. This had to end and end now.

Opening her purse, she pulled out some cash and put it on the table. "That's my share of the bill and tip. Goodbye, Markus."

Exiting quickly into the wet street, she just hoped she hadn't made an enemy there. She needed to speak to Cal more than ever. She sent him a text. So long as he replied, that would be fine. *Just keep him safe and look after his brother.*

# 16

"Stop moping." Aunt Laurie's voice was sterner than usual. "It's all you've done for days."

Hattie glanced up from the shelf she was restocking with miniature crew people. "I'm not moping."

"Then what would you describe it as?"

She sighed and looked at the crewperson in her hand. It looked like Cal. "Just missing him. He's been gone for over two weeks and only sent a couple of texts."

"That would be because there was a rubbish phone signal in the part of Denmark we were in." The familiar deep voice had her spinning around.

"Cal!" She was up on her feet and across the room in a flash, arms outstretched, and a huge grin on her face. "You're back."

He grabbed her and lifting her off her feet, spun her around before kissing her soundly. "Now that's what I call a welcome. I missed you, too."

"Missed you more." She suddenly caught sight of the wheelchair behind him and the two women standing just beyond it. She wriggled to be put down. "Cal...there's someone there. Please, put me down."

Cal smiled and obliged. "This is my brother, Carter, his wife Rose, and my sister, Jess. Guys, this is Hattie."

"We kind of worked that one out for ourselves,

Cal," Carter said with a chuckle so much like his brother's. He held out a hand. "It's a pleasure to finally be able to put a face to your name and meet you in person, Hattie. He's done nothing but talk about you for days."

Hattie shook his hand. "How are you feeling?"

"Better. It's going to be a while before I'm back on the bike though. I'd love to catch up and learn about you some more, but I'm tired. We only came in to collect Cal's pager since he's meant to be on duty this week. Only once he learnt you were here, he insisted on coming to see you before he did anything else," Carter answered.

"Do you blame me?" Cal hugged her again.

"I don't." She snuggled into him. "It's a shame its Wednesday and you'll be training all evening. Otherwise we could catch up and spend the evening doing nothing."

Cal nodded. "I know what I'd rather be doing." He rolled his eyes at Carter who sniggered behind him. "I meant catch up with Hattie, rather than go out in a boat and train," he grinned.

Carter grinned back. "Course you did. You live for training."

"Excuse me? And you don't?"

Hattie looked from one to the other, not sure quite how intent they were on fighting. The tones were teasing, but the looks they gave each other belied that.

Jess winked at Hattie. "Ignore them. They tease each other like this the whole time. Why don't you and Laurie come over to Dad's tonight about seven? We can get to know each other and chat without Cal interrupting us."

Hattie smiled. "I'd like that, thank you." She

looked at her aunt.

Aunt Laurie smiled and nodded in agreement. "We'll be there. I'll get Hattie to make some of her apple cakes."

"You'd better not eat them all." Cal grinned. "I like them." He kissed Hattie again. "Better go. See you later."

"You too." She watched from the door as Cal pushed the chair over to his truck.

"Well?" Aunt Laurie's soft voice came from behind her. "What does your heart tell you now?"

"Same as before, but I'm still not sure if it's what God wants. I need to pray a few more days."

*Even though I promised him a week or so and it's been two. This may well be the biggest decision in my life and I don't want to screw it up.*

****

Cal struggled to concentrate on training, his mind on other stuff, as he piloted the lifeboat across the water. Mainly Hattie. As pleased as she was to see him, she hadn't given him an answer. Maybe she wanted him alone to tell him; he just wasn't sure when that was going to be. Or she hadn't decided. Or the answer was no.

A hand tapped his shoulder. "Earth to Cal."

He glanced at Phil. "Sorry. You take her for a bit."

Phil nodded as they swiftly changed places. "So what's up? Is it Carter?"

"No, yes, well kind of. Jess met Hattie this afty and invited her over for a chat with her, Carter, and Dad."

"Without you being there?"

"Jess's idea. It's kind of asking for trouble. I mean,

who knows what they're telling her."

"Knowing your sister, she'll tell her all your deep dark secrets most likely. And drag out the baby photos and then come up with all the embarrassing things you've ever done in your entire life. Hattie will be fine. How serious are things between the two of you?"

"Pretty serious. I know how I feel about her. Just not sure she feels the same way."

"Ask her."

"I did. Still waiting on an answer. I'd hoped she'd give me one when I saw her earlier, but she didn't."

"When did you see her?"

"I popped into the store when I picked up my pager. I introduced her to Carter and Jess at the same time."

"Cal. You've been gone, virtually incommunicado for two weeks. You saw her for all of two minutes earlier, surrounded by other people. What chance did she have to say anything?"

"True."

"So take her somewhere nice tomorrow. And ask her then."

"Target spotted," Sam called. "One buoy with tag."

"Then let's register the tag and head home. Tom wants us to practice a beach landing."

"Oh, those are always fun," Sam grinned. "I might have to fight you for it."

"I don't think so," Cal said. "I'll do it."

The radio cracked. *Ray of Hope* this is Penry Island LBS, do you copy over?"

"We read you."

"Coastguard requests launch to a yacht in distress, ten miles south of your position."

"On the way."

Sam grinned at him as the boat turned on to the new course. "It's been a quiet week without you. No shouts at all. Trouble follows you."

"Cheers for that." Cal looked at Phil. "Step on it."

****

Cal grinned at Hattie over the glass of soda at lunch the following day. "So we get there and the bloke is cold and hungry and wants a lift home because he's a paid up civilian member of the RNLI."

"You're kidding." She shook her head slowly.

"Nope. Sam's like on his high horse and quoting *'we're not the AA'* at him."

Hattie laughed. "What did you do?"

"I refused on the grounds that while we were faffing about here with him, someone else could be in real danger. Only two hours later we get called out again. To the same bloke, same yacht, with the same request. Only wait for it, he insisted he couldn't read the dials on the nav unit in the dark. This time we hauled him aboard and towed the boat back to the nearest harbor. Otherwise we'd have been called in and out to him all night. We didn't tow him to the harbor he wanted mind you, as his car was several miles along the coast and he had no way of getting to it, but never mind. He was safe and on dry land and our task was done. We then headed back to base and washed the boat and refueled her."

"Did you charge him?"

"No. The French charge for towing and rescues, but we don't."

"Maybe you should. Especially when you're used

as a taxi service or the sea going equivalent of the road rescue people."

He chuckled. "I'll suggest it. Are you still on for the dancing lesson tonight?"

"Try stopping me. I've missed those. I didn't see the point in going without you."

He smiled. "How did it go last night with Jess, Carter and Dad?"

"I wondered when you'd get around to asking me about that." She took a long drink. "Actually we got on really well."

"Is that it?" He raised an eyebrow.

She laughed. "What more did you want to know? Other than you were a very cute baby."

"Oh, they didn't?" Mortification filled him.

She held his gaze, her face straight, then she grinned. "Gotcha!"

"Brat."

"Takes one to know one. They did offer to get the baby photos out to show me, but I said next time. I want to see your face when I look at them."

He sighed as his pager went off. Disappointment flooded him. "I wanted to ask—"

"It'll have to wait until later. Go. Save the world, well whoever is in peril on the sea. I'll be around for dancing if you're back in time."

"The crew thinks I'm jinxed. They didn't have a single callout while I was away."

"Nah, not jinxed. Just a disaster magnet."

He rolled his eyes. "Just whose side are you on, woman?"

Hattie thought for a moment then laughed. "My own."

He stood up. "You promised me an answer to my

proposal."

"And you'll get one, when I've decided. Now *go on now go, walk out the door*…"

"OK," he grinned "I'm going before you sing anything else at me. But you owe me an answer."

She nodded. "And I'll give you one. On Monday."

"I'll hold you to that." He kissed her and ran out of the door.

# 17

Hattie looked out of the car window as Aunt Laurie drove to church on Sunday morning. The forecasted storm had come in stronger and sooner than predicted. The Harbor Authority had taken the unusual step of closing the harbor to all inbound and outbound shipping.

Aunt Laurie glanced at her. "I've never known the harbor closed. Not since the great storm of nineteen eighty-seven. This one could get just as nasty. The Met Office issued a severe weather warning. They say the winds could reach gale force ten if not stronger."

"Cal won't be training in this, surely?"

Aunt Laurie shook her head. "Not sea training, no. They'll do first aid or some such thing on the safety of dry land. Mind you, if they get called out they'll take it on a case by case basis. The inshore boats can take up to a force seven. Over that, it's up to the helm officer. He and LOM or DLA have the final say as to whether they go or not."

During the two hours they were in church, the wind picked up even more. Tree branches and leaves littered the roads. Advertising hoardings blew off buildings and walking upright was impossible. Cal met them at the cottage which was warm and welcoming out of the storm.

"It's really bad out there," he said hanging up his jacket. "The waves are topping fifteen to twenty feet already. They've warned shipping to stay away from the coast."

"I'm not surprised. Are the bridges closed?"

"The road bridge is, yes. There isn't a train due until five o'clock tonight. They'll make a judgment call then most likely. So we're effectively sealed off from the outside world right now. Phone lines are down in some parts of the island."

"That doesn't sound good."

He smiled. "Sometimes no phones can be a good thing." He looked at Aunt Laurie. "Something smells good. Can I carve for you?"

"In about twenty-five minutes once the veggies are done. You two young people go in the other room and talk."

Hattie followed Cal into the lounge and sat on the window seat, watching the storm through the window. "So much damage," she said quietly. "Would you go out in this?"

"Only if there was no other way," Cal said. "The Navy would respond as well, but no one would be stupid enough to be out. There was enough warning this time."

"What about people being blown off cliffs and piers and so on?"

He laughed. "Would you be out there?"

"No, but I'm not some crazy reporter for the TV news." She winked. "I'm a…Actually what am I? Other than a nothing right now?"

"Hmmm." He looked at her thoughtfully. "Maybe a Nothing with a capital N."

She laughed. "Sounds good to me."

He lowered his voice. "If I didn't know better, I'd say there was some serious matchmaking going on here."

"You mean Aunt Laurie?"

Cal nodded. "Yeah. Not that I mind your company. Actually I quite enjoy it."

"That's good, because I do, too."

"Enjoy your own company?" he teased. "Probably a good thing."

"Oy." She hit him playfully on the arm.

He laughed and gently tugged her towards him, kissing her cheek. "Behave woman." He sat next to her on the window seat. "So, when do I get my answer? Did you tell her?"

"I might have, but she'd have asked you over anyway. She likes having you around." She snuggled against him. "And stop asking. You said I could have as much time as I wanted and I told you I'd let you know tomorrow. I shall have to call you Mr. Impatient."

He clutched her to him as the wind howled through the glass, with a banshee-wail. A roof tile clattered against the pavement before it went flying down the street in several pieces. "Not one of your aunt's roof tiles, I hope."

"Hopefully not, but I know a man who could probably fix it if it was."

"Oh?"

"Yeah and he's not too far away either." She winked. "I hear he's a dab hand with a hammer and nails."

He chuckled. "I'm a carpenter, not a roofer. But yeah, I know a man who can."

Aunt Laurie came in and flicked on the radio. "You should listen to this," she said quietly. "The storm is making the national news."

Dinner was eaten in the lounge with the radio still playing. Reports came in from up and down the coast of damage to power cables, phone lines, and some flooding on the other side of the island. Rain pounded the windows, blurring the distant lights of the mainland. They spent the afternoon playing scrabble and Pictionary.

The lights went out at four and Aunt Laurie lit hurricane lamps and candles. It gave the cottage an almost Christmassy feel to it, with the storm raging outside. All they needed was fairy lights and carols, but there was no electricity to power the lights or the stereo.

Just before five, Hattie moved closer to the window. She blinked hard, not sure if she was seeing things or not. It looked as if the bridge was moving, but surely that wasn't possible. "Cal, look at this."

He came over to her side. "Look at what?"

"The rail bridge."

"What about it? Is the train trying to cross?"

"I don't know about that. The bridge looks as if it's moving."

Cal frowned. "Can't see from here, as the light isn't good enough and the rain's obscuring the glass."

Hattie ran to the front door and flung it wide open. She stepped out into the porch, the wind and rain buffeting her instantly. The creaks and groans of the bridge could be clearly heard above the tumult of the storm. Waves crashed against the sides of the ironwork sending spray high into the air.

Cal pulled his phone from his pocket, dialing fast.

"Who are you calling?"

"The station master. See if he can stop the train from crossing from the mainland." He paused.

"Answer the phone, will you? Finally. Jake, it's Cal Trant. Has the 503 left?" He froze. "Seriously? Call him back, the bridge is moving in the wind."

Hattie grabbed the binoculars from the shelf by the door. Her uncle had always kept them there and her aunt had never moved them. She scanned the bridge and pointed. "Look, see those lights almost at the far end of the bridge? That has to be the train."

"Call him back!" Cal yelled into the phone. "I'm telling you the bridge is moving!" He paced as he spoke. "Then try again."

"It's too late," Hattie whispered. She pointed to the slow moving lights on the bridge and watched mesmerized. They kept moving until they were half way across, in what the locals termed the high girders. Maybe he'd make it.

The whole bridge shuddered, visibly moving as a huge wave knocked against it. Metal screeched and twisted with a loud creak, swiftly followed by a noise unlike anything she'd ever heard before. A long metallic groan, a whoosh of water that shot up almost in slow motion into the sky as the wind howled and moaned.

As the spray cleared, Hattie's eyes widened and she rubbed them, not wanting to believe what she was seeing. The central span of the bridge, along with the lights of the train, was gone.

For a moment Hattie stood there, too shocked to speak or think. Then she looked at Cal. "It's gone. Cal, the bridge has gone. Where's the train?"

"I don't know." He reached for the binoculars from her motionless hand and searched. "It's not there."

"Oh no...Oh, Lord, God, please help them..." she

whispered.

Cal reached for his coat. "Dial 9-9-9. I'm going down to the lifeboat station before they page me. Laurie!"

Aunt Laurie came running out. "What is it?"

"The bridge has gone. The 503 was on it. I have to go."

Hattie grabbed the phone, dialing with trembling fingers. "The line's dead. I'm coming with you. I'll call from your mobile on the way."

"What can you do?"

"I don't know." She grabbed her coat. "But I can't sit here and do nothing." She took the phone from his hand and dialed as they ran to his truck.

"Operator, which service do you require?"

"All of them," she had to yell to make herself heard over the storm. "The Penry Island rail bridge is gone. So's the train."

# 18

Huge arc lights cut through the dark, illuminating the bridge with its gaping hole. Naval, coastguard, police and lifeboats navigated huge waves as they searched the water looking for survivors. Hattie stood on the shore, the yellow reflective jacket she'd been given barely keeping her warm.

She'd made tea and sandwiches for the rescuers and the few survivors they brought ashore. Blue flashing lights from the emergency service vehicles behind her lit the sky as the wind still downed trees and hurled debris around them.

At two in the morning Cal brought the lifeboat ashore to be refueled. He looked shattered. After speaking to Tom, he came over to find her. "Hey, you slept any?"

She shook her head. "No. Have you?"

"I've just been ordered to. Blue watch is going out for the next couple of trips, before I take over again. There are still folks out there."

"Let the others take over. Four hours sleep or so should help, you look exhausted."

"So do you, but yeah, we all are. See you later." He headed past her into the lifeboat station to find somewhere to lie down. Or at least that's where she hoped Cal was going. She was tired herself, yes, almost beyond tired, but all she had to do was make tea and coffee, and provide warm blankets and a hug when needed. It wasn't as if she were out there in the boats doing the bulk of the rescue work.

She looked around and then headed back inside. She busied herself between working and watching the boats searching under the bridge.

As the pale light of dawn slowly broke on the horizon, she made her way to the door of the boat house. The local TV crews milled around, mixing with the rescue teams. The storm was starting to die down, meaning help was finally going to reach them from the mainland. In her hand she clutched the first coffee she'd made herself all night.

It seemed to be more retrieval than rescue. The boats and crews working on recovering bodies, with just body bags coming ashore, with the last survivor having been pulled from the water a good three hours previously. The mood was one of dejection and sorrow, yet they kept working, determined to bring every last passenger back to dry land.

Cal staggered out from a side room, helmet in his hand.

She looked at him worriedly. "You still look shattered. Did you sleep any?"

"Not really. You?"

She shook her head. "Time for sleep later."

He pointed to her cup. "Is that coffee?"

"Yeah." She handed it to him and watched as he drained the cup in a few swift gulps. "You look like you needed that."

"Yeah, I did." He handed her the cup back. "Thank you. I should get going."

Hattie impulsively gave him a one handed hug. "Be careful out there, Cal. Just because the storm's easing, doesn't mean the danger is passed or the waves are any smaller."

He kissed her cheek. "I will. And you should get some rest."

Aunt Laurie came over to her. "I'll see she lies down for at least an hour. Now you go and be careful out there. Storms easing, but that doesn't mean the danger is passed."

Cal nodded. "Hattie just told me the exact same thing. Don't worry. I'll bring them all back if it's the last thing I do."

\*\*\*\*

Dawn turned to daylight as Cal docked the boat onto the tractor to refuel. Clouds scurried across a leaden sky as the full extent of the horror began to unfold. A gaping hole sat in the middle of the bridge where the high girders used to be. The roof of one carriage protruded from the water where it had landed on top of another. At least Cal assumed that's what had happened to it. He prayed it would hold for the few minutes it would take him to get back out there.

He hadn't wanted to come back to base at all as his was the only boat that could get close enough to pull the woman off the wreck itself, but the fuel gauge was on empty. He'd promised her that he'd return and he just prayed he'd be in time.

The wind pushed the water against the bridge, which creaked and moved in the strong gusts. The beach was littered with the remains of personal effects. A forensic crew, covered head to toe in white overalls, slowly moved down the shore, photographing every small piece before collecting it in clear plastic bags.

Cal stood on the boat, overseeing the refueling.

Hattie watched him. He longed to hug her, to assure her he was all right and to make sure she was, but he didn't have time. Not if he were going to get back out before that carriage finally went under.

Tom came over. "Cal, we're standing down. The engineers think more of the bridge is going to fall and want everyone to steer clear until someone's checked it."

Cal shook his head. "The other team heard someone as they got close to the wreck, so I checked it out. She's in the carriage that's just above the water line. We're the only boat that can get in close enough to get to her. I promised we'd go back."

"It's not safe."

"I'm not leaving her to die, Tom." He raised his voice. "We delay, or wait until they say it's safe, and that carriage could go under. It's my decision. As helm officer I have the right to launch on my say so. I want to go."

Tom frowned, and nodded at last. "But I do not agree with this decision and I will note it as such in the log."

"That's fine." Cal nodded. He glanced at the rest of his crew. Sam, Trevor and Phil met his gaze unwaveringly. "If you guys want to stay here, that's fine with me."

"You need us," Trevor said.

"We all go," Sam echoed.

"All or none," Phil agreed.

"Thank you." Cal looked at the shore crew. "Let's go. We've wasted enough time." He held his breath as the DODO moved back into the water. He prayed again that they'd find her, and that the carriage would hold long enough for them to pull her to safety. She'd been so scared, of dying, of them not coming back. He had to make it.

He aimed the boat into the breaking waves, accelerating rapidly. He glanced at Trevor. "Rope up. She might not have the strength to catch the rope herself."

"Aye."

Cal turned his attention to the controls, steering the boat to where he'd last seen her. Arriving at the carriage there was no sign of the woman. Where had she gone? Had someone else pulled her off? "Tom, has someone else found her?"

"Negative." The reply cracked over the radio.

"Roger that. Going in closer."

"Cal, don't be a—"

Cal flipped off his radio, leaving the others to communicate back. The waves grew rougher the closer he got, tossing the boat into the remains of the bridge. The impact threw them all to the floor of the boat. "Everyone all right?" he asked, pushing himself upright.

"Aye," came three responses.

"Found her." Trevor yelled, diving over the side of the boat at the same time.

Cal trusted the others to do their job, while he held the boat as steady as he could. They depended on him just as much. The whole point of being a team—four individuals working together as one. He kept praying as they worked. They needed God's help just as much as they needed each other.

"Got her," Phil yelled and tapped him on the shoulder. "She's alive. Her name's Ellie."

"Thank You, Lord." Cal turned the boat and headed back to shore. Behind him came a horrendous tearing sound. He glanced over his shoulder to see the train carriage vanish beneath a huge wave. He accelerated, but the edge of the wave picked up the small lifeboat, tossing it under the bridge.

At that instant, a large piece of metal framework fell, catching the stern of the boat. The boat tipped over backwards, almost in slow motion, tossing them into the icy, tumultuous water.

Forced under the water by the falling ironwork, Cal struggled to get free. He kicked desperately, pushing side the debris until he broke the surface, his lungs burning. He took large swallows of air, looking around for the others. The lifeboat was nowhere to be seen, presumably somewhere on the bottom of the sea or on its way down.

Phil and Sam broke the surface beside him. "Cal?"

"I'm fine. What about you two?"

They both nodded.

He looked around, desperately trying to locate the others. "Where's Trevor? What about Ellie?"

"I don't know."

Cal dived down searching for them. The water was murky, filled with debris and mud kicked up by the falling ironwork.

As he surfaced for air, he found himself being hauled aboard a navy RHIB. "I have to find them," he yelled. "Trevor's still down there."

"We'll do it. Let's get you back to shore."

"No…" He struggled to get free. "I can't leave them."

"Let us handle it now." The officer held him firmly, a steel look in his eye that Cal knew only too well.

The other lifeboat surged past them, heading to

the bridge. Another navy craft headed in from another direction. Cal sat back in defeat, tears burning his eyes. The RHIB headed quickly back to the shore, landing on the beach itself like he'd seen done in television programs, and he himself had done in training a few nights previously.

The navy officer helped him out and someone put a blanket around his shoulders.

He shook it off and looked at Tom as he came running over. "I have to go back out there and look for Trevor."

"No. I'm standing you down."

"Trevor is out there!" Cal yelled, frantic with worry and guilt. "I have to go and find him."

"You need to stay here. The crews from Porthness are on scene now. As is the navy and coastguard. Search and rescue will be here as soon as the winds die down sufficiently. Go home."

"Not until Trevor is safe." Cal tried to head back to the boat, but Tom caught his arm and shook his head.

"Stand down. That's an order."

"Not while Trevor is missing."

"I'm not saying it again." Tom narrowed his eyes. "You stand down or I will relieve you of duty."

"Cal!" Hattie's voice cried out across the beach.

"Fine," he muttered. "But I want it noted that I do not agree with this decision." He pulled off his gloves, shoving them into his pocket. Yanking off his helmet, he swallowed hard, bile rising in his throat.

Hattie reached out for him. Her eyes were bright with barely contained tears. "Cal, are you all right? When the boat vanished I thought..."

"I'm fine. I just need a minute." He hugged her quickly, then headed inside and into the crew changing area. He sank onto the bench and buried his head in his hands.

Was this his fault for insisting on going back out? Was he too close to the bridge or the wreckage? Should he have left that woman, Ellie, to die? No, he shouldn't have. He was doing his job, but his job could have cost the life of one of his own.

Stripping off, he stood under a hot shower. His eyes burned and the lump in his throat threatened to choke him. A huge sob welled up and overtook him. Then he heard footsteps outside and he reigned in his emotion, swallowing hard. There'd be time for that later. Perhaps.

He toweled off and dressed, before heading towards the office to write his report. He could hear Hattie and Laurie talking and paused at the bottom of the stairs to listen.

"I have to go to him." Hattie's voice was broken as if she were crying.

"Give him a few more minutes." Laurie sounded just as upset, but more in control. "He needs…"

"He could have died out there…"

"Yes, and men react differently to us women. Trust me on that one. He'll be down when he's ready."

Cal headed up the stairs and sat at the desk by the window, pulling open a file to start writing up his report. His vision blurred. What was he doing?

Guilt filled him.

He'd made Hattie cry. He'd left a man out there to die. He'd failed in his duty of care to a civilian. He'd defied orders and risked the lives of three men and for what? And he'd upset the woman he loved.

This was his fault. And no matter what the result, he had to put his hand up and own it.

*Forgive me, Lord. Because as long as I live, I will not forgive myself for this. What kind of a man am I? Not one that should be out there, that's for sure.*

His gaze returned to the window. He could see the bridge and the boats surrounding it. Bags and cases were being pulled from the water, along with larger pieces of debris.

Men in fluorescent jackets walked out along the bridge, checking it. How would they raise the train? Or would they just leave it there, as the water was deep enough so it wouldn't pose a hazard to shipping.

His attention was caught by the lifeboat coming back in. There was another figure in the boat. Pushing back the chair, he leapt to his feet and ran to the door, his exhaustion forgotten. He took the stairs at full pelt, and stood with Tom and the others on the beach.

Hattie crept up beside him and slid her hand into his. He clung to it tightly, feeling like he was drowning all over again. "I'm sorry I snapped at you," he whispered. "Just didn't want to leave him out there."

"It's OK. I understand."

With bated breath he watched as the tractor towed the boat up the shingle towards them.

Justin stood up in the boat and helped the woman over the side. *They found Ellie, thank You, Lord. But what about Trevor?*

His heart sank as Bert and Roger bent, and then stood, lifting a motionless figure in lifeboat uniform from the bottom of the boat.

*Nooooooo…..*

# 19

Hattie woke to the sound of hammering and sawing coming from downstairs. She glanced at the clock and sat bolt upright in shock. One twenty. The muted light from the other side of the curtains meant that must be afternoon. She hadn't meant to sleep that long at all. Had she slept through her alarm? She'd only wanted a couple of hours. She got up and pulled her robe over her pj's. Whoever was banging was making way too much noise.

Making her way to the kitchen, Hattie flicked on the kettle and picked up the note propped against it. *Hattie, I've gone to work. Cal's here, doesn't look like he got much sleep if any last night. Make sure he drinks something at least. See you at five.*

Pulling her robe tighter around her, she headed towards the source of the noise. She stood in the hallway transfixed at the sight that beheld her.

Cal stood in the den with his back to her. Stripped to the waist with sweat trickling down his back, he ripped out the old doorframe, his arm muscles rippling.

She leaned against the wall, taking in the view, unconsciously tugging her robe tighter. "Morning."

Cal looked up and shot her a wry smile. "Afternoon, actually. Did I wake you?"

"I had to get up anyway. I hadn't intended to sleep this long. How are you?"

He shrugged. "Here. How are you?"

"Doing OK. How's Trevor?"

"He's in a coma."

Her stomach twisted. That accounted for the distraught look and the way he threw himself into his work. "Is he going to be all right?"

"I don't know. They don't know. I shouldn't have gone back out. There were other crews. Tom wanted to stand us down. If I hadn't gone out there, if I hadn't insisted, launched on my own authority—"

"You can't second guess yourself, Cal. That woman wouldn't be alive if it weren't for you."

Cal hit the door frame extra hard, splintering it. "I lost the boat." He pulled the wood away, puncturing his sentences with bits thudding on the floor, his voice taut with barely suppressed emotion. "I lost Trevor. I lost all those people I never reached in time. He was my friend and I. Lost. Him."

Hattie caught hold of his arm. "Cal, you pulled a dozen people out of that train wreck Sunday night, if not more. You rescued a shed load of other people this year, including me. That's dozens of people who would have died if it weren't for you and countless other crews up and down the country who go out in horrendous weather."

"Trevor—"

"—was doing his job," she finished. "Just like you he put his life on the line to save others. Just have faith he'll be all right."

"And if he isn't? Hattie, his wife, Miriam, is expecting another baby. His kid might never know him because I screwed up."

"Then let's pray that God over rules and heals him." She held his gaze, then grabbed his hands tightly in her good one and prayed with him.

"Thank you. Least I'm not meant to be out there for two weeks. Give me time to pull myself together."

"What will you do?"

"What I normally do. Work. Right now, that's putting this place to rights for Laurie. That reminds me." He reached into his back pocket and pulled out a sheet of folded paper. "How's this?"

She took it, his scent filling her.

He held her gaze, then reached for his tee-shirt, pulling it over his head and tugging it over his chest. "Sorry."

"Don't be," she said looking at the paper. The design was exactly what she'd asked for and the quote more than reasonable. If it was right. "Is this for all the shutters or just the missing ones?"

"All of them."

"OK. It sounds great. Thank you."

"You're welcome."

"What will happen about the lifeboat?"

"They've sent us a temporary one from the repair fleet." She must have looked as confused as she felt because he carried on. "When a boat needs repairing for whatever reason, they send out a spare, so we can continue to operate. For every six boats built, one goes into the relief fleet. It arrived yesterday, so we're fully serviceable."

"That's good."

"Only temporary though."

"Then we fundraise for a new one."

"Yeah, right."

She pulled her robe tighter. "How'd you manage to make a double positive sound so negative?"

"Practice. Hattie, you know what a new lifeboat

costs. Fundraising will take years. We don't have that kind of time."

"I'll think of some ideas."

"If you want."

She reached out, taking hold of his hand. She didn't understand his reaction at all. She'd thought he'd be pleased she wanted to help. "You've gone from loving your job to almost hating it. So you had a bad day at work. It happens."

"You have a bad day and we get burnt toast or underdone venison. If I have a bad day, people die!" he snapped, pulling away from her.

The doorbell rang. Hattie tugged her robe tighter and went to answer it. Maybe she should have gotten dressed before coming downstairs. The postman offered her a letter and she signed for it. Closing the door she looked at it. From Penny.

She walked to the stairs and sat on them, opening it. A bankers draft fell into her hand. For way more money than she ever thought she'd see in a lifetime. Tears fell slowly down her face.

Cal came into the hall and reached her side in a few short strides. "Hattie, I'm sorry." He looked downcast, shoulders drooping. "I didn't mean to make you cry."

"You didn't. You may infuriate me sometimes, but I'm not crying because of you."

"Oh. You're not?" He sat down on the stairs beside her. "Then why are you crying?"

"I just got this from Penny." She showed him. "She says it's what her accountant says I'm owed. Seven years back pay, plus the money I originally put into the lodge. She said I could sue them if they don't pay me."

"Why would you want to sue them?"

"I don't know. I wouldn't. I just want out of there," she whispered. "I want a job here, a life well away from all the stress. It's all such a mess and I don't know what to do anymore." She buried her head in her hands as his arm slid around her shoulders.

"Do about what?"

"Markus has been in contact with Steve."

Cal visibly bristled. "Really? When did this happen?"

"He did it while you were away. I was going to tell you, but never had the chance. He said he told Steve where I was and that he's asked Steve and got his permission to marry me." She sighed. "It doesn't matter how many times I turn him down, he doesn't listen. I just want it to end."

He hugged her. "Then maybe find that great guy you like and elope. Or accept my offer and then Markus can't bug you over it anymore."

She smiled as he kissed her cheek. "Maybe I should." She looked down at the paper in her hand. "How about I pay for Aunt Laurie's repairs with this?"

"She's paid up front. If I refund it, she'll want to know why. And you need to talk to your brother."

"I'll take that under advisement." *Or maybe I just buy a lifeboat with the money. Or put it towards the fundraising for a bigger one.*

"Do it, Hattie. Life is too short to bear grudges or to be estranged from your twin. Like it or not he's part of you."

She straightened. "I should get dressed. Can't sit around like this all day."

The phone rang. "No peace for the wicked," she sighed. "Hello?" Her breath caught and she closed her eyes. "Hello, Steve."

"Hattie. I heard you were staying with Aunt Laurie. The Penry Island bridge disaster is all over the news. Are you both all right? I tried ringing several times over the past day and got no answer."

*Oh, right, it's Tuesday, isn't it?* "Yeah, we're both fine. We helped out all Sunday night and most of yesterday with the rescue and clear up, got home very late last night. Plus the phones have been out because the wind brought all the lines down, so even if we'd been in when you rang, we wouldn't have gotten the call."

"What do you mean, you helped with the rescue?"

"Aunt Laurie works at the lifeboat station, so we were down there, making tea and coffee and so on."

"But you're all right?"

Was that concern in his voice? She twisted the phone cord around her finger. "I'm fine. Aside from my arm. I broke it in an accident the first week I was here."

"Maybe you should come home."

"I'm not coming back. I told you that." She paused. "I'm looking for work here on the island."

"I need you here." His voice rose in anger. "I need the money back. I know Penny sent it to you."

"Is that the real reason you rang?" she asked quietly. For some reason she wasn't surprised, even though her heart was breaking. "For the money? You didn't really want to know how I was at all, did you?"

"It's my money, Hattie. I want—need it back."

Hattie pulled the phone away from her ear and looked at it for a moment, then slowly put it down, cutting off the call.

*There's no reasoning with him like this, Lord, Please*

*calm him so we can talk about this properly. I don't want the money, especially if it means that much to him, but I'd rather know why it does. What's he gotten in to? Is he in trouble of some kind?*

She looked at Cal. "All he wants is the money and a slave in his kitchen. I don't matter to him at all. I'm going to get dressed. Then I'm going for a walk. Need some air."

"Want some company?"

"Yeah, that'd be nice. Give me five minutes."

****

Cal held her hand as they walked. She hadn't said a word since they left the cottage. All he could do was be there, he knew that much from having a sister.

Her mobile rang as they reached a bench overlooking the sea front. Small figures swarmed over the bridge. Huge cranes were being wheeled into position to raise the wreck. The beach was taped off and littered with debris.

"You should answer the phone," he said gently as it kept ringing.

She pulled it from her pocket and looked at the screen, before slumping down onto the bench. "It's Steve. Don't want to speak to him." She raised her arm and made as if she were going to throw the phone into the sea, but he caught her hand.

"Let me talk to him." He sat next to her and took the phone from her hand. "Hello, Mr. Steele. This is Callum Trant. We met when…"

"I know who you are. Why have you got Hattie's phone?"

"We're out for a walk and she didn't want to

speak to you."

"Why not?"

Cal reigned in his automatic sharp response. "She's upset. She has a lot going on right now and could do with your support, rather than you hounding her over money."

"How dare you? Just because you're…"

He cut him off. "Hattie was almost killed her first week here, did anyone tell you that? Just cut her some slack."

"What? Markus never mentioned it. Why wasn't I told?"

"I have no idea. You'd have to ask him about that. She was out on Markus Kerr's boat in a storm and the yacht sank. We rescued them. Hattie broke her arm."

"*You* rescued her?"

"As part of a team. I work on the lifeboats. We responded to their distress call."

"I see. May I speak to my sister?"

Cal held out the phone to Hattie. She sighed, but took it. He looked away as she spoke, not listening to her side of the conversation. Instead, he looked out over the bay at the recovery work being undertaken. The crane lifted a carriage onto a huge barge, water pouring from it.

In the sunshine, it was difficult to imagine the horror of two nights ago, but the evidence of it lay all around them. The broken bridge, strewn wreckage and personal belongings which covered the coastline, was nothing compared to the brain-numbing, heart-rending, soul-chilling anguish, which came with having lost his boat and landed Trevor in the hospital. Possibly killed him.

Hattie hung up and put the phone away. "He

wants to come over and see me."

"He'll have to drive."

"Yeah, told him that. He'll leave after breakfast and get back in time for the evening meal, hopefully. Although he did say they had no one staying right now. Not sure how he managed that one, but anyway." She paused. "He said he'd come tomorrow."

She pushed to her feet and Cal took her hand, standing with her. She glanced at him as she began walking. "Don't ask me how I feel about this, because I don't know."

"If you want I'll be there with you. There isn't anything that I wouldn't do for you. I'll keep you safe, no matter what."

Hattie stopped and looked at him. "Did you mean what you said?"

"I always mean what I say." He looked at her, slight confusion running through him. "If you want me there, I'll be there."

"No, about marrying me. I mean, so much has happened since, and I know I promised you an answer, but—"

How many times did he need to say it? He'd say it a million times if he had to or shout it from the nearest rooftop. "Yes, I meant it."

He held her hand firmly and got down on one knee. "Hattie, I love you. Will you marry me?"

The sparkle in her eyes and the way her face lit up said it all. "Yes, yes, I'll marry you."

He rose, wrapped his arms around her and kissed her, with as much passion as he could. Nothing mattered, except her and him and the relationship they had.

# 20

Hattie pushed open the door to the shop, a huge grin still plastered over her face. Cal's hand tightly in hers, she made her way to the counter and looked at Aunt Laurie. "Hi."

"Hello, you two. What can I do for you?"

She looked at Cal and then back at her aunt. "Do you sell confetti?"

Aunt Laurie looked at her for a moment, before shooting around the counter, and enveloping them both in a massive hug. "Oh, my, congratulations. I'm so pleased for the both of you."

Hattie hugged her back. "You're the first person we've told. I'm on cloud nine right now."

"You both look over the moon. About time we had something good happening around here."

Cal nodded. "And Markus best keep his distance now."

"Oh, speaking of which, Steve rang." Hattie took a deep breath. "He wants to...no let me rephrase that, he *is* coming over tomorrow."

Cal pushed his hand through hair and then ran his fingers over her face. "I should get back to work. I'll see you later, yeah? I have a few errands to run later if Laurie doesn't mind me knocking off early tonight."

Aunt Laurie winked at him. "I'll make an exception just this once. And that's Aunt Laurie to you, if you're marrying my niece."

He grinned. "Thank you, *Aunt* Laurie. I'll see you later, Hattie."

She smiled, her heart doing somersaults inside her. "Count on it."

He kissed her and then headed out.

Hattie watched until she could see him no longer. Her aunt's voice registered on the edge of her hearing but she had no idea what she'd said. "Sorry, didn't hear you."

"I asked about Steve."

"He just wants the money back. All of it, but he can't have it because the accountant says it's mine. He was more worried about that than me. Even when Cal told him about me having broken my arm and almost dying the first week I was here, all he wanted was the money."

"I'm sorry, dear."

She shrugged. "At least I know where I stand now, and yes, it hurt, but I love him regardless. However, I've got more important things on my mind."

"A wedding, perhaps?"

She laughed. "Other than that. I was thinking about organizing a fundraiser for the lifeboat here. Put the money towards a new boat." She caught the look and shook her head. "I was going to do it anyway. They saved my life. I want to give something back. Raise awareness to what these guys do out there every day."

"OK. So what kind of things were you thinking?"

"A week long thing. A bake sale, car washing, beat the goalie, and something huge to finish." She paused and then grinned. "How about a date a crewmember? Both boat crew and shore crew. We could auction them off either to the highest bidder or do it by raffle."

"Won't that cost money?"

"Not if we charge so much a ticket and get a sponsor to donate the dates. Maybe contact Cal's old team mates, raffle a few of them too. Or I'll use some of my money."

"Maybe you should talk with Steve first…"

"Whatever I do has nothing to do with him. It's my money, only I don't want it so I'm giving it away. Either this charity or another one. I want to do this. I owe them my life."

"OK. Talk to Tom about the fundraiser. He'll be able to arrange dates and promotion and so on."

"I'll go and do it now." She grinned. "I'm getting married…"

\*\*\*\*

By the time she and Aunt Laurie got back to the cottage, Cal had finished for the day and gone off to run his errands. When he got back an hour later, Hattie hugged him tightly as if she hadn't seen him for days instead of a couple of hours.

He pulled back slowly and then pulled a small black box from his pocket. "If it doesn't fit, the jeweler said he can adjust it. I explained about your wrist." He opened the box.

Hattie's eyes filled as she took in the sparkling diamond and emerald ring. "Oh, Cal, it's beautiful."

He took it from the box and slid it onto the ring finger on her right hand. "Just until you can wear it on the left," he said. Then he folded his arms around her and kissed her. Hattie wasn't sure how long he kissed her for before Aunt Laurie's teasing voice echoed across the hallway.

"Do I need a bucket of water?"

Cal broke the kiss slowly and glanced up, a broad grin on his face. "It might be an idea. You have one extremely hot niece here."

Hattie's cheeks flamed and she held out her hand. "Look, it's beautiful."

Aunt Laurie admired it. "It certainly is. Cal, you have exquisite taste."

This time Cal blushed. "Thank you."

"You're welcome. Do you have any plans for tonight?"

"No I don't, unless you count dinner for one in front of the TV. I was planning to take Hattie out to celebrate tomorrow night."

"Good. Then you can stay and help us."

"Help with what?"

"Hattie will fill you in while I cook dinner."

Hattie looked at her. "Whose idea is it anyway?"

"Yours. Now tell him." Aunt Laurie winked and headed into the kitchen.

"But I thought…Fine, OK, I'll tell him." She hung her jacket up and sat to take off her shoes.

Cal put his hands on his hips, a comical expression on his face. "Will someone please tell me what's going on? You're not planning on getting married wearing lifeboat uniform are you?"

"I wasn't, but now you mention it I'll wear the uniform and you can wear the dress." She grinned, propping one knee over the other to unfasten the Velcro on her new sneakers. Her broken arm meant tying shoe laces was impossible. "I spoke to Tom before we came home. I'm going to start organizing a whole week of fundraising. The idea being that we hopefully have enough to buy a new boat at the end of it. Or at least put a down payment on one."

Cal just stood there, staring at her. His eyebrows shot into his hair and his whole body stiffened. "Is this just because I saved your life the other week or are you trying to make me feel better?"

"What?" She paused with her left shoe in her hand.

"The boat has only been gone a couple of days, not even that."

"So? Tom liked the idea."

"It's too soon."

"It's never too soon. Cal, right now people are talking about the lifeboat. It's in the news. It'll be easier to fundraise now than in six months' time. And you said yourself the boat replacement is only temporary and fundraising could take years. So the sooner we start, the better."

"Yes. Yes, I did, and yes, it can. Doesn't rule out the fact it's too soon. If anything, the money raised now should go to Trevor's wife and kids. I appreciate you wanting to get involved in things, Hattie, but really there is a time and a place and this isn't it."

She pushed her shoe back on, irritated. "Fine, you just sit there and feel sorry for yourself. I have to do something to help and this is what I want to do."

Pushing upright, she flung open the front door and headed out into the dark, not bothering with a coat.

How did they get from over the moon, happy as pie and getting engaged one minute, to having their first argument the next?

She didn't understand his reaction. Why was he so anti this idea? Tom had thought it a good one and of course some of the money would go to Trevor's family if worst came to the worst. She hadn't expected this type of reaction from Cal. She thought he'd be pleased she was getting involved in his life at the lifeboat station, not dismiss it out of hand.

How could she be his wife if she couldn't support him in the little things like this? Or by taking an interest in what he did?

Reaching the village church, she found the door unlocked. She pushed it open and went inside. The organ was playing, and a book lay open on the table at the front. Hattie walked slowly up the aisle and looked at the book. It was full of messages of condolence for the people who died on the train. She signed it and then went and sat down in one of the pews.

Her attention was caught by a huge stained glass window. A street lamp illuminated it from the outside, making it the only window visible against the dark night. It depicted a small lifeboat, being tossed on huge waves as it gave aid to a stranded tanker. Two men in lifeboat uniform watched down on the scene from above.

"That's my grandfather."

She jumped slightly, not having heard his footsteps. "Oh…"

"Sorry, love. I didn't mean to make you jump. Here, put this on. You'll catch cold otherwise." Cal put her jacket around her shoulders as he spoke, and then sat beside her.

"But it's a memorial window."

"Yeah." He took a sharp breath. "He and one other crewman were lost in that rescue. Along with the boat."

"I don't understand." Hattie twisted in the pew to

look at him, trying to read the expression on his face. "You said they rescued the people on the ship, that he was awarded an MBE for his part. But if he died, then how?"

"Yeah, they rescued the crew and then went back to secure the ship so it could be towed once the storm abated. Their boat never made it back to shore. He got the MBE posthumously. Gran collected it from the palace."

"He went back, just like you did."

Cal nodded. He slid a hand into hers, holding it tightly.

"How old were you when he died?"

"I was nine, but I remember it like it was yesterday." Myriad emotions crossed his face, his eyes glistening in the lamplight. "Gran was distraught. The whole town turned out for the funeral. I remember it was a horse drawn carriage, huge black horses and a glass hearse. There was a spray of white flowers spelling his name in big letters. It stopped at the house, and at the lifeboat station. The church was packed, so much so that the congregation spilled over onto the pavement outside." His voice cracked.

"It's OK."

He visibly struggled for control. "Sorry. I've never spoken about this to anyone. He told such wonderful stories about the lifeboats, played in the park with us. He built us a slide for the back garden. Things were never the same after he died. A lot of memorials sprung up all over. There was an appeal and fundraising for a new boat. They named it after Grandad. But Gran got nothing. She struggled to make ends meet for years afterwards."

"Why did you join up?" She rubbed her thumb

over the back of his hand, trying to keep him talking. That was why he was anti funding a new boat.

"Grandad was my hero. He helped save people and I wanted to do the same. He made the rescues sound exciting and worthwhile."

"He died a hero, doing what he believed in."

"Like Trevor," he whispered.

"Trevor's not dead."

He looked at his hand in hers. "His unborn child might never know him because of me. Because I made the wrong decision."

"But Trevor made the decision to respond to the pager, to join the lifeboats in the first place. Was your grandfather the helm officer?"

"No. Going back wasn't his decision either."

A new voice came from the doorway. "It was mine."

****

Cal turned and swallowed, hoping he looked better than he felt. "Mr. Garrett."

The old man moved slowly over to them, leaning heavily on the cane. He lowered himself into the pew in front and regarded them through his glasses. "I blamed myself for a long time. I lost the boat, the crew, and my friends. I felt I had betrayed those I considered my family."

"How did you cope?" Cal asked. "You stayed with the service." Hattie started to get up, but he didn't let go. He needed her here, couldn't do this without her. "Please, don't go."

"OK." She sat back down.

Mr. Garret held his gaze. "My faith, friends, and

the counseling the service provided. Take them up on that, by the way. I had nightmares for weeks afterwards, second guessed every shout and every decision I made for a long time, too. And asked myself the same questions I expect you are right now."

Cal looked down, afraid he was going to throw up. "It was my fault. I got told to stand down, but I went back."

"Your lass is right. We all know the risks, but saving lives is what we do. If you hadn't gone back, what would have happened to Ellie?"

"She'd be dead," he whispered.

Mr. Garrett nodded. "And I would have lost my granddaughter and unborn great grandchild."

Cal's head jerked up, his mouth opening in shock.

"She told me you kept your promise. You came back. That meant so much to her. You also pulled her husband from the water a while before. She thought he'd drowned. Nick thought the same thing about her."

Hattie squeezed his hand. "See…"

Mr. Garrett smiled. "Because of you and your decision to go back, I still have my family. Trevor wouldn't want you to beat yourself up over that. Your gran told me the same thing at Sid's funeral. She looked me in the eye and told me to man up and get back out there. She told me when God pushes you to the edge of a cliff, trust Him fully because two things can happen. Either He'll catch you when you fall, or He'll teach you how to fly. She said that Sid was flying with the angels now and that God had caught me because I still have people to save."

The dam within Cal broke. Tears fell like rain. He was dimly aware of Hattie wrapping her arms around him, holding him, but he also felt God there, comforting him and assuring him that everything was under control and He had caught him.

# 21

Hattie sat on the bottom stair looking over to where Cal was sanding down the new doorframe.

He glanced at her. "Penny for your thoughts."

"They aren't worth it."

"OK, a quid then."

"Not even that. Ha'penny perhaps. I was thinking about Steve. Maybe I just go out. That way I'm not here when he arrives in a bit."

"Coward." He wiped the wood down with a cloth and ran his hand over it. "Running away doesn't solve anything."

She scrunched her nosed up at him. "Don't care. I love my brother, but really don't want to see him right now."

The doorbell went. "Hattie, can you get that?" Aunt Laurie called from upstairs. "I'm trying to make the beds."

"OK." Hattie pushed up and headed to the door. She opened it and for a moment she was tempted to shut it again. *Help me be nice to him, Lord.* "Hi, Steve." She held out her arms to him for a hug.

He ignored them, staring at her. "Hattie."

She dropped her arms, and moved to one side. "You'd better come in. Aunt Laurie is just making the beds."

Steve stepped over the threshold and stopped short at the sight of Cal coming into the hall.

Hattie smiled, her heart turning cartwheels at the sight of her fiancé. The tight shirt did nothing to hide his six-pack. "Steve, this is my fiancé, Cal. Cal, this is my twin brother, Steve. I know you two already know each other, but figured I'd do a proper introduction."

Cal held out a hand and smiled. "It's nice to finally meet you formally. Hattie talks about you a lot."

"Fiancé?" Steve's eyes remained ice. His hand barely made contact before he dropped it. Hattie was about to call him on it when his phone rang. "Excuse me."

Cal moved to Hattie and slid an arm around her. "It's all right," he whispered.

"No, it isn't. He's being downright rude."

Cal gently turned her face to his and kissed her. "I said its fine, love, and I meant it."

Her heart fluttered in her throat and her breath caught. He'd called her that in the church, but she'd thought she'd misheard him. "What did you call me?"

"Love," he repeated. "Because you are." He fingered the engagement ring on her right hand. "I can't wait to see this on the finger it belongs on."

Hattie smiled. "Actually in some European countries they wear it on the right anyway. But I can't wait to wear it on my left hand. It's beautiful. Can't believe you got the size right."

"Just a good guess. Just bear in mind your left ring finger may be a different size."

Steve hung up. "I have to go. I've got some business to attend to. I've got a meeting with Markus Kerr."

"Oh?" Her heart sank. "I thought you'd come to see me, not Markus."

"You'll keep. This is business and a potential

investment. It's important."

"Thought I was," she whispered, tears burning her eyes. She blinked them away, not wanting him to know how deeply hurt she was. "Nothing changes does it?"

"And when I get back, we'll discuss the return of my money." Steve headed out, shutting the door behind him.

Hattie just stood there. "I don't believe that just happened. He didn't even want to see the ring."

Aunt Laurie came down the stairs. "Was that Steve?"

"He came, he saw and he left." Hattie sucked in a deep breath. "He's gone to see Markus on 'business'." She put brackets around the word business.

"I thought he was coming to see you?" Aunt Laurie hugged her.

Hattie hugged her back. "So did I, but I was wrong. What's the betting he'll still try to marry me off to Markus?"

Cal raised an eyebrow. "Wait a sec. You're already getting married. To me."

"And we told him that, just now. But Steve has some ulterior motive here. Everything is business and has a price. Markus already said Steve approved his proposal." She pushed her hands through her hair. "Steve never listens to anything I say, anyway."

"Don't worry about him."

She turned to Cal and hugged him, then ran a hand down his face. "I'm marrying you and nothing is going to stop me from doing that."

He leaned into her touch, catching her fingers with his lips. "Good. Maybe we elope."

"Or just post the banns today and marry in three

weeks' time in which ever church can fit us in."

Cal's eyes widened. "Are you serious?"

"Very." She held his gaze. "If it has to be in a registry office, then so be it. Or we catch the next flight to Vegas and get married in twenty-four hours."

"Where will we live?"

"Your place." She smiled. "This was your idea. Don't you back out on me now."

He chuckled. "I'm not. So when do we go to the registry office?"

Hattie looked at Aunt Laurie. "Is three weeks all right with you?"

"It's your wedding, sweetheart, so do whatever makes you happy. Three months would be better— give me time to find a hat and dress to match." She smiled. "But if you *do* decide to elope, take me as a witness."

"You're on." Hattie looked at Cal. "How about now?"

"Vegas or the registry office?" he quipped.

"Both." She grabbed his hand. "Come on."

Cal hung back. "First, can I borrow your phone? I need to speak to your dad. His is the only permission I need."

\*\*\*\*

An hour later, they arrived back. Hattie hung up her jacket and followed Cal through to the room he was working on. She looked at the door frame he'd been working on painting and pointed. "You missed a bit."

"Honestly, woman, we just got back indoors having booked the wedding and you're criticizing my work already."

Hattie laughed and put a thumb on his head, pressing down with a gentle touch. "I'm just keeping you in your new and rightful place."

"It's a good thing I love you." He laughed.

"Definitely a good thing."

Cal put an arm around her and pulled her in for a deep, mind blowing kiss. When he pulled back he smiled. "It sure was a blessing running into Pastor Kenny like that and booking the church after we left the registry office. Are you sure you don't want to get married in Headley Cross?"

"I'm sure. I don't even have to register the wedding there as I'm living here now which is also a good thing. I'll ring Pastor Jack at some point, see if he can come up and take part in the service somehow. Maybe he'll marry us and Pastor Kenny can preach or the other way around. I'd like him involved somehow."

"Sounds like a plan. Give him a ring now."

Steve appeared in the doorway. "So you're hanging out in here. I've been waiting for you to get back."

Hattie looked at him. "We had important business to attend to." She threw his own words back at him.

He looked scathingly at Cal. "If you don't mind, I want a word with my sister. In private."

She scowled. "Don't you talk to Cal like that. He's my fiancé. That makes him family. Whatever you have to say to me, can be said in front of him, because I'll only tell him later anyway."

Cal hugged her. "It's OK, love. I need to go and get some nails. Forgot to pick some up when we were out." He kissed her soundly. "I won't be long."

"Love you." She watched him head across towards the door.

"He's only after one thing," Steve said. "And I don't mean just your money."

"How dare you!" Hattie smacked him. And instantly regretted it. She might be angry at him but they weren't children any longer and the anger in Steve's eyes frightened her.

He raised his hand to return the blow.

Cal caught it before it made contact with her face. Hattie hadn't even realized he was still there. His eyes blazed fire and his voice was low and threatening. "You hit her, or lay one finger on her, and I will have you arrested. Is that clear?"

Steve looked at him. "Crystal."

"Good. And for your information, I don't need Hattie's money. I have enough of my own." He let go of him. He leaned against the wall, pulling Hattie into his arms. "Are you all right, love?"

"I'm fine." She leaned against him, safe in the knowledge he was protecting her.

"Good." He looked at Steve. "I'm staying right here. So talk away."

"That's *my* money."

"Is that why you came?" Hattie asked. Yes he'd said it, but part of her didn't want to believe it. "To get the money back?"

"Of course. That and to catch up with Markus."

"Penny just gave me what the accountant said I was owed."

"She *what*?" Steve's face froze and then hardened, his eyes glittering with barely concealed anger.

Oh no, had she dropped Penny in it now as well? She hoped not. "Then I guess you'd better go take it up with her," she said quietly. "Just don't hit her."

Shock flitted on Steve's face for a moment before belligerence replaced it. "I..."

Hattie lowered her voice. "You gave me two hundred quid a month. I couldn't afford to leave and you liked it that way. It took me years to save enough for the car. Even longer to go anywhere or do anything and then you'd cancel it for me or make me cancel it. If you ever employ anyone else, you'll have to pay them properly."

"I don't want anyone else. No one else cooks like you do."

Hattie put her hand on her hip, Cal's arms still securely around her. "Tough cheddar. There is no way I'm coming back. Besides Cal's work is here. So this is where we'll live."

"With *him*?"

"Well obviously. We're getting married."

"No, you're not. Not to him."

"I'm wearing his ring. We've posted the banns, booked the church, and told Mum and Dad." Her voice wobbled. "I thought you loved me, hoped you'd be happy for me."

"I do love you."

"Then why can't you be pleased I finally found someone who loves me?"

"He's beneath you."

She shook her head. "A few weeks ago you were raving about how wonderful he was, and now? You love money more than me. Money and power and profit. Because Cal is a carpenter now and not a footballer, you don't want to know him. He's so much more than that. He's the man I love and the man I'm going to marry."

Cal's arms tightened around her. His lips brushed the back of her neck and she felt the rivers of energy pour through her. His breath was warm on her skin as he spoke. "I think you should leave now, Steve."

"You can't tell me what to do!" Steve spat.

"Maybe Cal can't, but I can. I've heard enough out of you." Aunt Laurie's icy voice filled the small hall. It matched the hard look in her eyes. Hattie had never seen her aunt look so angry and upset. "Leave. Now. And don't come back unless it's to apologize and then congratulate your sister properly."

For a moment, it looked as if Steve was going to argue. Then he flung open the door and stormed out, letting it slam behind him.

# 22

For the rest of the afternoon, Hattie threw herself into helping Cal with the carpentry. He gave her some sandpaper and asked her to sand down the new frames ready for priming and painting. She attacked them with gusto, discovering she actually enjoyed it.

Cal glanced at her. "So this fundraising you were talking about?" he began.

She looked at him, pushing a dusty hand through her equally dusty hair. They hadn't spoken about it since they'd argued. He'd apologized and they'd avoided the topic ever since. "What about it?"

"I think it's a really good idea. How about combining a bake sale with a coffee morning? You might sell more that way and get more people in."

"Sounds good. And maybe a boat pull."

"How's that going to work?" he asked.

"Uh, I don't know," she giggled, winking at him. "Pulling a boat along the sand perhaps?"

"I suppose you think that's clever." He paused. "Hey, we could put Tom in stocks and pelt him with wet sponges. People could pay to do it."

She smiled. "Now you're getting the idea. Maybe we have a car wash as well." She rubbed the frame hard for a moment. "Then the auction to finish off."

"What auction?"

"Something like a raffle, or a proper auction with the highest bidder winning, I'm not sure how it'd work yet. The prize would be to date a lifeboat crewmember. All the boat and shore crews are up for grabs."

Cal threw the sponge he was using at her. "Oh no. I'm not for sale."

"Why not? It's for a very good cause."

"Because my fiancée is a jealous woman and she might slap someone if she didn't win me. I've seen her right hook and it's a pretty mean one."

"Don't tempt me. But I was thinking something pretty innocuous, so the wives and so on don't get upset by it. And maybe get some of your footy mates to come and be auctioned too."

"That part of my life is over."

"Cal, surely you keep in touch with some of them."

"I'm not part of that world any longer."

"I was just thinking we could have a beat the goalie stand, too. The kids would love it. At least think about it for a little bit, if nothing else." The phone rang and she reached for it. "Hello?"

"Hattie, its Steve. Markus said he'd take us out on his boat so we could talk. Just the two of us. That way we can sort things out."

"I don't think so."

"Then meet me for dinner. We do need to talk. And don't even think about bringing *him*. Markus will act as an impartial referee."

*Markus impartial? Do me a favor and don't make me laugh.* "No."

"Please, Hattie."

"I said no. I have nothing to say to you that I want to say in front of anyone else, thank you very much."

"It's just dinner. You'll be perfectly safe with me, you know that. And we really do need to talk without

Aunt Laurie throwing me out this time."

"One minute." She sighed and looked at Cal. Covering the mouthpiece she scowled. "Steve wants to have dinner with me tonight so we can talk. Him and me, apparently. With Markus to referee. Is that OK?"

His face creased for a long moment before he nodded. "Go."

"Are you sure? If you don't want me to go, then say the word and I won't go."

"You don't have to obey me until after the wedding, love," he said lightly.

"I know. It doesn't hurt to practice though."

He nodded. "It's fine. Go talk to him."

"OK." She uncovered the phone. "OK, fine."

"Great," Steve said. "I'll pick you up at six." The phone clicked off.

"He's picking me up at six. So much for him being back in Headley Cross in time for the evening meal tonight. There's something going on. I just wish I knew what. And I don't like the idea of Markus being there." She took a deep breath, wishing Cal had forbidden her to go.

"Just be careful, hon. Take your phone and if you need me to come pick you up either call or text me where you are. I'll be there soon as I can."

"Thanks, love. I will."

\*\*\*\*

Hattie looked at Steve as he pulled in front of a huge sprawling house. "This isn't a restaurant."

"No. It's Markus's house. He's arranged this, so we can talk in private."

She shook her head. The slight unease she'd felt

ever since Steve suggested this, increased tenfold. "No. Take me home."

"Stop acting like a child, will you? We've known Markus for years. Let's just have dinner and talk."

The front door opened and Markus walked down the steps and across the graveled driveway to greet them. "Steven, I'm glad you came."

"Hello, Markus." Steve shook his hand warmly. "I told you I'd get her here."

Hattie's heart sank further. She should have put her phone in her pocket. This was sounding more and more like a set-up, rather than a conversation between brother and sister.

"Come on in. Dinner's just about to be served. Cook has done herself proud tonight." He smiled. "Hello, Harriet."

She refused to shake his hand, instead pushing her hand through her hair making sure he got a good look at her ring. "I thought we were meant to be talking on our own, Steve."

"And we will be. Over dinner." He gripped her arm and led her to the house. "And you will be polite to Markus, is that understood?"

She nodded slightly, not saying another word as Markus led them into the house. The huge yawning hallway had doors opening off each side. They walked past three before entering an equally enormous dining room.

The massive table had three places laid around the top end. A red table runner offset the white linen. A huge candelabrum sat as center piece. Crystal glasses and silver utensils glinted in the candlelight.

Markus looked at one of the servants. "Tell Mrs. Edwards that we're ready now." He pulled out a chair for Hattie. "Here you go, Harriet. Steven, you're opposite, and I'm sitting between you."

"As referee?" Hattie asked.

Steve scowled at her.

"Now, now, play nice. At least let's get the soup out of the way before you start fighting." Markus sat and flicked his napkin out in a swift motion before laying it across his lap. "I've chosen the wine carefully to go with the meal."

"I don't drink," Hattie said. She looked at the servant hovering behind her. "Just juice for me, please."

Markus narrowed his eyes and then nodded. "Give Harriet the apple juice. It's the cloudy one if that's all right?"

She nodded. "I prefer that one." Creamy liquid filled her crystal wine glass and she picked it up. First hurdle sorted. The juice was cool and refreshing and she quickly drained the glass. As soon as she put it down, it was refilled.

The servants in livery served the soup. Hattie waited until they were alone before taking a small sip. Cold celery soup had never been a great favorite of hers. "So, why are we here?"

"We're celebrating your engagement," Steve said.

She raised an eyebrow, careful to keep her tone level. "Then why isn't Cal here? You specifically told me to come alone because you wanted to talk without him here, but that makes no sense now at all. In order to celebrate an engagement you need both halves of the couple present, right? So, I ask again. Why isn't Cal here? After all I'm marrying—"

"Markus," Steve said pointedly. "You're marrying Markus."

Her spoon dropped into the soup, sending the thick green liquid splashing over the edge of the bowl and onto the pristine white table cloth. Surely she'd heard him wrong?

Her mouth hung open for a moment before she found her voice. "Excuse me? I'm marrying Cal, you know that. We've posted the banns, booked the church. And like I said, we've told Mum and Dad. Cal even asked Dad's permission."

*Lord, he can't be serious about this. We've posted the banns. Nothing can stop Cal and I from marrying. Unless You don't want us together. Overrule here and work this out for Your good.*

"No you're not. You're marrying Markus. It's all agreed. You'll have to untell them." Steve looked at her. "Hear me out."

"I'd rather hear it from Markus." She fixed a pointed glare on him. "I told you no. Several times. I thought you understood."

Markus wore a placating expression on his face that she didn't fall for. "Things changed. There is a way for you to own half of Rainbow Lodge."

"That's assuming I want anything to do with it. Steve already tried to get me to go back and work with him. I told him no, too."

"Harriet, listen for a moment."

"I'm through with listening." She stood up. "I'm going home."

"Sit down!" Steve glared her way.

"I'm fine standing up," she said sharply. "I'm not being railroaded into anything. I'm old enough to make my own decisions. That includes who I'm going to marry, where I'm going to live and what I'm going to do for the rest of my life."

Markus looked at her. "Steven is prepared to let me buy into the lodge. A dowry if you will. I'll own half of it and as my wife, you'll share that ownership. In return, you and I move there and help run it much the same as you were before."

"No way." The words were out before she could stop them. "I have done the working for next to nothing thing to death, thank you. And why would you think I'd want to marry you and return to being a slave at the lodge?"

"I like you. You like me. We've been friends for years. Steven and I get along as well. It makes good business sense."

"And you have money to burn." She looked at her brother. "This is all about money, isn't it? If it bothers you that much that Penny sent me some, I'll give it back. Every single penny of it..." She paused. "I'll get the bank to transfer it back in the morning. What I've never had I shan't miss."

She picked up her bag and shouldered it. "I'm marrying Cal. If you two want to go into business together, that's fine. Just keep me out of it. Steve, I'll give you the money back, all of it. I'll arrange a bank transfer in the morning." She repeated herself in the vain hope it'd sink in this time. "Then I'm going to marry Cal and we're done, you and I."

"Would marrying Markus be so distasteful?" Steve asked.

"For goodness sake!" she snapped. She waved her right hand at them. "See this? It's Cal's ring. I don't love Markus. I never have, and before you suggest it, no, I will not grow to love him. Now I'm not saying another word on the subject. I'll call a taxi, have it meet me on the main road."

"Harriet, wait..." Markus began.

She headed toward the door but as she took a step everything spun. "I'm going home..."

"No, stay." Steve's voice seemed to be coming from a great distance as the floor came rushing up to greet her.

# 23

Cal arrived at the cottage at the usual time to find the key under the mat and a note on the kitchen table. *Gone to work. See you tonight. 'Auntie' L.* Short, sweet and to the point, and typical Laurie. He headed into the den and looked around. He'd have to try to work quieter this morning. Unless Hattie was already up and gone in with Laurie.

Although if so, he would have hoped she'd sign the note as well. He whistled as he mitered a length of baseboard. Thoughts of Hattie floated through his mind: Hattie working beside him, dancing with him, bringing him coffee. The way she wanted to help, to get involved in every aspect of his life. He'd never had a woman get under his skin and affect him the way Hattie did.

He was definitely blessed to have her in his life and to always, God willing, have her there. Jess had laughed the previous evening and told him he was rushing into things, marrying so soon. But he didn't care. It was the right thing to do. He loved her. Nothing else mattered.

He fixed the new skirting boards to the walls, pausing only when he heard the front door open and close. Heavy footsteps crossed the hall. Hmmm, too heavy for Laurie and definitely too heavy for Hattie. He stood and wiped his hands on his jeans. "Hello?"

The footsteps stopped.

Cal moved to the door. "Who's there?" There was no answer. He grabbed the hammer and pushed open the door. "Identify yourself."

The figure turned. "Cal, are you trying to kill me?"

"Rob, you sneak up on me again and I just might. How did you get a key?" He lowered the hammer, his heart pounding fit to burst.

"Laurie gave it to me. You wanted a hand with the coving according to the job book."

"Ah, yes, thank you." He headed back into the den.

"Are you OK? You seem distracted." Rob paused. "And what's this I hear about you getting married?"

Cal grinned. "The tribal drums at work again I see."

"It's all over the village. Jess told Alba in the corner shop..."

"And that's better than taking an ad out in the *Courier*. Yes, it's true. I asked Hattie before Carter's accident, and she said yes yesterday."

Rob slapped him on the back. "Congrats, mate. When's the big day?"

"Three months."

"Wow. You two aren't hanging about. Why the rush?"

"Long story, but it was that or elope." He paused. "Though I still think the latter's a better option."

His cousin's face creased. "Elope?"

"Long story."

"Then you can fill me in while we do the coving." Rob grinned. "But seriously, coving? That's so old school."

"It has to match the rest of the house."

As they worked, he filled Rob in with all the

details, grateful for the help and support as they finished the gently curved surface that transitioned from wall to ceiling.

"For what it's worth, I think you should elope. Keep the church date and get married twice. I mean, it doesn't have to be in a church to be in God's sight, does it? A beach or the blacksmith's shop in Gretna Green would work just as well." Rob grinned as he held the coving in position. "Or Vegas. You could have an Elvis wedding."

"Uh huh."

Rob howled with laughter. "You just had to do that, didn't you?"

Cal shrugged his shoulders and tossed his head back. "Uh huh."

The door opened and Laurie came running in. "Cal, has Hattie rung yet?"

The blood in his veins froze, the humor of the moment dying as he took in the look of utter panic on her face. "No, why? I thought she was with you. Isn't she?"

"No. Steve called to say they were headed back to Headley Cross for the rest of her things. She was going to call before she left there to come back."

"I haven't seen her. I thought she was with you."

Laurie looked at him. "She didn't come home last night. I said Steve rang. They drove back there after dinner."

"How's she getting back?"

"Steve said he'd put her on a train, and then she'd get a cab over from the mainland once she got to the coast."

"When was the last time you spoke to her?"

"Last night. I said goodbye when Steve picked her

up."

"Have you tried ringing the lodge?"

"There's no answer. Hasn't been all day." She paused, fear in her eyes. "What if he's hurt her? If he wants the money back and she refuses…"

"He does. He also wants her to marry Markus. He told her that several times."

"I knew something was wrong yesterday. Steve wasn't acting right." Laurie wrung her hands. "What do I do? Should I call the police?"

"And tell them what? Her brother might have abducted her?"

"Might be an idea."

Cal looked at her and took a deep breath, trying to calm the worry filling him. "Not yet. I'll drive up to Headley Cross now. It's a two hour drive, three at the most. I should be there before they lock up tonight."

"But if they're not answering the phone…"

"I'm going." He hugged her. "And I'll find Hattie and bring her back. I promise. You've got my mobile number. If she rings or turns up here, let me know. Likewise I'll keep you posted when I find her."

****

Cal drove like a madman to the mainland and then up the dark motorway to Headley Cross. He prayed the whole way that Hattie would be all right and there was a simple explanation. Fear knotted his gut and sat like a choker around his throat. Had Steve done something to her? Had he and Markus conspired and hurt her or worse? Or was there a simple explanation? *Whatever it is, Lord, keep her safe.*

He pulled up outside the guest house. Lights

shone from most of the windows and he locked the car before heading up the path. He pushed the door open and rang the bell. Part of him hoped Steve was there. More than that, he hoped Hattie was.

The internal door opened and Penny came out. "Oh, Mr. Trant. Hello."

"Hi. I'm sorry to arrive unannounced, but I'm looking for Hattie. I was told she was here."

"No, she's not I'm afraid. I can get a message to her if you like."

His spirits lifted a little. "Do you know where she is? It's really important that I speak with her."

"She's on holiday."

Cal held her gaze, but didn't want to give her too much information at once. He needed to know what she knew. "She told me she'd quit. We've talked a lot the past few weeks."

"Then you probably know she's been staying with her aunt."

"I've just come from Laurie's house. Steve was there last night. He said he was bringing Hattie here. It's imperative I speak with her."

"Has something happened to Laurie?"

"Other than being worried about Hattie, she's fine." He lowered his voice, aware of the guests in the lounge. "Look, Steve turned up yesterday, demanding in no uncertain terms that Hattie return all his money. He then took her to dinner. No one has seen or heard from her since. Now if you know anything, or know where she is, I suggest you tell me. Laurie is talking about calling the police."

"I haven't seen Hattie in weeks. Steve left here on Saturday morning to go and see her. He was on the island during that huge storm. I was so worried."

Cal frowned. "I'm sorry? He rang yesterday to say he was coming up. It's a two hour drive."

"He left here on Saturday." She whispered the words, her brow furrowed. "I haven't seen or spoken to him since."

He pulled out his mobile and dialed quickly. "Laurie, it's Cal. Is Hattie back yet?"

"No. Is she not there?"

"No she isn't and nor is Steve. I'm on my way back. We'll decide what to do then. Try not to worry."

"Easier said than done."

"I know. I'll be back in a couple of hours." Cal hung up and pulled out a card. "When you see either of them, ask them to call me or Laurie, please. It's urgent."

Penny took the card. "It sounds like Hattie means a lot to you."

Cal nodded. "She does."

She sucked in a deep breath, worrying her bottom lip. "Is Markus missing too? Maybe they left together."

"What?" The lump in his stomach tightened and it was hard to breathe.

"Well, they are getting married. Markus said so himself."

"No, she's marrying me in three months. Markus asked, but she turned him down several times."

"Markus said they'd been engaged since she got to the island."

"What?" His heart stopped and sank. Now he knew Hattie was in danger. Markus was obsessed with her and obviously didn't take her "no" as an answer. But why was Steve encouraging the man's delusion?

"Aunt Laurie knows about this, right? Hattie would have told her at least."

"Like I said, Hattie is marrying me. Laurie knows all about that. So do Hattie's parents. They're happy for the both of us."

"Oh, but Markus was so sure about this. And Steve seemed really happy for the both of them."

"Yeah, right. If Hattie does come back here, or when you speak to Steve, tell him to come and see Laurie." He turned and headed slowly to the car, his footsteps heavy and his heart in his boots. "Now what do I do, Lord?"

The instant answer came. *Save her.*

He got into the car and started the engine. He'd head back home and see if she was there. If not he and Laurie needed to do something.

# 24

Hattie slowly opened her eyes. Bright light assailed them, making the hammering in her head worse. She shut her eyes tightly for a moment, before squinting around the room. Where was she? She didn't recognize anything.

She felt sick. The way the room sloshed and swayed set her head pounding and her stomach turning. She ran a tongue over her parched lips. Her hands were heavy and leaden and wouldn't move properly. It was only as she raised them and looked at them, she discovered they were bound with duct tape.

*Duct tape? What's going on?*

She sat up and glanced around. She was on a boat. She could hear water lapping somewhere and the movement was the waves under the hull. No engine sounds so must be docked somewhere.

But where? She didn't even remember getting on a boat. She closed her eyes, trying to remember something, anything. Why would someone want to put her on a boat and tie her up? What had she done?

The boat lurched, sending Hattie rolling to the floor. She cried out involuntarily as she landed hard against the edge of the cabinet. Pain ripped through her shin and blood oozed through the long jagged tear in her slacks. "Nice one, Hattie," she told herself. "At least you won't have broken your wrist again. Not with the cast on, anyway."

She glanced down at her feet. "Where are my shoes?" Looking around she couldn't see them. "Curious. All I need now is a white rabbit and today will be perfectly confusing. And why am I talking to myself?"

She paused. "Maybe because you work things out better aloud than thinking. But sitting here isn't going to get you out of here. Besides, no one kidnapped Alice. Now, move."

Grateful her hands were tied in front of her and not behind her, she caught hold of the cabinet and pulled herself to her feet and stood for a minute, fighting to get her balance. Her leg took her weight, so it wasn't broken, just cut. Perhaps there was a first aid kit somewhere.

The deck beneath her feet had a slight list to it which didn't help her balance any better. Her head spun and the sea-sickness increased.

Hattie slowly walked to the door and tried it. It opened. That didn't make any sense, but then none of this did. Why tie her up and yet leave her in an unlocked room? Whose boat was this anyway?

The boat lurched again and she staggered into the corridor. Her confused mind couldn't make sense of it.

*Oh, think, Hattie. The only person you know with a boat is Markus…*

Distorted images danced in her mind. She and Steve had dinner with Markus. She'd tried to leave, but when she stood she'd felt incredibly dizzy and fallen. Then Markus picked her up and…

Nothing. Then there was nothing.

Had they drugged her?

She glanced at her hand. Cal's ring was gone. No—surely she hadn't lost it. She pulled herself back into the bedroom and looked for it. Not an easy task with her hands bound. It wasn't anywhere obvious. Maybe if she found a knife, cut the tape from her hands she could look easier.

Something cold and wet ran over her bare feet. She glanced down. Water ran across the floor from the open doorway. Water? That wasn't a good thing on a boat. Maybe someone had left a tap running or something.

Leaving the search for the ring for a moment, she headed to the door. She had to untie her wrists. The list was a little more pronounced now. Stumbling into the kitchen, galley she corrected, she pulled open all the drawers until she found a knife sharp enough for her purpose.

She wedged it into the drawer and slowly rubbed her wrists against it. The tape seemed impervious at first, then finally it gave and she was free.

OK, so now what?

*Find something to bandage that cut first. Then find a radio. Find out where you are. If you're docked then just get off the boat and call for help.*

There was a first aid kit on the galley wall. Pulling it down, she emptied the contents on the table and used the sling to tie over her leg. She debated taking some aspirin for her headache, but decided against. If she had been drugged, they might react with whatever she'd been given and kill her. Not a good move.

She took a deep breath and started walking through the boat until she found a ladder leading upwards. It led to a small bridge. Climbing the ladder wasn't easy, but she managed it.

Her heart sank as she stood on the small deck and looked around.

There was nothing but open sea in front of her though the small window. On the control panel, there was no radio, just bare wires where it had been ripped out. The door to the deck swung open and she headed through it. From which ever direction she looked there was no land.

The boat was lower in the water than it should be. Fear coursed through her, turning her blood to ice. She'd been abandoned and left to die.

"Lord, God, help me. What do I do?"

# 25

The morning sun streamed through the kitchen windows of Laurie's cottage. Cal sipped the tea that Laurie asked, no insisted, that he drank. He hadn't slept, spent the night sitting on Laurie's couch, and felt sick with a mixture of worry and exhaustion. His hands shook, the lump in his throat tried to throttle him every time he tried to swallow, and he wasn't sure the tea would stay down long.

He put the cup down. "There is no way she'd consent to marry Markus. Not willingly."

Laurie looked at him. "What if she had no choice?"

"You think he'd put a gun to her head? Force her into it?"

"I don't know." She sounded just as upset as he was. "I don't understand it. She was so happy about marrying you. There's no reason for her just to up and change her mind. I know Steve can be pushy, but even he wouldn't stoop this low."

"I wish I knew. I should have gone over there last night as soon as I got back." He pushed the chair back and stood. "I'm going to see Markus. Ask him outright."

"And if she is married to him?"

He sucked in a huge breath, hissing it out between his teeth. Nausea rose in his throat. "See if it's what she really wants. If it is, then I accept it and wish her all the best."

Laurie's hand covered his. "Can you in all honesty do that?"

His heart broke within the confines of his chest. "I…" He struggled to control his voice. "I have to. I love her and if that means letting her go in order for her to be happy, then I will."

****

The drive to Markus's house was short, but seemed to take a lifetime. Steve's car was parked out the front, next to Markus's and Cal pulled up next to it. His battered red truck looked out of place next to such luxury. His feet crunched on the gravel and then thudded on the stone steps. He pressed the bell, the clanging chime resounding beyond. What would make this scenario perfect would be a butler complete with tray and liveried uniform answering the door.

The huge door swung open. A butler in a black suit stood there. Had things not been so serious, Cal would have laughed. "I need to speak to Markus."

"Mr. Kerr is busy."

"I don't care. I need to see him now. It's an emergency." His voice rose, and he struggled not to lose his temper. At least not yet.

The butler nodded and vanished closing the door again, not inviting him inside. Cal paced on the doorstep. As he paced, he became more and more frustrated.

Finally Markus appeared, holding the door open, just enough to carry on a conversation. "Good morning, Callum. A little early in the day for a social call, isn't it?"

"Where's Hattie?"

"How should I know where Harriet is?"

"Don't give me that. No one has seen her since Steve took her to dinner two days ago."

"And this is my business because?"

"She told me you were going to be there as well. Playing referee between her and Steve or words to that effect."

Markus laughed shortly. "That's what she told you, was it? I had wondered how she'd explained coming over here. I can assure you that things between her and Steven are as good as they ever were."

It was all he could do not to push Markus against the wall and slap that smug look from his face. "I spoke to Penny last night. According to her, you and Hattie are getting married."

"Oh, I get it now. You're jealous. Well, my fiancée is fine, thank you."

"What?" It was more of a strangled cry than outrage.

Markus smirked. "You've come here out of a fit of the green eyed monster, because the best man won. I do apologize for not inviting you to the engagement party. It was a spur of the moment thing."

"I need to see her."

"That's not possible. She's sleeping right now."

He frowned. The man was lying to him, but which bit was a lie? "Then ask Hattie to ring Laurie when she wakes. She's worried sick."

"Laurie? Oh, right, you mean Mrs. Dillon, her aunt. I'll ask her. But Harriet's determined to make a clean break."

Cal glanced past him to the suitcases just visible in the hallway. "Are you going somewhere?"

"On a cruise for our honeymoon. After that it

depends on what Harriet wants."

Cal changed tactics. "Is Steve here?" he asked, knowing full well he was. Not only was Steve's car here, he could see his reflection in the mirror in the hallway.

"Steven went home. I'll have Harriet call her aunt at some point before we leave."

Markus was lying through his teeth. More than ever convinced Hattie was in trouble, Cal simply nodded.

He turned and headed back to his truck. Driving a short way down the road, he pulled over and parked. He got out and doubling back on foot, sneaked back up to the house. The drawing room window was open and he hunkered down beneath it.

Markus's voice floated through. "Be careful with that. I don't want it broken."

"Did he leave?" Steve's voice was unmistakable.

"Yes, he did. But he did have a point. You'd better ring Mrs. Dillon before she sends the cops over here. You don't want that."

"*I* don't? It's not just me involved here. You're the one who set all this up."

"Once I get my money back, all this is over."

Footsteps and rustling accompanied the voices. Cal risked a peek through the window. They were packing something into crates filled with straw.

"I almost had it," Steve replied. "Until my idiot of a wife got the accountants in and they gave it to Hattie."

"We just need to keep Harriet occupied a few more hours for the money to transfer over to my account. Then it's all over."

"What about the lodge?" Steve's voice was closer

to the window and Cal ducked back down again.

"I'll take care of it. It's not like we need it anymore."

"I don't want to do this any longer. I want my life back."

A car drove up and Cal ducked into the bushes. There was a long silence then, just as he was about to creep away, Markus's voice floated back through the window.

"That was the lawyer with the forms. I told him I'd get Harriet to sign them, then I'll drop them off."

"I'll sign them." The pen scratched on the paper. "There."

"Nice forgery."

"When can I see her? What have you done with her? You haven't harmed her have you?"

"It's a little late for brotherly love, don't you think?" The papers rustled as Markus gathered them up. "Sorry, Steven, by the time anyone finds her, it'll be too late. That ship sailed a long time ago. Jacobs, see these are filed with the solicitor immediately."

There was a pause, then Steve spoke again. "Markus?"

"You are just as involved, Steven. If the police get wind of this, I will know it came from you and then I'll have to kill her slowly. Got it? Good. Then let's get out of here."

Cal pulled back and ran to where he'd parked his truck. As he drove, a sudden thought hit him. *That ship sailed a long time ago.* He reached for the phone and turned on the hands free mode. He dialed the harbor master.

"Harbor master, Dan Green speaking."

"Hey Dan, it's Cal Trant. Are there any boats due

out today?"

"Let me check for you."

"Thank you." He pulled up at the lights, his fingers tapping on the steering wheel.

"No. There's nothing due out today."

"What about any of Markus Kerr's boats?"

"Nope, nothing scheduled. He won't be back for a while according to this. He left last night for France."

*He can't have.* He tried to contain the panic starting to fill him. His voice deepened, taking on a note of urgency. "Which boat? Was it definitely him?"

"I'll check, but it's his signature on the form here."

"It's really important. Was he alone?"

"Nope, he had some woman with him. A cute blonde, actually. She looked a little worse for wear, but he said they'd been celebrating and the champagne didn't agree with her. They left yesterday at twenty hundred hours in the *Cape of Good Hope*."

"Are any of his other boats missing?"

"No, just that one. But like I said he sailed yesterday."

"You still have the CCTV footage?"

"Of course, you want me to hang on to it?"

Cal swung off the main road and headed into the estate where Laurie's cottage was. "Yes, I do. Can you fax a copy of his shipping plan across to the lifeboat station? Along with a couple of stills from that CCTV footage, if possible please. I need to ID the woman with him. Thank you. I'll be in touch." He hung up.

Two minutes later, he parked outside Laurie's and ran up the path. The door opened as he got there. He filled her in quickly. "Markus was lying. I'm not sure how he got back without the harbor master knowing, unless he docked somewhere else."

"What do I do?"

"Ring the police, and report Hattie missing. I'm going to the base to alert the coast guard. Have the police meet me there. Maybe we can track the boat." He hugged her and hurried out.

# 26

Cal pulled into his parking spot and ran to the Ops room, not bothering to lock his truck.

Tom glanced up as he ran into the room. "Cal, what are you doing here?"

"I need to trace a boat. I have reason to believe Hattie's been kidnapped."

"I'm sorry? Say that again, only slower this time."

"Hattie's missing. No one's seen her since she had dinner with Markus and Steve, day before yesterday. I've just seen Markus. Now, according to him, he's leaving today on a cruise, *with Hattie*. He also said several other things that didn't add up. The two of them getting married for one thing."

"I thought Hattie was marrying you."

"She is. However, I spoke to Dan, the harbor master on duty this morning. According to him and his records, Markus and a blonde woman left for France last night on the *Cape of Good Hope* and haven't come back. And none of his other boats are scheduled to leave today. But he said the blonde woman was worse for wear."

Tom pulled over the charts. "What was his course?"

"Dan was going to fax over some stills from the CCTV footage and the shipping…" He broke off. "Perfect timing. There it is." He ran to the printer and ripped it off.

His stomach plummeted and his gut twisted as he took in the photos. Markus had his arm tightly around Hattie, who looked more than worse for wear. She was leaning against him, her head on his shoulder. He'd taken her.

He took the papers over to Tom. "He took her. We need...I need to find her." The two of them poured over the map, comparing that to the shipping plan. Cal sighed. "This is hopeless. He left eighteen hours ago. The boat could be anywhere. Besides, Markus has kidnapped Hattie and then abandoned her. Would he really file a legitimate shipping plan?"

"You don't know that for sure."

"Yes, I do. This photo proves he left on the boat with her. I spoke to him not more than an hour ago. He's still on the island. And he said she was here, too."

Tom reached for the phone. "I'll request a helicopter to go up and look. Maybe the navy has seen them. I'll ask." Before he could call out, the phone rang.

"Penry Island Lifeboat Station." He listened and then nodded. "Consider it done." He hung up. "Fisherman spotted a boat adrift about twenty miles off the coast. They aren't answering radio hails and it seems to be low in the water. Coastguard wants us to attend." He paused. "It's the *Cape of Good Hope*."

Cal took a deep breath, his hands cold and numb. "Page the watch. I'll go and change."

"You're not on duty. It's white watch this week."

"I don't care. I'm here, page the rest of white watch, but I'm going as lead helm. You better get Laurie in. And the police."

"Why?"

He headed to the stairs, calling over his shoulder.

"Because Markus is not on that boat. And I'm betting that only Hattie is."

\*\*\*\*

The water had reached the upper decks now. Hattie splashed back to the bridge. Everything below was flooded, but she wouldn't have been able to fix it even if she had the tools and the use of both arms. She'd gone below to check the pumps and not only were they smashed beyond repair; there were a series of small holes in the side of the boat. The boat would have taken it's time to flood, but there was no stopping it, even if the pumps had been working.

She was going to drown.

It had to have been deliberate. But then she knew that as the radio and all the electrics had been torn out or removed. The boat had been ransacked, but she guessed that was also deliberate. The only thing she couldn't work out was why. She went back on deck. The sun shone and the sea was flat calm. There just wasn't anyone in sight apart from a few seagulls that swooped and cried mournfully overhead.

The boat was sinking by the head, so she clambered to the stern. Maybe someone would come if she could hang on long enough. She tripped over a wooden box. The lid slid to one side, displaying the flares. Sending up a prayer of thanks and a fervent wish that someone would see them and come to her aid, she lit one.

\*\*\*\*

Jim from White Watch tapped him on the

shoulder. "Cal. Flare. Nine o'clock. A long way off. If that's her then she's drifted a fair way."

Cal turned the boat and sliced through the waves. "What if it's not her?"

"It's a boat in distress, we can't ignore it."

"I know that, Jim."

"Cal, chill. If it's not her, we call it in and they send out the other boat to search for her. Chances are Hattie won't be on the boat anyway."

"She was seen getting on it."

"Aye," Jim insisted. "But if Markus got off then perhaps she did, too. The boat appears abandoned."

Cal tilted his head. "Maybe, but someone let off that flare. There's another one."

A huge explosion lit the sky in front of them. The sound roared across the water towards them, the waves rippling outwards tossing the small lifeboat high in the air. Ignoring the curses and exclamations around him, Cal increased speed, time now being of the essence. *Oh, God, keep whoever it is out there safe just a few more minutes.*

He hit the radio mic and called it in. "Penry Island ILS, this is *Seagull*. Large explosion approximately five miles ahead. Request helicopter support and police and fire service."

"Roger that."

Cal tried not to dwell on the fact it was most likely Hattie out there. But it was hard. No matter how firmly he told himself it didn't matter who it was, he had a job to do, Hattie's face swam before his vision. He could feel her arms around him, her lips on his.

Tears burned in his eyes. He couldn't lose her, not now, not after all this. Was it wrong of him to hope it was a different boat?

As he reached the scene, pieces of wood and fiberglass floated on top of the water. Charred remains of what was once a boat. Some of it still burned. A piece of the hull bobbed on the surface of the water with the word *Cape* still visible.

His heart sank further, a pounding in his ears. He was dimly aware of Jim behind him confirming on the radio that it was the boat they were looking for and they were now searching the wreckage for bodies.

Tom's voice came over the radio. "Markus just reported the boat stolen. He claims he wasn't on it last night."

Cal growled. "We know he's lying. We've seen the pictures the Harbormaster sent over. He still has the original CCTV footage of him and Hattie taking her out last night."

He scoured the water as he piloted the boat. Where was she?

Something caught his eye. A motionless figure floating face down a hundred yards away. There was too much debris to get the boat through fast enough. Jumping up he glanced behind. "Jim, take her." He dived over the side, swimming as quickly as he could over to the figure. Definitely a woman. Was that Hattie?

He reached her and turned her over. His blood ran cold. Was she breathing? "Hattie..."

No reaction. He felt for a pulse. Slow, but there. He leaned down to start breathing for her. His lips covered her cold, blue ones, breathing deep into her lungs, his legs working to keep them afloat. One breath, two breaths...

"Come on Hattie, please..."

Her eyes flickered open.

*Thank You, God. She can't have been face down for long.*

His hand ran down her face as he started back to the lifeboat. "Hattie..."

"Am I dreaming?" she whispered.

"I wish you were, love. Just hold on. I'm taking you home."

# 27

Hattie eased herself onto the sofa, holding in the sigh as Aunt Laurie fussed around her, tucking a second blanket across her legs.

"Can I get you anything, dear?"

"You fuss too much. I'm fine, thank you. Cal is right in the next room if I do, anyway."

Aunt Laurie nodded. "And no getting up to help him."

"I promise. I'm going to sit right here and catch up on all the TV I missed the three weeks whilst I was in hospital." She tapped the laptop next to her. "Then I'm going to finalize the fundraiser. You and Cal did a great job with it, but—"

"It needs the Hattie touch." Aunt Laurie laughed. "Have fun."

"Have you heard from the police yet?" Hattie asked quietly. She laced her fingers together, the all too familiar nausea rising at the thought of what happened. She couldn't remember all of it. Just bits and pieces of Markus's hands—on her—horrifying memories she wished she could forget. She remembered a little of the boat and going into the water. Then Cal was there.

"DS Johnson rang just before you got up."

"Has he found Steve?" she asked. No one had seen Markus since Cal had pulled her from the water. A fact she only found out yesterday. And as no one had mentioned Steve either, she had to assume they were together somewhere. Or Steve had just gone away to sulk as was his custom when he didn't get his own way.

"He didn't say. He said he and another officer will be coming to talk to you later. Now, I'll be in at lunch, so you don't need to get up and make yourself anything to eat."

"OK. See you later." Hattie sat until she heard the car start up and drive away. Taking a deep breath, which for the first time in a while didn't hurt, she pulled up to her feet. Aunt Laurie was lovely, but she fussed way too much.

"Sit down." Cal's voice echoed from the other room.

She glanced around but there was no one in sight. "How do you know I'm standing up?"

He looked around the door at her. "I know you. And if I didn't, your reaction gave it away."

She picked up the notebook, pen and phone, and walked slowly towards him. "I'm not an invalid."

"I beg to differ. You've been in hospital the past three weeks with pneumonia. This is only your third day home and your first day out of bed. The doctor said to rest."

She kissed him to shut him up, satisfaction filling her as he responded. Then she sighed as he threaded one hand under her knees, the other around her shoulders and swung her into his arms. "Cal—"

"Rest."

"Fine. Then I'll sit in the other room and watch you work." She leaned against him as he carried her, her heart beating in time with his. "I'm sorry."

"What for, love?"

"This mess."

"It's not your fault."

"Steve's my brother and Markus is, well, I thought he was my friend." She sighed. "I don't remember what happened that night. So if our wedding needs cancelling..." Tears pricked her eyes and slowly tracked down her cheeks.

He probably didn't want her now. And she didn't blame him in the slightest if he didn't.

He set her down on the chair in the den and hunkered down in front of her. He cradled her face in his hands, his thumb wiping away her tears. "Hattie, I love you. And I intend to marry you in two months and one week just as we planned."

"But, I remember Markus..." She couldn't finish

"Laurie didn't think you were listening to all the test results that the docs ran, and let's face it there were so many of them. And you were pretty sick for a while there." She nodded numbly as he spoke. His thumbs wiped away more tears. "Love, nothing happened. He didn't touch you. And even if he had, it wouldn't change the way I feel about you."

She held his gaze. "Really?"

"Really." He kissed her. A mind numbing kiss that would have blown her socks off had she been wearing any. A kiss that made her forget everything except the fact he loved and wanted her.

When he broke off, she leaned into his arms. "I love you."

"I love you, too."

"Glad you do."

He looked at her notepad then up at her. "Is that the fundraiser stuff?" As she nodded he grinned. "Then guess what?"

"What?"

"We have a beat the goalie stand."

"Do we?"

"Sure do. And ten footballers ready to be raffled." He paused. "And I have organized a special guest to draw the raffle and he's agreed to be raffled as well. Or we auction him on the night."

"How did you manage that?" she asked amazed and in awe that he'd have done something like that.

"I have my ways," he grinned.

She tilted her head. "By the way, you have to promise not to be jealous if I win someone else."

"That depends on who wins me. I mean Alba does chat me up every time I see her."

"Pfft. She chats every bloke she sees up. Don't know how Fraser puts up with it. Hey…" She winked at him. "What if old Miss Wright gets you?"

Cal laughed. "She's eighty-seven and in a wheelchair."

"You could take her dancing. Waltz the chair around the ballroom floor. It'd really make her day."

Cal nodded. "Take her to a tea dance. I might just do that anyway, even if she doesn't win me."

Hattie laughed. "Wonderful. Oh…that's it. Where to take all the dates. A huge tea dance at the Palladium with their orchestra. That way everyone wins the same thing and no one can get jealous." She reached for the phone. "You're brilliant."

He pretended to tip his non-existent hat at her. "I do my best."

She laughed and turned her attention to the phone.

\*\*\*\*

Cal kissed the top of her head and let her talk on the phone as he went back to work. It had been touch-and-go the last three weeks and he'd feared he'd lose her on more than one occasion. She'd spent twenty days in hospital, sixteen of those fighting for her life in intensive care. This was the first time Laurie had left her alone, and only because he'd promised to watch her.

Once out of ITU, Hattie had planned the fundraiser from her hospital bed. He had to admit, she did have a flair for organization and the flyers she'd designed were fantastic. Getting his old friends to agree to help was a piece of cake. They'd all seen the news of the bridge disaster and the loss of the lifeboat and were glad to do something to help—even offered match tickets as another prize for the auction. And convincing his longtime friend, Kevin, to help out was a doddle. The hard part was going to be keeping who he was from Hattie.

So much money had already poured in to the Bridge Disaster Fund and the new lifeboat fund that they really didn't need Hattie's fundraiser, but he wasn't telling her that. The money raised from it would go to the RNLI regardless. She needed something to focus on to take her mind off everything else.

He answered the doorbell and let in the two police officers. DS Johnson, he knew as he'd been to the hospital several times. The other officer, tall with dark hair, he didn't know.

Hattie appeared at his side. She smiled and moved to the other officer, hugging him. "Nate. Fancy seeing you here."

Nate hugged her back. "Hey, Hattie. How are you

doing? I hear you've been pretty sick."

"Yeah, I'm better now. It's nice not to have to eat hospital food."

"I bet."

She turned to Cal. "Cal, this is DS Nate Holmes from Headley Cross. He's also an elder from my church."

Cal shook his hand.

She turned back to Nate. "Why are you here?"

"This ties into a case in Headley Cross I was working on."

"Oh." Hattie took a deep breath. "Hello, Sgt. Johnson."

"Miss Steele. Can we talk?"

"Sure."

Cal started back to the den, but Hattie grabbed his arm. He looked at her, worried by the fear in her eyes. "Love?"

"No more secrets, Cal. Come with me. I need you."

"Sure." He held her hand and went into the lounge with her. He sat on the couch.

Hattie sat as close to him as she could and didn't let go of his hand. She shook and swallowed hard, a sure sign she was uncomfortable and overly anxious. He'd keep an eye on her and if it got too much, he'd call a halt to this interview.

DS Johnson looked at her. "We arrested both your brother and Markus Kerr yesterday."

"Arrested?" she whispered. Her hand tightened on Cal's, turning his fingers white. "You found them?"

"We've known where your brother was for some time."

"Why wasn't I told he was all right?"

"Steve was in protective custody. We couldn't tell anyone. As for Markus, we got a tip off and followed it. They've been charged with kidnapping, fraud and theft. Markus has also been charged with murder and attempted murder."

"I don't understand. Murder?"

"Hattie, I'm sorry. Penny's dead," Nate said gently.

"What? She can't be..."

Cal put his other arm around her, holding her firmly. He could feel her whole body trembling.

"The lodge had been shut for the past two weeks. Yesterday it was destroyed in an explosion. Early indications are that it was gas—probably where it has been left turned on somewhere in the building. The firefighters found her body in the basement. She'd been there some time by the looks of it."

Hattie swallowed hard and the color drained from her face. "I'm going to be sick..." She got to her feet and bolted from the room.

Cal gave her a few minutes then got up. "I'll be right back." He headed out to the downstairs bathroom. Huge sobs came from within. He tapped on the door. "Hattie, love, it's me. Let me in."

She opened the door and he gathered her into his arms, holding her securely. "Why...?"

"I'm so sorry, love. I wish I knew." Her knees buckled and he gathered her into his arms. "I've got you." He carried her back through to the lounge and sat on the couch with her, his arm protectively around her.

"Sorry..." she whispered.

"It's OK," Nate said gently. "It's never easy news to give or receive."

Hattie shook her head. "Was she...how did she?"

"She was shot. It would have been quick, she wouldn't have known anything."

"It's my fault."

Nate frowned. "Why do you say that?"

"Because I told Steve that it was Penny who brought in the accountant." She sucked in a deep breath. "If I hadn't left and quit working there because he kept cancelling my holidays and not paying me, she wouldn't have tried to get the money for me."

"It's not your fault." Nate's voice took on a firm tone. "They'd been under investigation for a while. It was only a matter of time before we caught them." He paused. "They have been laundering money through the guest house for years."

Hattie looked at him and then at Cal. "That's why I wasn't paid," she whispered.

He ran his fingers over her arm as he hugged her.

Nate carried on speaking. "When Penny got the accountant in to try to pay you, he audited the accounts and raised the alarm."

Hattie paled so fast, Cal feared she'd pass out. "Hattie?"

"I'm OK," she whispered. She shook in his arms and he pulled her closer.

He kissed the top of her head. "Just take your time, love," he said. "I'm sure the officers will go at your pace here." He shot them a warning glance. "She's only been out of hospital three days. This is her first day out of bed. If need be we can do this another time."

Hattie took a deep breath. "Steve wanted me to marry Markus. He kept going on and on about the money and needing it back. I didn't understand why the money was so important. Why don't I remember anything?" She paused. "I remember bits and pieces, but nothing concrete."

"There was a vast amount of rohypnol in your bloodstream when you got to the hospital. Which is why you don't remember."

"Oh... Maybe he was waiting for me to accept being married to him before he did anything. Or just hoped I'd drown and solve the problem that way." She pushed a hand through her hair. "If he couldn't shut me up by marrying me, he'd shut me up by killing me. A wife can't be made to testify against her husband, right?"

Nate nodded. "She can give evidence voluntarily, but we can't subpoena her to testify, no."

"So why didn't he...?" she broke off, not wanting to think it, never mind say it.

Cal looked at her. "Least he had some morals then. Or he just wanted you to remember it."

Nate shook his head. "Steve stopped him. He agreed to the kidnapping, but it was simply to get what he assumed was the laundered money back from your account. He wasn't going to let Markus touch you without your consent—which you were in no position to give after Markus drugged you. Steve even put you in the car, so you couldn't be traced to the house. But from Steve's testimony, Markus shot him. When Cal turned up and confronted Markus, Steve had a change of heart and tried to call this all off. However Markus had already rigged the boat you were in to sink."

Hattie shivered. "How could he even go that far?"

DS Johnson resumed the questions. "Is there anything you can remember? Anything at all, no matter how small?"

She closed her eyes and shook her head. "No. It explains a lot. Why there always seemed to be a lot of money around, but stuff never got done. Or why he never let me see the accounts." She sucked in a deep breath. "Is there anything left of the lodge?"

"It was completely destroyed. I'm afraid the insurance won't be valid as the building was bought using illegally gained funds."

The rest of the color drained from her face. "So, the money sitting in my account, that he was so desperate to get back…? Is that laundered as well? Am I under suspicion too?"

"No," Nate said. "There are two sets of accounts. The money from the paying guests and then the other. Penny only knew of the one account and paid you from that. And gave back your original deposit."

"So it's from legitimate guests?"

Nate nodded. "Yes. Literally the seven years wages he owed you." He shrugged. "It was even in the books as Hattie's wages. He just hadn't paid it to you."

Cal could see and feel the relief filling her as Hattie slumped against him. He hugged her securely. "So she can keep it?"

"Yes. And if she wants to press charges over not being paid…"

Hattie shook her head. "No. What's going to happen to Steve and Markus now?"

"They've been remanded in custody until trial." Nate looked at her. "For what it's worth, Steve isn't being charged with attempted murder or Penny's death. Both he and Markus agree he had no part in that. When Steve regained consciousness in the hospital, he reported what had transpired, but by that point Cal had found the remains of the boat and called in the coastguard and police."

"I don't remember much after dinner. When I woke up on the boat, the water was already coming in. There were holes in the pump room. The radio was gone, except a few wires. I found a box of flares. Lit a couple then there was a huge explosion. I thought I was dead."

Cal hugged her tightly. "I'm glad you're not."

"Me too."

"You're safe now," Nate told her. "They've been refused bail and won't be getting out any time soon. Are you prepared to testify in court if needed?"

"Yeah."

The two officers stood. "If there is anything else you remember, let us know."

Cal saw them out and then went back into the lounge. Hattie sat curled up on the sofa, crying. He sat beside her and wrapped his arms around her, holding her close. Her whole body shook with the force of her sobs.

Finally, she calmed down enough to speak. "How could my own brother do something like this?"

"I wish I knew, love. "

"Everything was a lie."

"Not everything," he said, rubbing her back gently. As she raised her face to him, he smiled, wiping away her tears with his thumb. "He still loved you enough to protect you from Markus."

She shook her head. "He went along with it. He didn't care about what I wanted, he never did. Just the money. I don't want any of it. Despite what the police said about it being legitimate funds, I don't want it."

"What will you do with it?"

"Give it away. I was going to do that anyway, at

least some of it..." She broke off and smiled wryly. "Maybe a third to the church, a third to the fund for Trevor and the rest to the fundraiser, if that's OK with you."

"Whatever you want to do with it, love, is fine with me."

She leaned against him. "How can you still love me after all that he's done?"

"Because you are not your brother and even he isn't beyond saving. Just keep praying for him. We can do that now if you like."

"I would," she whispered.

# 28

Hattie spent the week of the fundraiser, happily running back and forth between Aunt Laurie's house and the lifeboat station where all the various fundraising events were taking place. The coffee morning had been a fabulous success, as were her apple cakes. She'd ended up taking orders for more. Maybe Cal was right and she should open a patisserie, or at least find a job in one.

Raffle tickets were also selling like hot cakes. She half wished she'd gone with the auction and raised more, although not everyone was flush with money and this way even the pensioners could feel they were doing their part.

As promised, the footballers had turned up and posed for photos as well as playing a charity match against the lifeboat crews. To the crowd's amusement, the match had to be halted for a couple of hours as the lifeboat was called to a shout. A stranded horse which had thrown its rider, then panicked and swam out to sea.

The crowd was able to watch the rescue as the lifeboat crew tried to lasso the horse several times, before finally catching it and gently towing it back to shore. Once the boat was cleaned and refueled, the football match continued.

The visitors eventually won sixteen goals to nil—which was probably a good thing as they were donating a hundred pounds for every goal they scored.

Later that afternoon, Hattie glanced around the dining room of the Grand Hotel, sited on the sea front, opposite the lifeboat station where she was holding the final event, the grand dinner and raffle. "Does it look all right?"

Cal glanced around. "It looks amazing."

"Are you sure?" She turned around looking at the tables with their flowers and place settings. "Does it need more balloons?"

"Any more balloons and it'll blow away in the breeze. Don't worry."

"What if no one comes?" She gnawed her bottom lip, unable to shift the feeling that the evening was going to be a complete disaster.

"Hattie, you invited everyone who bought a raffle ticket to a free dinner. They'll come."

She nodded. "I'll just go and check on the food."

"No, you won't. You've done enough. You and I are going to go for a walk and get some air." He took her hand, pulling her from the building. "I haven't spent time with you for ages."

"Yeah, you have."

"Not alone. We've done nothing but fundraising or planning the fundraising for the last few weeks. And before that you were in the hospital."

She pulled her jacket around her. It was dark now and the wind was starting to get up. "Do you think they'll repair the bridge or rebuild it?"

"I think the plan is to rebuild the missing section. They'll build new base columns so it'll be a few feet to one side or the other of the original one."

"At least we're not totally cut off. We have the road bridge." She looked at him.

He nodded. "And the floating bridge. We're fortunate that was still around."

She grinned. "I can't believe you haven't been on it yet. It's fun."

"You have a strange definition of fun, woman."

"Seriously, it is. It runs on cables and huge chains and gets pulled from one side of the water to the other."

"I know how it works." He rolled his eyes. "I also know how old it is."

"Then you know how safe it is. Over a hundred-years-old and never had an accident. You can't say that about anything else. It doesn't seem possible that it's November. The time seems to have flown by. And every day I love you more. I didn't think that was possible." She changed the subject.

He nodded. "Aye, time flies when you're in love. It'll soon be Christmas and I haven't even started shopping yet."

"Soon be our wedding," she said. "And I haven't even shopped for a dress yet."

He grinned. "Then you'd best snap to it. I've got my outfit organized."

She laughed. "Your uniform, I hope."

"Now I need to find something else," he moaned, poking his tongue out at her.

Hattie laughed. "If you're going to be a diva, perhaps you'd better wear a dress and carry a handbag."

"Not unless it's pink," he retorted.

She laughed so hard, she could hardly reply. "The bag or the dress?"

"Both." He rubbed his thumb over the back of her hand. "I like seeing the ring on the right hand now."

"That's my left hand and it's been there a while. You just haven't noticed." He'd bought her a replacement one. The original having never turned up. She assumed it had gone down with the boat.

"Oh, I noticed. I notice everything about you." He kissed her, slowly at first, then deeper, warming her entire body, until she was sure she glowed. He broke off and leaned his forehead against hers. "Do you think you could live here?"

"Nowhere else I'd rather be."

"People are arriving." Aunt Laurie's voice washed over them. "You two need to come inside and change."

****

Hattie smoothed her long pale green dress down, wondering if it were too much. She'd bought a strip of raffle tickets, but knew the chances of her winning Cal were remote to say the least. As much as she'd like that, she half hoped Miss Wright, the wheelchair-bound oldest church member, would win him. He at least would make sure she felt like the only woman in the room at the tea dance.

It seemed as if the whole island were there. She stood in front of the microphone and looked out over the packed hall. People from the mainland had come too, representatives from the rail company, the media and the RNLI head office as well. Even the local Member of Parliament was there somewhere. Did she look as nervous as she felt?

So long as she could get through this without throwing up. She hated public speaking. She always had.

"Thank you—" The microphone howled and she

paused whilst they adjusted the sound level. "Thank you all for coming. It's been a wonderful week, with a lot of different things going on. I've had a lot of fun, and I hope you all did too. Tonight should be fun as well. The raffle and auction will be taking place after we eat. Even if you don't win a date with one of our—can I call them prizes?" She smiled at the response she got.

She held out a hand and gestured for them to stand. "Actually, can our prizes stand up?" The clapping grew louder as all three watches of the lifeboat and shore crew stood, along with all the footballers. Hattie waited until it died down before she continued. "The raffle is being sponsored by the Palladium and all the 'dates' will be at special tea dance coming up at the end of the month. If you don't win a date tonight, and have always fancied a tea dance, Mr. Sanderson, from the Palladium has said that you just need to bring your raffle ticket along at any of the tea dances in January, February, or March next year and he will let you and a partner in free. Mr. Sanderson, could you stand please?"

He stood to more applause.

Hattie paused again to wait for the clapping to die down. She wondered if reading the weather forecast would garner the same response right now. She was half tempted just to try it and see.

"And now, before we begin properly, I have one more very important announcement to make. Can I extend a special welcome to Trevor? Not back to active duty yet, but home from the hospital and the proud father of a bouncing baby girl born at four-fifteen this morning, weighing in at nine pounds fifteen ounces. Mum and baby doing fine. Dad's going home for his last night's sleep in a while after this."

She grinned. "He's also agreed to be raffled and thinks by hiding at the back I won't see him. Trevor, on your feet."

More applause filled the room as a beetroot red Trevor stood, waved and then sat down again.

"All that's left for me to do is to say I hope you have a pleasant evening, enjoy the food and the company. Pastor Kenny will give thanks for the food and then the staff will serve it."

She made her way to her table and slipped into her seat, blushing at the attention. She slid a hand into Cal's. His family and Laurie sat with them.

Pastor Kenny stood and gave the blessing.

As the food arrived, Carter grinned over at Hattie. "I hear you planned the menus and gave the hotel staff your recipes?"

"Yeah." She took a small bite, hoping the chef hadn't added anything. She'd been careful not to include anything that could set off Cal's allergies.

"She's being modest," Cal said. "She designed the dishes herself. The hot trifle is a particular favorite of mine."

"*Hot* trifle?" Carter and Jess chorused at the same time.

Hattie laughed. "That's exactly what Cal said the first time he was given it."

Cal nodded. "Trust me, it's peng, you'll love it."

Jess rolled her eyes. "Peng? That's what my class of teenagers say all the time."

Jim Trant, Cal's father, frowned. "And what is peng when it's at home?"

"It used to be wicked when I was their age. Then it became cool. Then sick and now peng."

Jim shook his head. "What's wrong with using proper English? In my day…"

Cal kept his face straight and looked his father in the eyes. "We know, Dad. When you were young, several hundred years ago, you said spiffing, ace, brill, super and wore shorts even in the middle of winter. Not to mention got the bus to work, bought dinner, a new suit, took Mum to a dance and still had change from a fiver."

Jim glared at him over his fork. "Now then you young whippersnapper…"

Carter picked up his glass, stuck his little finger out, and put on an affected accent. "I say old chap, don't forget the jolly hockey sticks and the fact that Great Britain used to close all day on a Sunday and again on a Wednesday afternoon. The whole country has gone to the dogs since they stopped doing that."

"Well, we would go to the dogs if we didn't have to go to work," Cal finished.

The whole table burst out laughing. Hattie loved the way they all teased each other, but there was never any malice in it. Her hope was one day she and Steve could have a relationship like Cal's family did.

The main course arrived. Hattie became even more nervous. The special guest Cal had promised hadn't yet arrived. "What if he isn't coming?"

"He'll be here, love. Maybe the traffic is bad." Cal's phone beeped and he glanced at the message. "He's here. Is he sitting with us?"

"Yes, hence the empty place at the table."

"And there I was thinking you'd had one laid for the Unseen Guest," Laurie said.

"That too. It's also why our table is right at the back. So your mystery man stays a secret a little longer."

"Clever woman." Cal stood. "Come meet him, love."

"Excuse me." She stood and took Cal's hand, walking with him to the lobby.

A tall dark-skinned man, shining eyes and no hair stood there. She caught her breath recognizing him instantly. Surely, she was wrong. It couldn't be...

He moved forward and enveloped Cal in a massive bear hug, almost sweeping him off his feet. "Cal, my man, how are you?"

"I'm good, Kev. How are you?"

"Training, running, more training, you know how it goes." He grinned and then held out a hand to Hattie. "And you must be the woman who finally tamed the ultimate wild boy."

"I'm trying to." She took his hand, admiring his firm grip. "Hattie Steele."

"Kevin Wells."

A flash of fan girl squee washed over her. It *was* him, the fastest man Britain had ever produced. He was world famous, someone she'd watched race on the TV numerous times, win countless gold medals, and he was standing here shaking her hand, attending the little fundraiser dinner she'd put together. *Wow. Wow. Wow.*

Somehow, she found her voice. "Thank you so much for coming tonight, Mr. Wells."

"Please, call me Kevin. Mr. Wells is my father. And it's a pleasure to have been invited. I'm sorry I'm late. The traffic was horrid, and it's so windy they were restricting travel on the bridge. They closed it after me. So I'll need a hotel or something tonight. Perhaps I could get a room here."

"Rot," Cal said. "Laurie will no doubt insist on you staying with her. And if she doesn't you can stay at mine." He winked at Hattie. "He and Laurie go way back."

Kevin grinned, a hint of a blush showing. "Pear trees, wasn't it?"

"Least we started asking after that though." Cal laughed. "Come on and eat whilst it's still hot. You haven't missed much."

Hattie watched Kevin talk easily with the others as he ate. Her view of celebrities was radically undergoing a rethink. Like Cal, he wasn't the least bit affected by his fame and talked easily about his life and faith. He teased Jess mercilessly and Hattie knew by the way Jess blushed that she had a huge crush on him. But then that wasn't hard—the guy was gorgeous.

Kevin smiled at her, with perfect white teeth she was instantly jealous of. "So, Hattie, how did you and Cal meet? He wouldn't tell me no matter how many times I asked him."

"He stayed at a guest house I worked in. We met again when I came to live with Aunt Laurie."

"You're Laurie's niece? Wow. It really is a small world after all."

Hattie smiled. "I had no idea Cal worked on the lifeboats until the yacht I was on sank and he turned up to rescue me. The rest, as they say, is history."

Kevin grinned. "Ah, Cal always was a chick magnet."

"Chick magnet?" Cal spluttered. "I prefer totally irresistible to women."

Carter roared with laughter. "Chick magnet."

"Even at school, the girls were fighting over him in the playground."

Cal blushed. "Can't help being cute," he muttered.

"That's 'Cute', capital C," Hattie told him. "I was just wondering how you two met. Athletics and football seem a world apart."

"School," Kevin told her, still laughing at Cal. "We lived here until I was thirteen then moved to the mainland, but I commuted over the bridge to school every day. I did athletics, Cal did football. We sat next to each other in maths. He'd say 'when I grow up I want to play football for England.'"

Cal grinned. "And Kev would say 'I'm going to win gold in the Olympics.' Not only did that, but got the world, commonwealth *and* Olympic records."

Kevin grinned back. "I may be the fastest man on the planet, but it pales into comparison with what you and your mates do out there each day on the lifeboats."

Hattie tuned out the conversation as she noticed how the wind howled outside, tossing torrential rain against the windows. Lightning flashed and she counted to fifteen before the answering thunder came. A fair way off, nothing to worry about.

Cal nudged her. "You OK, love? Not spooked by the storm?"

"A little, but I'll be fine."

"Time you got the ball rolling out there."

Nodding, she stood and made her way to the mic at the front again. "Wasn't dinner great? Let's show our appreciation for the chef and the staff who cooked and served it." She paused as applause drowned out the storm outside.

"It's now time for the raffle, so if you've all got your tickets ready..." She grinned as people waved them at her. "Without further ado, I'll get the instructions out of the way first. In this bowl are numbered ping pong balls. Each one corresponds to one of our thirty-five dates. A list of each one and their number will come up on the screen in a second. In the other bowl are all your raffle tickets. In the event of a 'double date' we'll draw again. Now let me introduce you to our special guests, who'll be doing the draw. First is Carter Trant, current Tour de France champion. Despite the crutches he assures me he can still dance. He'll be drawing the ping pong balls."

Carter stood and made his way to the front. Once he got on stage he did a twirl. *"Yes, ma'am, I can boogie..."* he sang.

The audience laughed and applauded with delight.

She clapped along with them. "See. And our other special guest, who has also kindly agreed to throw his name into the hat tonight, is current British champion and Olympic one hundred meters gold medalist Kevin Wells. He'll be drawing the raffle tickets."

She made her way back to her seat as thunder crashed again. She wrapped her arms around her stomach as Kevin and Carter began to speak.

Cal slid an arm around her. "What's up, love?"

"The storm's really bad."

"Just relax a little. We still have power, and it's just a storm. They happen all winter. Not always with thunder, but wind and rain, yeah."

Lightning flashed again. Hattie counted silently. *One one thousand. Two one thousand. Three one—* She jumped. "That was barely a mile away."

"You're missing the raffle," he whispered. "You won't know who you've won."

"You'd better win me or a little old lady," Hattie whispered back.

"Ditto."

"I don't want a little old lady thank you very much."

He laughed.

Carter got people to stand as their number was called out. He was about half way through when Cal's number came up. Cal stood and grinned at Hattie.

She fingered her blue tickets. The chances of winning anyone was remote, she knew that and had only entered herself because Aunt Laurie had insisted.

Cal did the obligatory twirl, looking very fit in his tux and bow tie.

Kevin reached into the bowl. "And the winner of the dashing Callum Trant is blue—"

A pager went off. Cal reached into his pocket.

Hattie's heart twisted and her stomach sank. *No, not tonight...*

He looked at the pager and then at her. "I have to go. Don't stop on our account. Keep going."

More pagers went off and across the room, the men and women of Red Watch shore and boat crew stood, saying brief and hurried goodbyes.

Cal leaned down and hugged her. "I love you. I'll see you soon."

She grabbed his hand. "I love you, too. Be safe."

He nodded and hurried from the room. As they left, applause rippled and then resounded. Hattie watched with fear mixing with pride. That was her man going off to save those in peril. They were all superheroes in ordinary clothing, though none of them would admit it.

Carter looked over at Hattie and she nodded to him. "Carry on," she mouthed.

He nodded. "Well, it looks as if someone needs the

guys and gals more than we do tonight. I've been told to carry on, so we'll do that. We're making a list of who wins who anyway and we can put pictures up of the dates instead of making them stand if they're not here. But first I'd like to invite Pastor Kenny up here, to pray for all those who've just left us and for whomever it is out in that storm that needs help tonight. Pastor?"

Pastor Kenny stood and nodded. "Let's pray. Lord God, we know that you are in control of all things, even the storm that is currently raging around us. We ask Your protection on those crewmembers of Red Watch who have just left. We don't know what dangers they will face or for how long they will be gone. Guide and guard them and, if it's Your will, bring them home safely. We also ask comfort for those left behind and for patience for those awaiting rescue or help. In Jesus' name, amen."

Kevin nodded as he sat down again. "Thank you, Pastor. So as I was saying the winner of the dashing Callum Trant. And I know he's dashing because he just dashed out the door..." he paused as everyone groaned, "...is blue seven one five."

No one said anything. Aunt Laurie nudged her. "Hattie, check your tickets."

"Blue seven one five," Kevin repeated.

Hattie looked down at the strip of tickets in her hand. Blue seven twelve to seven sixteen... She'd won him. She raised a hand. "He's mine."

Carter laughed. "Think we all know that Hattie... oh my bad, you mean you're the holder of blue ticket seven one five." He grinned and made a note.

They continued with the draw until it was finished. Carter grinned. "And now the hotel staff has laid on some music and there's dancing for anyone who wants to for the rest of the evening. Or feel free to sit here and chat until about ten when we end."

Hattie sat still, the bad feeling in her stomach growing.

Aunt Laurie touched her hand. "You all right, dear?"

"Worried."

"We all are, but it's something you need to get used to if you're going to marry him. He's not going to change what he does."

"I don't expect him to. This is what he does." She took a deep breath. "I should go and circulate. See you later."

An hour later, she was doing the final tidying up. Tom came in and over to her.

"Hattie."

She glanced up, her blood freezing at the look on his face. "What is it?"

"The boat's back."

"I'm going over there."

He put a hand on her arm. "No...they're going straight back out again. Sit down."

"I don't want to sit down." She shook his arm off. "Tell me what's wrong."

"There was a child in the water. Cal dived in and rescued him. Got the child into the boat and started to clamber back in himself. The boat was hit by a huge wave that knocked him off. There's been no sign since. He's missing."

# 29

*Missing… Missing… Missing…*

The word echoed round her mind. No matter how hard she tried to think of something else, she couldn't. She sat in the Ops room of the lifeboat station, still wearing her pale green evening gown. She had found Cal's tux hanging in the crew changing area and wore that in an effort to keep warm.

Cold tea sat in front of her, in Cal's mug. It had his name and a childish stick figure in uniform painted on it. She'd gone through the whole range of emotions in the last two hours. Anger, fear, tears…

Now she was numb. Just wanted to know where he was. She'd prayed so much. Asked why, then asked that God protect Cal and bring him home. Both lifeboats had gone out, with relief crews. But she knew they'd bring him back. They'd keep looking until they found him. He was one of their own and they wouldn't leave him behind.

"They're back!"

The shout had her on her feet and running for the stairs. Tom met her half way up. He gently took hold of her arms.

"Let go. I have to go to him."

"They haven't found him. The search has been called off until first light."

"Noooo…" The anguished cry was torn from the depths of her soul. "You can't do that."

"It's not my decision. It's too rough. The boats are getting swamped, the choppers can't fly, and we could lose more men. The Navy has a patrol boat in the area, and they'll keep an eye, but we can't do any more until morning."

"He's out there somewhere. You can't just leave him. He could be dead by morning."

"Hattie, Cal would make the same decision."

"No, he wouldn't. He didn't want to stop looking for Trevor. You kept going then, why not now?"

"We *will* find him. As soon as it's light."

Tears streamed down her face. Pulling away from Tom, she ran outside into the storm and down onto the edge of the beach. She stood there, waves crashing over her feet, facing the sea, crying to the Only Hope she had left. "Why? Why take him now? After all we've been through?"

A quiet voice, full of peace echoed in her mind. *The eternal God is our refuge and underneath are the everlasting arms.*

\*\*\*\*

Cal struggled to keep his head above the water. He had no idea where he was or how far from the lifeboat he'd been swept. The current was strong and that combined with the wind, rain and raging storm had left him half drowned and fearing for his life.

Something red appeared in a break in the waves. A buoy. Maybe if he swam to it, he could hold on, stay afloat a while longer.

Swimming hurt. The waves crashed over his head, pushing him under. He reached the buoy and held on. His fingers, cold and numb, struggled to keep a tight enough grip.

Words from Psalm twenty-two filled his mind. *Do not be far from me, for trouble is near and there is no one to help.*

Cramps ripped through his legs and he let go of the buoy, crying out in pain. A wave pushed him under and for a moment he was afraid he'd stay down and never come up again. He was so tired, couldn't fight the storm any longer.

Hattie's face floated in front of his eyes. He leaned back into his jacket and closed his eyes. *Be with her, Lord. Whatever happens, Thy will be done.*

\*\*\*\*

First light of dawn began to light the eastern sky and the search and rescue mission finally resumed. Hattie had spent the night alternating pacing the shore and checking the Ops room for updates which never came. She watched both lifeboats launch and the coastguard helicopter fly overhead. She'd begged to be allowed to go, but Tom refused.

As the boats disappeared from view, she turned and trudged back into the crew changing area. Cal's spare bunny suit was hanging on his peg. Cold, she pulled off her dress and slipped into the bunny suit. She zipped it up, his scent washing over her.

Tears filled her eyes. "Where are you, Cal?"

She looked at the pile of old uniforms they'd used for photographs during the week. For a small payment, the public had been able to dress up in full lifeboat crew uniform and have their photo taken on board the lifeboat itself. She had to do something. She'd go stir crazy if she had to sit around for any longer. They'd wasted five hours as it was.

In that instant, the idea was born. Rummaging through them, she found one that would fit her and pulled it on over the bunny suit. The boots were too big but she'd manage. Not bothering with the life vest, she put Cal's tux back over the whole ensemble.

Turning around, she grabbed a backpack, containing a rope and first aid kit, a torch and checked the inside pocket of the tux to check Cal's phone was still there. It was. Good. She'd need it.

She grabbed a couple of bottles of water and shoved them into the backpack. Then she headed back outside to find Aunt Laurie looking for her.

"Hattie? Where are you?"

"I'm here."

"I made you some..." Laurie's voice trailed off as she took in her outfit. "Where are you going?"

"I can't just sit here. I'm going to go along the coast line."

"Why?" Aunt Laurie pressed the hot drink into her free hand.

Hattie gulped the scalding liquid, not caring if it burned her throat. It might be a while before she had another drink, even if she really didn't have time to spare. "The current here drove the debris field inland rather than out to sea right? So it stands to reason that anyone lost at sea would be dragged the same way."

"I don't see what that has to—"

Hattie sighed. "It has everything to do with it. No one is searching the beaches. So I will. I have Cal's phone. If they find him then ring me. If I find him then I'll ring here."

"You can't go alone."

"There is no one else free. I'll be fine. Just pray."

She gave the cup back. "I love you. See you later."

Before anyone could stop her, Hattie headed down the beach to the shore line, using the torch to light her way. She followed it to where the cliff edge met the beach and cautiously edged around it. There was a slight beach at the bottom of the cliff, more at low tide, but the tide was gradually coming in. There was a chance she'd get cut off by the tide, and have to wait it out on the cliff itself, but hopefully it wouldn't come to that.

The wind howled and tore at her hair and her jacket. It pulled the breath from her and refused to give her the next one. It tugged Cal's name from her lips and tossed it like chaff into the distance.

Water spray stung her face and hands as the coldness dug into her body despite the layers of clothing. She stumbled, pushed into the cliff face by the rushing waves. She kept going, the oversized boots hampering her movements almost as much as the weather. A wave came in hard and fast, drenching her to the waist.

Her feet slid inside the boots, making walking hard. She hadn't had this much trouble walking since she borrowed her mother's high heeled shoes for a school play when she was ten. The wind made her eyes water. Rain kept falling, as constant as the prayers that fell from her lips. The faint dawn overhead, became an angry, grey sky. Finally, the sun rose enough to light the sky and she could see clearly, well as much as she could in the storm, and she turned off the torch and put it in the back pack.

A hundred yards further on, she stopped. A new rock fall blocked what little beach there was. *Please, God, don't let him be under that.*

"Cal," she yelled. There was no answer. Going around the rocks wasn't an option, not unless she wanted to be dragged out to sea and then tossed back against them. Just like in the kid's song, she had to go through it. Or in this case over it.

The slippery rocks cut her hands to shreds. Her feet slid and caught on Cal's jacket. Losing her balance, she fell, tumbling down the other side and landing in a heap on the sand. She lay there for a moment, winded, trying to get her breath back. If the rescue services could see her now, they'd probably laugh. Some rescuer she made. She shook her head, irritated at the way her mind was working, trying to distract her from what she had to do.

It was lack of sleep. Deep down, she knew that. Wiping the sand from her face, she pushed upright. Cal needed her. She checked the phone was still in the jacket. The last thing she wanted to do was lose it and not be able to call for help when she found him. *And yes*, she told herself, *that is when and not if*. There wasn't the slightest doubt in her mind that he was still alive and out there.

The rain eased off, the wind dropped. *Thank You, Lord. Did you rebuke the wind and the rain, telling them to be quiet, like You did all those years ago? I would ask that You change the course of the tide, but that's not possible. Too much relies on the tides and so on. Let me find him.*

She started walking again, hugging her chest, ignoring the pain slicing through her. The cliff bent around to the left, hardly any beach for her to walk on. The waves lashed high against it and it took every ounce of courage she had to wade around it.

There was something just ahead, lying next to the water. "Cal," she yelled.

The figure stirred.

She waded faster, feet sliding on the sand one minute and being sucked down deep the next. "Cal..." *Please, God, let it be him. Let him be all right.* She dropped to her knees beside him and turned him over.

His eyes flickered open. "Are you an angel?" he muttered.

"Cal, its Hattie. It's going to be all right." She dragged him away from the water's edge, to the base of the cliff and onto an outcrop of rock. There was so much blood. It left a trail on the sand before an incoming wave washed it away.

"Have you come to take me home?"

"Yes. Where does it hurt?" OK that was a stupid question, but she needed to know how much he was aware of what was going on. He'd lost a lot of blood and if she didn't do something, he might just end up bleeding to death.

"Everywhere. Are you an angel?"

"You wish." She pulled the first aid kit open and rummaged around the contents until she found a roll of gauze. She tied the bandage as tight as she could around his leg. Cal cried out in pain. "Sorry..." She cradled him against her body, trying to keep him warm. Pulling the phone from her pocket, she dialed Aunt Laurie's phone, praying she'd have it switched on.

Aunt Laurie answered on the second ring. "Hello?"

"It's Hattie, I found him."

"Thank the Lord. Let me give you to Tom."

There was a brief pause as he came to the line. "Hattie, its Tom. Where are you?"

"A beach somewhere, back's against the cliff. Cal's

hurt badly, he's bleeding, not making much sense. The tide's coming in fast. Not sure how long we can stay above water. There's nowhere to go."

"Which direction did you go?"

"East. Not sure how far. Walked about an hour I think, hard to tell. There's a new rock fall. It's just past that. We're on a ledge, but the water's reached us—"

A huge wave crashed over them, snatching the phone from her hand and tossing it far out to sea. She wrapped both arms around Cal, holding him tightly. The pain in her ribs returned with a vengeance. She'd have her fair share of bruises after this. "Cal, talk to me."

He stirred. "Hattie?"

"Yeah. Still not an angel."

"Thought you were."

"Nope. Just a woman looking for a bloke she won in a raffle." His eyes glazed for a moment and she shook him. "No you don't. You stay awake, you hear me?"

"You…won…me?"

She pulled the cap off the bottle of water and offered him some. "Sure did. You and me and a night of dancing. Although some people go to great lengths to avoid it."

He took a small sip then turned away. "Makes us even…"

"What does?"

"You…rescuing…me…"

"Not quite. You still owe me that date."

"More than one…" His eyes slid shut.

"Remember the sermon on Sunday? What Pastor Kenny preached on from Zephaniah? It's one of my favorite verses. *The LORD your God is with you, He is mighty to save. He will take great delight in you, He will quiet you with His love, He will rejoice over you with singing."*

"Sang it afterwards," he whispered. "My God is mighty to save..."

The water lapped higher now. She pulled him as high as she could, holding him tightly. She didn't want to drown, but there was no sign of the promised rescue. "Least I'm with you," she whispered.

There was nowhere left to go. The water reached his chin. She held him tightly, unable to pull him up any higher. "I love you."

He looked at her, his eyes focused for a moment. "It's OK... I love you." The water rose, covering his mouth.

"I'm sorry..." she sobbed.

A voice called her name. She glanced up to see the lifeboat appearing on her left. "Hurry..."

A splash and two swimmers appeared by her side. Strong arms took Cal from her, lifting his head back above the water.

Then someone took hold of her, taking her to the safety of the lifeboat.

# 30

*Three months later*

Hattie stood, surrounded by more than two hundred and fifty people on the shore by Penry Island Lifeboat Station. The brisk February wind blew her neatly done hair, here, there and everywhere. Cal appeared next to her in his uniform. He'd spent the Sunday morning training as usual, taking the new boat through her paces before her official launch that afternoon. His hand took hers, his thumb running over the wedding band she wore under her engagement ring.

She smiled at him. "I've never been to a boat launch before, never mind done one. Except for the excerpts on the television when the Queen does a new cruise ship or something, I have no idea what to do."

"It's a cinch. It'll be exactly like the launches you see on the TV. You say 'I name this lifeboat' and so on and then hit her with the champagne. And it had better break or else its bad luck."

She grinned. "But we don't do luck."

"Try telling that to this lot. Sailors are an inherently superstitious lot."

"These are all volunteers. Hardly any of them come from diehard sea going families anymore."

"Doesn't matter." He hugged her. "I love you."

Hattie hugged him back. "I love you, too."

"Are you sure you want to name it after Steve? He doesn't want to see you, and he won't accept your letters. It's as if he hasn't forgiven you for testifying against him."

"He hasn't. But, despite everything that's happened, he's still my brother. And I forgive him. I love him, Cal, and that won't ever change. Maybe one day things will be different." She sucked in a deep breath. "I'm still going to the prison on Wednesday. He'll probably refuse to see me again, but I have to go."

He nodded, hugging her tightly. "We'll both go. Put up a united front and show him that he's still part of our family, no matter how hard he tries to run. God hasn't given up on him and nor have we."

"Thank you." She hugged him back. "All we need now is Tom and we can start here. Maybe he got lost."

Cal laughed. "More likely he's stealing one of your apple cakes."

Tom came running out. "OK, Red Watch, get in the boat. You're on a shout. Speedboat in difficulties, four miles to the north-east."

"You're kidding," Cal said.

"Nope. Go, now."

The driver jumped into the tractor and started it up, while Cal and the rest of red watch scrambled up the ladder, starting the engines of the lifeboat.

Pastor Kenny stepped up to the microphone. "I know we still need to name her officially, and I'm not going to do that. But I want to pray and ask God to bless the lifeboat on her maiden rescue voyage."

Hattie kept her eyes on the boat as the tractor drove down the shingle and into the sea. She'd seen this done countless times now, but it still enthralled her. She raised a hand in farewell, as Cal headed from the DODO and out into open water. Less than a minute later the second boat followed them.

Tom looked at everyone. "Let's start the party without them," he said. "Tea and coffee will be served now, and we'll name the boat when they come back."

"Won't have enough cakes for that," Hattie commented to Laurie. "Actually, I'm not sure I made enough anyway. I didn't realize so many people would turn up."

Laurie smiled. "It's because it's *our* boat. We all helped raise the money for it. OK, the name is yours because it was your idea, but the boat belongs to the whole island."

Hattie's gaze shifted from the empty DODO, to the bridge. New columns would soon start to rise from the shadow of the old ones, and the familiar high girders would be rebuilt. This time next year was the plan, but whether that would happen was anyone's guess.

Choosing to forgo the tea, and making sure there were enough people to serve without her, Hattie sat on the sea wall, gazing out at the water.

Carter sat next to her. "He'll be back."

She looked up. "I know. Just part of me will always worry a little. Even on a calm day like this." She smiled. "How's the training going?"

"It's good to be back on the bike. Doc says I should be ready to start competing again in a week or so."

"That's great."

"Not as great as seeing the change in Cal. He's really settled down since you came on the scene."

She tilted her head. "You're one of the few people who said we didn't rush into marriage."

Carter shrugged. "Sometimes you just know when

Mr. or Miss Right comes along and then there is no point in waiting, especially when God's nudging you that way as well."

Tom came over. "They got there."

"Already?" she asked glancing at her watch. A mere six minutes had elapsed since the boats launched.

Tom nodded. "Cal is taking the couple to Yarbrough ED in the lifeboat, so they can be checked over. The RHIB is bringing their speedboat back to the harbor. They should all be back within the hour."

"So allowing time to clean up and refuel, about two hours or so before we can restart?"

"Something like that." He grinned at her. "So, are you working permanently in the shop now?"

"Alongside the catering, yeah." She grinned. "Course the café might not take off and…"

Carter elbowed her. "It's a brilliant idea. A beachside café, right next to the lifeboat station. What's not going to work about it?"

"It's seasonal. Might not get many visitors in the winter."

"Trust me. Advertise your cakes and they will come."

\*\*\*\*

Once the boats were cleaned and refueled, the crew resumed their places on the beach. Hattie swallowed hard, now the moment had come she was terrified.

Cal took her hand. "You'll be fine. Short speech, break the bottle and there you go."

Tom finished his speech and invited Hattie up to the mic. Trying to stop her knees from buckling under her, she stood in front of everyone. "I name this lifeboat the *Steve and Penny Steele.* May God bless and protect those who crew her and the lives of those she saves."

Taking the champagne bottle in her hand, she swung it hard. It hit the side of the boat and shattered. She grinned at Cal.

The phone in the main building rang. Tom ran inside and was gone about a minute before coming back out. "Red Watch…" he began.

Cal grinned. "No rest for the wicked, or those in peril on the sea." He hugged Hattie as the shore crew swung into action once more. "Save me a cake. Love you, see you later."

Hattie kissed him. "I'll be waiting right here. Same as always. Go do what you do best. Save lives."

Cal looked at Tom. "Where to?"

"Fishing trawler in difficulties. Ten miles northwest."

Hattie watched as the lifeboat launched and cut through the waters, heading off across the brightly lit waves.

# Hattie's Apple Cakes

2oz margarine
3oz sugar
4oz SR flour
1 egg
¼ teaspoon cinnamon
¼ teaspoon nutmeg (optional)
1 tablespoon milk
3oz chopped apples

Beat margarine and sugar together.
Add egg and beat again.
Mix in flour, cinnamon, nutmeg and baking powder.
Add milk and mix all together.
Add chopped apple.
Stir well.
Divide into 12 cake cases.
Mix a little cinnamon, nutmeg and sugar and sprinkle over each cake.
Bake 15 minutes gas mark 7 / 220C / 435F

## Hot Trifle

Fill the bottom of an oven proof dish with stale sponge or broken pieces of sponge fingers.

Top with a tin of fruit and the juice.

Make half a pint of custard and pour over the fruit.

Make a meringue with 2oz sugar and 1 egg white

Spoon the meringue over the custard and fluff into small peaks with the back of a teaspoon.

Bake on a very low heat ¼ gas/ 110C / 225F for 1½ hours

Thank you for purchasing this White Rose Publishing title. For other inspirational stories, please visit our on-line bookstore at www.pelicanbookgroup.com.

For questions or more information, contact us at customer@pelicanbookgroup.com.

White Rose Publishing
*Where Faith is the Cornerstone of Love*™
an imprint of Pelican Ventures Book Group
www.PelicanBookGroup.com

May God's glory shine through
this inspirational work of fiction.

AMDG